SUSAN MOODY, a former Chairman of the Crime Writers' Association, is the author of the Penny Wanawake detective series, and also the suspense novels *Playing with Fire*, *Hush-a-Bye*, *House of Moons* and *The Italian Garden*.

Praise for her previous mysteries featuring Cassie Swann:

TAKEOUT DOUBLE

'There's some brilliant motivational legerdemain. Fun, even for the card blind'   *The Guardian*

'Classic openers to some quite stunning finessing. Swann's way is my way'   *The Sunday Times*

'A bedrock of romance and humour adds interest . . . A good read set among the eccentricities of village life'   *Today*

GRAND SLAM

'Cassie Swann is back in spades . . . Clever, cosy-sinister bluffing and ruffing'   *The Sunday Times*

'Very amusing and entertaining'   *Sunday Telegraph*

'A satisfying traditional read, full of good humour'

The Times

KING OF HEARTS

'Gripping detective fiction'   *Daily Mirror*

'An amusing and deftly professional piece of work

Daily Mail

'Susan Moody's female investigator is unusual – and delightful Cassie Swann, bridge professional, always comes up trumps'   *Peterborough Evening Telegraph*

Also by Susan Moody

Take-Out Double
Grand Slam
King of Hearts

Doubled
In Spades

Susan Moody

HEADLINE

First published in 1996
by HEADLINE BOOK PUBLISHING

First published in paperback in 1996
by HEADLINE BOOK PUBLISHING

10 9 8 7 6 5 4 3 2 1

ISBN 0 7472 4625 4

Typeset by
Letterpart Ltd, Reigate, Surrey

Printed and bound in Great Britain by
Cox & Wyman Ltd, Reading, Berkshire

HEADLINE BOOK PUBLISHING
A division of Hodder Headline PLC
338 Euston Road
London NW1 3BH

Doubled
In Spades

♣ 1 ♣

'He's trying to kill me,' she whispered. Tears rolled thinly down her pale cheeks.

'Sorry?' Cassie put her head closer to Naomi's.

'I know he is . . .'

He? Cassie looked round the ward. Nobody in it looked homicidal. Nor were the beds occupied by anyone male. The only man in sight was a good-looking young doctor standing by the door exchanging clipboarded information with the ward sister. 'Who is?' she said.

'John. He's . . .' Propped against pillows, her thin face drained of colour, Naomi seemed not to have the strength to finish the sentence.

'Your husband?'

Naomi nodded.

'And you think he's trying to kill you?'

'Not think . . . know.'

'Why on earth would he want to do that?' Cassie felt uneasy. It was not simply the hospital atmosphere, with its intimations of mortality, its brisk smells overlying an uglier odour of apprehension and the anticipation of pain. There was also the fact that Naomi appeared to believe what she was saying.

'. . . wants a younger . . . someone to give him children . . .'

1

Naomi managed. Still recovering from the effects of sedation, she licked her dry lips with a white-furred tongue.

'Don't say such things,' Cassie said. 'Don't even think them. John loves you. He only wants the best for you. We all do. When I spoke to him about coming to see you here, he kept saying how much he'd missed you and that he couldn't wait for you to get back home.' She figured the lie had therapeutic value and was therefore worth telling. In actual fact, the conversation she had held with Harris prior to making this visit had contained neither of these sentiments. She had no idea what he really felt about his wife. With some couples, it was easy to determine either passion or dislike; with the Harrises, the only thing she could have reliably said about their relationship to each other was that they were married.

Disbelief spread slowly across Naomi's face as though it was being painted on with a brush. She frowned. Wetting her lips again, she struggled to speak, though at first the effort appeared to be too much for her. Finally, she said: 'Of course he did.'

Cassie took Naomi's narrow hand in hers. Dark spots showed on the sallow skin, not freckles but the beginning of age. 'Why didn't you tell us you were going in for a hysterectomy? You should have said something. I didn't even know you were in hospital until I telephoned about setting up a game of bridge and your husband told me.'

The tears trickled again. 'I suppose this is better, in a way,' Naomi murmured. 'At least now there's no hope left . . .'

'Naomi—'

'You've no idea what it's been like. So awful. What we've put up with . . .' The sentence floated away, adrift on a tide of awkward suggestion: rectal thermometers, sperm counts, ovulation charts.

'There are worse things than not having children,' Cassie said gently.

'Not if that's what you want.' The effort of talking was obviously exhausting the other woman. 'If it's *all* you want.'

'There are other things to strive for.'

'No!' Naomi struggled against the covering sheet. 'No! I wanted a child. I want . . .' She turned her head restlessly on the pillows.

'But you and John have so much going for you.' Another lie. Cassie had no idea whether they did or not. They certainly seemed to, but other people's relationships were always inexplicable to outsiders and the public face of any marriage did not necessarily mirror the private one. Although she had nothing against him, John Harris had never struck her as a particularly nice man. Maybe Naomi felt the same way. Maybe she wanted children because she needed something to love. Or to be loved by.

'Had.'

'What?'

'We *had*,' Naomi said, her tongue too big for her mouth. 'We used to have things going for us.'

'I'm sorry.' Cassie wished she had been more aware of the marital problems, the baby problems. She and Naomi had played bridge together for two or three years on a more or less regular basis, and not until very recently had it occurred to her that there might be a reason why Naomi wore that perpetual frown of worry between her brows, why she seemed so discontented.

'If you could look into the future . . .' Naomi muttered.

'How do you mean?'

'When you're young . . .'

'Yes?'

'. . . wouldn't do things, would you?'

'It's probably best in the long run that we can't,' Cassie said. 'See what's going to happen to us, I mean.'

Naomi's fingers scrabbled, dry as scarabs, across Cassie's hand. 'I wish that . . .'

'What?'

'. . . I was more like you.'

'Sometimes *I* wish I was more like me.'

'Strong. Fearless. I'm always . . . afraid.'

'Oh, Naomi.' Cassie felt like crying. 'Most of us are afraid most of the time. Including me. It's how you deal with it that counts.'

'Mmm.' Naomi suddenly fell asleep. Her mouth dropped open a little. Cassie waited a long while when tiptoed away.

She walked along the hospital corridor to the nursing station. Wards fanned to the right and left; a group of smaller rooms lay on either side of the passage, their large windows Venetian-blinded to the gaze of the world bustling by. The white-coated doctor was still holding his clipboard as she approached. A badge on his lapel announced his name. On impulse, Cassie stopped beside him.

'I'm a friend of Mrs Naomi Harris,' she said.

'Yes?' A bleeper protruded from the breast pocket of his coat. Pushing it further inside, he waited politely, head on one side.

'I just wondered how she was.'

'Absolutely fine. No reason why she shouldn't be,' the doctor said heartily. He took Cassie's elbow and steered her towards the reception area. 'Perfectly fine, or will be, once she's recovered her full strength. A certain amount of emotional resistance to overcome, perhaps.'

'Understandably.'

4

'Of course,' he said, male, not understanding in the least. 'If you want to be of any help to her, the best thing you can do is persuade her that she made the right decision to have the operation.' He moved into jocular mode. 'After all, what use is the baby-carriage when there are no babies to fill it?'

Cassie pulled her arm away from his fingers. 'Nobody asks sterile men to have their dicks off, do they?'

He raised his eyebrows, smiling, unaware of her anger, thinking she was joking. 'Perhaps not an entirely apt analogy.'

'Good enough, though. After all, what use is a baby-making *machine* when it's not producing the goods?'

He laughed, showed strong white teeth. His handsome face creased with tolerant amusement. 'It's a subject we could debate much further. For one thing, it has not yet been established that prior to the gynaecological problems, the husband was at fault.'

'Was the wife?'

'That seemed fairly clear, though I will admit that the root cause hasn't been determined to our complete satisfaction, either.'

'I see.' Cassie wanted to take issue with his uncaring tone about a distressed patient, his damnably patronising attitude, but his skin was clearly centimetres thick. Seething, she left, reminding herself as she did so that, as a taxpayer, she paid this man's salary and so was technically his employer.

The man was out there again, waiting for her. She stopped. Behind her, the automatic doors swished back and forth, open and shut, their mechanism activated by her presence. He was leaning against the side of his car, nonchalant, dark glasses hiding the direction of his gaze. But she knew he was looking at her. That he had followed her here.

5

She walked to her car and got in, locking the door, pushing down the knob with unnecessary force. Was she being paranoid? She wasn't rich or famous enough to have attracted her own personal fan. She hadn't had the kind of public exposure which would catch someone's eye, or have dragged her into anyone's private fantasies. Starting the engine, she debated whether it was the article which had appeared in the local paper a few weeks earlier that had brought her into this man's cognisance. There had been a photograph of her, unflattering, taken from the wrong angle, emphasising her chin. Hardly the stuff of dreams. But fixations were not based on any acceptable rationality.

If, indeed, fixation was what lay behind these more than accidental encounters. It couldn't be merely a coincidence that he was here today. He had obviously been waiting for her to come out. She fumbled in her bag for her sunglasses and put them on, stared into the rearview mirror. Sweat gathered in the hollow above her buttocks. To know she was here, he must have followed her.

Stalked her.

Stalk . . . Images tumbled in her brain. Stags, noble against the sky. Indian trackers. Men with slogan-painted headbands crawling through tropical undergrowth. Hard breaths and pounding hearts.

But this kind of stalker was different. This kind went after human quarry. High-profile people had them: they went with the territory, they were almost part of the contract. Film stars. Tennis players. Pop idols. Not ordinary citizens. Not women like herself, with jobs to do, places to go, ten pounds of unsightly fat to lose. Backing out of her parking place, she knew she was deceiving herself if she really believed that only high exposure attracted the attentions of the lunatics. There had been cases in the papers, women who had inadvertently imprinted themselves in the crazy fabrications of a weirdo or men pursued by deranged women. Phone calls, hundreds of them, night and day. Letters, rambling, making impossible claims and written in elaborate curling hands with gold ink or green. She'd read about it in a magazine. They even had a name for it: erotomania.

The man made no attempt to get into his own car and follow her. She had to pass him to get to the exit from the parking lot but he did not even turn his head as she went by. When she glanced in the rearview mirror, he was still there, arms folded across his chest.

Her hands were limp on the steering wheel. She forced herself to concentrate on the road but instead she found herself thinking about him. Her own personal erotomaniac. If that was what he was. It was about a month ago that she had noticed him for the first time, standing outside the public library in Bellington. She had barely registered the person sitting on the wall beneath the cast-iron lantern in front of the building until he got up and followed her down the street into the supermarket. He had collected a cart and pushed it behind her, not taking items from the shelves, simply stopping when she stopped, waiting, following again. At the frozen food cabinets, he had grinned at her as though they were joined in some doubtful complicity. It was only then that she really took him in. Since then, she had seen him several times. On each occasion, he had made it clear – or so it seemed to her – that he was there because she was.

Stamping on the brakes as a football from some street game rolled into the road from between two parked cars, she tried to laugh at herself. Ha ha. *Très* droll. They must be putting something in the water. First Naomi accuses her husband of

7

wanting her dead. Then Cassie Swann convinces herself that she is being hassled by a nutcase. If she had believed in a Divine Presence, she would have pointed out to It that she already had one psychopath in her life, thanks; she didn't need another. Though to be fair, Steve, the first one, the ex-prisoner who had been in her bridge class at HMP Bellington, and who had taken a fancy to her, had been lying dormant recently. It was some weeks since he last rang her up in the middle of the night, waking her from sleep in order that she might endure his obscenely violent whispers. Perhaps he had found some other unfortunate woman to torment. Better still, perhaps he was back inside somewhere, doing some more bird.

'He's trying to kill me . . .' Why would Naomi say such a thing about her husband? Was she suffering from some drug-induced hallucination? Turning left at the traffic lights, Cassie considered the Harrises. Their defining characteristic was that they were rich. Only the seriously well-off could have afforded to buy Bridge End, their perfect little manor house with its beautiful grounds; having bought it, only the seriously well-off could have maintained it at such an immaculate level. There was also a swimming pool, a tennis court, a boat down at Dartmouth. There was a house in Tuscany. And a London flat. They took expensive holidays, ran cars which looked as if they'd been bought yesterday. It all appeared idyllic.

But was it? There was the matter of their childlessness, for a start. Cassie had presumed it was by choice: only recently had she discovered that it was not. And the accidents to which Naomi was so prone: the time she had fallen down the stairs; the near-fatal car crash last year; the accidental overdose at Christmas; the occasion she had almost drowned in the pool. Each time she had laughed them off, said she was so clumsy, so forgetful, so careless. Perhaps they weren't accidental after all.

Perhaps she was right and John Harris really was trying to kill her.

Jesus.

Cassie looked into the rearview mirror again. There was no white car behind her but that meant nothing: there was no guarantee that the Peugeot against which the man had been leaning belonged to him. Negotiating the narrow country lanes between Bellington and Frith, she tried to think logically. Assuming that she was not mistaken in supposing that the number of times their paths had crossed in the past few weeks had been deliberately engineered, what did he want? Was this the downside of Care in the Community? Was he a loonie who had decided she was the woman he was destined to possess? Was he simply a lonely man looking for company? He was at the neutral midlife age when he might be recently divorced or a widower, a man new to the area and hoping to make friends. Or was there some other reason why he was trying to scare the shit out of her?

Because she had no doubt that he was. Naomi had called her fearless but she was not. She feared this man, not so much for what he might do as for what he had already done. He had diminished her. By frightening her, he had reduced her. It would be difficult to prove in any court of law that the smile he gave her in the supermarket, the way he had raised his eyebrows as they passed last week on the pavement outside Boots in Bellington, the casual flip of his hand as she ran for shelter in a sudden downpour, were in any way menacing. Yet she knew they were, and intended to be so. It was not the meetings in public car parks or outside municipal buildings which worried her. It was the possibility of other, more surreptitious encounters. Darkened hallways, empty streets, lonely dwellings set among fields and hedges. Houses like Honeysuckle Cottage,

9

unneighboured and far from help, should help be needed.

She drove down Back Lane and turned onto the bit of grass in front of the lean-to shed which acted as a garage when she could be bothered to open it up. She got out of the car. The sun blazed mercilessly down from a sky as matt and blue as a Wedgwood plate. The cottage needed cleaning and she'd set aside today for the job, but instead of pushing towards the back door, half-hidden under tendrils of insect-ridden ivy, she walked further down the lane. The air was dense with sweet country smells and gnats. And suffocating heat. Somewhere on the edge of the world a cuckoo hiccupped.

Three hundred yards along stood Ivy Cottage. Kathryn Kurtz, the cottage's American tenant, was just back from several weeks in the States, visiting her family in Nebraska. Wherever that was. Up in the top left hand corner, wasn't it? Cassie thought she must have been off sick the day they studied the United States at school. It always embarrassed her to read how drastically educational standards had fallen in recent years and how pig ignorant today's youth was, especially when compared with its Japanese counterpart. She was guiltily aware that today's youth wasn't the only one who didn't know precisely which side of India Calcutta was, *or* the name of the current Minister for Overseas Development.

Sitting under the long strands of honeysuckle which trailed from the thatch of Kathryn's porch was the white cat from the farm beyond her back hedge. For the past four months the cat had showed up daily outside the kitchen door of Honeysuckle Cottage and been treated like royalty. Now here it was at Ivy Cottage, cosying up to someone else, licking its whiskers over another donor's saucer of milk.

Dairy product slut. Cassie reached for the knocker. The cat began to wash itself with looselimbed elegance while Cassie waited for Kathryn to open the door. When it became clear that she wasn't inside the house, Cassie walked round to the back.

Kathryn was bent double in the knee-high yellow grass. 'Oh. Hi.' She sounded distracted.

'Still getting over that airline food?' Cassie asked sympathetically.

'What's been happening while I was away? Looks like the African veldt round here.' Kathryn straightened up.

'We've been experiencing a drought situation. It's the hottest summer since 1683. Or the driest, or both.'

'It only needs a giraffe or two and they could film the remake of *Zulu* out here.'

'Welcome back,' Cassie said. 'Did y'all have a good time in the States?'

'Fabulous, thanks. Particularly my mother.'

'Having her little girl back home after all these months must have—'

'The hell with her little girl. It was Giles she went for. She took one look at him and had the first orgasm she's had for fifty years.' Kathryn began walking back to the house. 'Coffee?'

Cassie made a negative sound.

'Let me rephrase that,' Kathryn said. 'Since it's only, like, five whole hours until the sun is officially over the yard arm, how about a glass of white wine? There's some cooling in the icebox.'

'Now you're talking.'

They sat in garden chairs on the uneven patio which some amateur bricklayer had installed several years ago. 'So your mother liked Giles,' said Cassie. 'That's good. And did Giles like her?'

'*Adored* her. Remember that scene in *Brief Encounter* when Trevor Howard first sees Celia Johnson across a crowded

11

railway buffet? It was exactly like that between the two of them. Love at first sight. Funny really. I love his mother because she's so unusual and he loves mine because she's so amazingly dull. Pure Stepford Wife: washes on Monday, shops on Thursday, visits the beauty parlour Friday.'

'How come she landed you for a daughter?'

'That's what *she* keeps saying.'

'Is she flying over for the wedding?'

'Try and stop her.' Kathryn snorted. 'And believe me, I did.' She was wearing a pair of earrings composed of miniature versions of familiar household objects. Without staring rudely, Cassie could make out a knife and fork, a teapot, a milk jug and a plate with a slice of bread on it, all made out of silver and agate, suspended from silver wire.

'When *is* the wedding?'

'Early fall, we thought. And by the way, in case I didn't say earlier, I want you to be my attendant. We both do.'

Cassie groaned. 'Do I have to?'

''Fraid so.'

'I'm so sick of dieting.'

'So don't diet.'

'Will I have to wear something frilly?'

'You do and I'll kill you.' Kathryn's face stretched in a chipmunk grin.

'Are you – uh – planning, as they say, to start a family?'

'Children? Oh please. I'll be thirty-eight next birthday. Kind of old to start mixing formula.'

'Not these days.' Kathryn was only a couple of years younger than Naomi, Cassie thought, but light years away in attitude. One so unconcerned, the other so desperate.

'Be honest, Cassie. Can you really see me as a mother?'

'I'm prepared to work at it.'

'Besides, Giles isn't keen on the idea. And who can blame the poor baby after what he went through as a child. I adore Mercy, as you know, but she wasn't the kind of mother you'd order out of the Nice Mommy catalogue.'

'What about honeymoons?'

'We can't really decide. In a way, visiting back home was a honeymoon, if it hadn't been for the zillions of relations coming round all the time trying to hide their disbelief that I'd finally hooked a husband.' Kathryn held up a hand. 'No. Don't tell me. I know it sounds prehistoric and non-PC, but it's the way my family thinks. Where I come from, not only does an unmarried daughter reflect badly on her parents, but it's her fault if the crops fail, the hens stop laying and the cows' milk dries up.'

'How about joining me in France? My godfather's been trying to persuade me to go over and housesit his place for a month, while he's away.'

'What's with persuade? I'd have been on the next plane over.'

'For one thing, I haven't got time, with the bridge business getting started. And for another, this house of his is completely isolated.'

'Sounds great.'

'I don't do good isolation.'

'How isolated are we talking?'

'There's a little town about six kilometres away. A pretty good *auberge* within walking distance. A surly handyman who shows up from time to time. That's about it, human-contact-wise.'

'Heaven,' Kathryn said wistfully. Then added the phrase which always made Cassie realise just how wise she herself had been to remain single. 'I'd have to ask Giles, of course.'

'Right.' Cassie changed the subject. 'Listen. If you started bumping into a stranger, time after time, someone you'd never seen before who suddenly popped up wherever you were, what would you think?'

'If I even noticed, if I gave it a second thought, I suppose I'd assume it was either a coincidence, or—'

'Or what?'

'Someone who'd recently moved into the neighbourhood. Someone who had the same tastes as I did. Or the same interests. Or worked in the same area. But why would you even bother to think? It happens all the time.'

'Yeah . . .'

'What else could it be?'

Cassie shrugged. 'You're probably right.'

Kathryn raised her eyebrows. 'What is all this, Cass?'

'You wouldn't immediately jump to the conclusion that he, this stranger who suddenly turns up wherever you go, this guy who waits for you when you go to the library or visit the hospital or go shopping, was a stalker?'

'A stalk—? You think he's *following* you?'

'It's probably my overheated imagination. Which is why I want you to tell me that I'm an idiot, that I'm overreacting. It's just that every time I go anywhere, he seems to be there too.' Cassie elaborated, feeling foolish. What had seemed obvious earlier now sounded ridiculous.

'You're an idiot,' Kathryn said, when she'd finished. 'You're overreacting. Some poor old guy smiles at you over the frozen chicken livers and you immediately start screaming sex maniac? Come on, honey. That's crazy.'

'Yeah. Probably. He's not a poor old guy, though.'

'OK, let's look at this logically. Have you met him some-where else and forgotten about it?'

14

'I don't think so.'

'Could he be one of your ex-cons, harbouring a grudge because you dissed him while he was inside? Or didn't explain some bridge convention clearly enough. Something like that?'

'As far as I remember, I've never seen him before in my life – until he began to show up four or five weeks ago.'

'Did something change around then?'

'Nothing that I can think of.'

'Could he be someone from one of your evening classes? Or someone you partnered in a tournament?'

'I'd have recognised him.'

'Maybe he's someone's husband. Some woman who caught the bridge bug and now is too busy to make dinner and iron his jockey shorts, so he blames you. You know what men are like.'

'That's a bit farfetched.'

'Maybe you beat him to a parking place somewhere. Or got the last ticket for a Rolling Stones concert. Or cut him up at traffic-lights.'

'You're not suggesting this is a subtle form of road rage, are you?'

'I'm trying to jog your memory. To see if you could've gotten up this guy's nose some time, perhaps without even realising it, and he's trying to get back at you for it.'

'Nothing. I've done nothing at all.'

'Maybe he's just shy. Maybe he likes the look of you and wants to get better acquainted. What's he like?'

'Somewhere between forty and fifty, I'd say. Tall. Fair-haired but balding. Rather . . . distinguished, actually. One of those interesting long faces.'

'Does he look like the type to come bursting through your back door waving a gun?'

'No.' Cassie hesitated. 'But—'

'Then I wouldn't worry about it. And talking of distinguished, how's dear Charlie?' Kathryn swung her earrings about.

'I can't see the slightest relationship between the two words,' Cassie said in her coldest voice.

'If Giles and I made it to France, would he be coming too?'

'Not with me.'

'That's a pity.'

'For whom?'

'All of us. You don't realise what a pearl among men he is.' Like so many of Cassie's friends, Kathryn displayed an inexplicable fondness for Charlie Quartermain. 'You never look at the real Charlie, only the appearance.' She sighed. 'Oh Cass: you're just so superficial.'

'At least it's only skin deep.'

But Kathryn failed to smile, and Cassie left shortly afterwards, feeling obscurely chastened.

♦ 2 ♦

Lunchtime was normally a time for rejoicing. A legitimate excuse to put something into her mouth, chew, appreciate and swallow it. Today, Cassie took the bag – the *giant* bag – of wheatgerm out of the larder and lifted down a jug of green olive oil. Set together on the kitchen counter, they looked only marginally less appetising than they tasted. Somewhere recently, she'd read that the American government had issued a statement associating weight loss with an increased mortality rate. That certainly made you think, didn't it? Right. About coffins mostly, swiftly followed by steak and fried potatoes. About spaghetti and hazelnut meringue. About devil's food cake and chocolate fudge sauce and profiteroles stuffed with almond cream and topped with caramel glazing.

Oh God . . .

What she needed was aversion therapy. Or perhaps the opposite. Therapy which would actually make her like the way she looked. She stared at her hands. Just look at those middle fingers. Sausages, or what? The rings she wore on her right hand, a plain gold band which had been her mother's wedding ring, and a hoop of small diamonds which had belonged to Gran, seemed all of a sudden to have become embedded in the flesh. In the past week she had put on three pounds: was it

17

possible that all the extra weight had gone straight to her fingers? She had a vision, compelling in its clarity, of herself being carted off to hospital to have the rings cut out of the gangrening flesh, of the surgeon's knife slipping, of her fingers rattling to the floor of the operating theatre. It would mean the end of playing bridge, unless she could find some sinister prosthesis: three stainless steel fingers attached to a wrist band, perhaps, or a completely unrealistic pink plastic job. Even then, people would avoid her. No one would want to partner her ever again. The prospect was too hideous to contemplate. She measured out the wheatgerm, poured in the olive oil, mixed the two together and then threw the whole lot into the trash.

Sorry. If it was to be stainless steel, so be it. Feeling much more cheerful, she scrubbed a baking potato and while it was circulating in the microwave, got a tub of sour cream from the fridge and went outside to cut chives from the earthenware pot beside the back door. At the end of the garden, a thick planting of creamy ramblers hid the vegetable patch where brown-edged lettuces drooped and tomatoes reddened among dry foliage. Beyond were fields full of petal-less buttercups slop-ing gradually upwards to a viciously cloudless sky. Bees moaned among the lavender heads. Birds made musical noises. How quaintly pastoral it was. How bucolic, even despite the ravages of the summer which had resulted in a straw-coloured lawn, shrivelled leaves lying defeated on crumbling soil, drooping shrubs. When the hosepipe ban was first imposed, Cassie had poured surreptitious buckets of water here and there, but the task of keeping the garden green had proved impossible.

She was about to return to the computer with a full stomach and a better frame of mind when someone knocked at the front door. She'd seen the man standing on the step before but—

'Hello. You're – uh—' Who the hell exactly *was* it?

'John Harris.' His voice was surly, on the edge of drunkenness.

'Of course.'

'You *are* Cassandra Swann, aren't you?'

'As far as I know.'

'The one who plays bridge with my wife? In fact, didn't you come to us for dinner once?'

'I did, yes.' And a bloody boring evening it had been, too: dreadful food, Naomi scurrying about in harassed housewife mode, and Harris being scintillating about golf, which he pronounced goff.

'Glad to find you at home,' he said. 'I've just been visiting Naomi, so I thought I'd drop in to thank you for visiting her. I gather you went to see her in hospital yesterday. Jolly nice of you. She needs cheering up.'

'I wasn't able to do much of that,' Cassie said. 'Why don't you come in?'

He followed her, still talking. 'She's pretty down, poor old thing. What can you expect, though? It's a question of coming to terms with it now, I suppose.' His eye fell on the bottle of whisky which Cassie had bought yesterday and not yet put away. 'Uh – any chance of a noggin?'

At two-thirty in the afternoon? On a working day? 'Help yourself.'

He did so. Generously. 'At least it'll be better than the way we've been living,' he continued. 'Trying to get Naomi pregnant: I can't tell you how appalling the last few years have been.'

Although she probably wasn't Harris's number one fan, any more than his wife had appeared to be, Cassie could not help feeling some pity. Just because he was a man didn't mean that

19

he hadn't wanted a baby as much as Naomi herself. For all Cassie knew, paternal yearnings could easily be as strong as maternal ones.

'I imagine she'll be pretty depressed for a while,' she said.

'Yes. But it'll be easier to cope with than what we went through before.' Harris drained his glass and picked up the bottle again. 'Expect you were already aware she'd been suffering some kind of woman's problem. If you catch my drift.'

'I didn't, actually. She never mentioned it.'

'Probably too embarrassed. The doctor's been recommending for ages that she have this operation, but until now, the stupid girl's been refusing to go along with it.'

'I can see why she might.'

'She thought it'd be the end of the world, said I'd stop thinking of her as – A Woman.' Harris injected a lethal amount of deep-voice scorn into the last phrase.

'And was she right?'

'Chrissake, I kept telling her it wasn't as if they were going to cut off her boobs or sew her up or anything!'

'That must have been reassuring.'

'Thing is, she couldn't bring herself to admit that she was never going to get pregnant. I mean, she's over forty now – too old for it, in my humble opinion. But she kept clinging to the fantasy that one sunny day she was going to wake up and find a sprog in bootees and a smelly nappy lying in a bassinette beside her.' He sagged onto one of the two couches set at right-angles to the empty fireplace. Sunlight filtered greenly through the small-paned windows, giving an emerald tinge to the shadowy room.

How would *she* feel if someone tried to remove her chances of ever having a baby, Cassie wondered? Not that she had so

DOUBLED IN SPADES

far had the urge. At least, not all that often. Sometimes, admittedly, her hormones went into overdrive and tried to persuade her that the only thing she needed to make her life absolutely perfect was an infant at the breast. Apart from those occasional blips, she had not thought too much about motherhood, beyond being grateful that her short-lived marriage had been childless. But choice was one thing, enforced impossibility was quite another. 'That's understandable, isn't it?' she said.

'Of course it is.' Harris swallowed again. 'What I couldn't come to terms with was why she wouldn't just accept it wasn't going to happen. I mean she's been trying for bloody years to have a child, without any success. And take it from me, it's not *my* fault.'

'How do you know?'

'What?'

'How do you know it's not your fault?'

'I've done all the bloody tests, that's why.'

'Poor Naomi. I wish I'd known,' Cassie said.

'You're a lot better off *not* knowing. You wouldn't believe the indignities and humiliations she's put herself through over the years – put us *both* through, for that matter. Having sex when you don't feel like it, because it's the right time of the cycle, wanking off into lemonade bottles, thermometers up your bum and in your mouth, Christ knows what.'

Hoping very much that the second insertion had not been immediately subsequent to the first, Cassie decided that if there was a man more insensitive, more thoughtless, more unpleasant that Harris, she'd like to meet him. Or, rather, she wouldn't. Not him, not any man who used the phrase 'having sex' to describe making love to his wife, as though it was no more than some mechanical function.

To her surprise, Harris's voice softened. He leaned towards

21

her, eyes afloat in alcohol. 'Poor old thing,' he said. 'I suppose
it all matters much more to the girls than it does to us men. I
tried to point out the good side. I kept asking her if, quite
honestly, our life is so bad, without kids. We've got – or we had
– a thriving business, nice cars, lovely house; we can do what
we like when we like; we enjoy doing the same things: theatre,
concerts, eating in good restaurants, holidays, usual middle-
class distractions. Not that we can afford any of it any more,
the way things are.'

This was the authentic whine of a member of that large band
of previously rich people who were now no longer so rich.
'Really?'

'This damned recession. The company's heading towards
the rocks, financially. Redundancies every week. Early retire-
ment, they call it.' He laughed harshly. 'That's a good one. And
even though I'm pretty senior, that's no guarantee I'll keep my
job. Washed-up, that's me.'

'You don't look it, John.'

'Overextended, that's what I am. Just keeping up the mort-
gages and paying the mooring fees is ruinous. If they let me go,
I don't know what I'll . . . Too old to be worth keeping on,
that's me, and too old to find another job that'll bring in even
half what I'm on at the moment.' He stretched an arm over the
back of the sofa and took another peg of whisky. Without even
asking. Damn nerve. That stuff was expensive.

'How perfectly awful for you both,' said Cassie. Naomi had
said absolutely nothing about any of this, last time they had
played bridge together.

'Both? Both, did you say? There's no bleeding *both* about it.
Naomi's fine, *Naomi's* just bloody fine, thank you very much.'

'Really?' Cassie tried to despise herself for the blatant way
in which she was leading him further into indiscretion. But she

22

knew so little about either Naomi or her husband that it would have taken a much more saintly woman than herself to attempt to stop Harris's flow. She wanted to learn more.

'Not a care in the world, has little Naomi.' Harris swallowed loudly. He was a dedicated follower of the school of male hairdressing which sprouted three long strands above one ear and spread them thinly over a balding pate in the belief that people would mistake it for a full head of hair. 'Apart from this little spot of gynaecological bother, of course. Anyway, I didn't come here to cry on your shoulder. Hardly know you, do I?'

'Not really.'

'Not on those sorts of terms. Not in the least. Thing is, Cash—' He was having difficulty with her name. '—Cassandra, just wanted to say thanks. Difficult girl, my wife. Doesn't seem to have the knack of making friends. So I wanted to let you know I appreciate you going in to visit her. Don't mind saying it was a real relief when she finally agreed to go through with it.'

'When was that?'

'Only a few weeks ago. I came home from the office one night and there she was, saying she'd thought it over and decided to get it done.' He struggled to his feet. 'Anyway, jolly decent of you to pop in.'

'How long's she in for?'

'Only a couple more days. She wants to get home, she says. We're having a live-in nurse for a week, by which time they think she'll be able to cope on her own, if she takes it easy.'

'I'll try and visit her again. And if there's anything else I can do . . .' Cassie wondered if she ought to invite him round for supper, a man on his own and all that, but decided that, in this case, *noblesse* did not *oblige*. It wasn't as if Naomi was a close friend.

'There's nothing, really,' he said. 'Thanks all the same. Unless—'

'Unless what?'

'—you know of a way to give her a baby.' He began to laugh, a horrible raucous sound which Cassie could still hear even after she had shut the door behind him.

Natasha was coming to visit later that afternoon. Cassie went into the new headquarters of the bridge sundries business which the two of them were setting up, and sat down in front of the computer. Chris, Natasha's husband, had ordered and installed the machines and then gone off to the States. 'Just follow the manuals,' he had shouted, as he disappeared behind the barriers at Heathrow. Cassie had been doing so. The trouble was that the computer wouldn't follow her. Still, it had some nice little extras. She spent a pleasant hour or two dragging various shapes onto a grid and then painting them all kinds of exciting colours. And another thirty minutes writing a letter-head in any one of forty-two fonts. *Every* one of forty-two different fonts, to be exact. Though this was a somewhat premature exercise, since neither she nor Natasha had been able to decide on a name for their fledgling company, and until they did so, a letterhead was unnecessary. Bridge Too Far, an offering from Chris, had been rejected loudly and with scorn. Bridge'n'Things, Natasha's suggestion, had Cassie sticking her fingers down her throat. Her own title – Frith Bridge Supplies – was, in Natasha's opinion, much too plain, and impossible to pronounce.

Meanwhile, there was the catalogue to design and pro-duce. And the computer to master. What she needed was the technological equivalent of a personal trainer. Someone who would come in and guide her through an intensive pro-gramme of cyber-exercises intended to facilitate her ability to make efficient use of the expensive equipment they'd lashed out on. Even with Chris's contacts, it had all cost a tidy sum. Hopefully, she pressed a button.

'You have made an error,' the computer flashed.

'I beg your pardon.'

'This is an incorrect entry.'

'It bloody is not.'

'Excuse me.'

'Excuse *me*.'

'Please try again.'

'Bollocks.'

Cassie brought up the menu, scrolled to Shut Down and double clicked on the mouse. The screen obediently went dead. That showed it who was the alpha dog round here and no mistake. It was also a step forward in her computer expertise. Last time she tried to switch off, a message flashed up telling her there was a serious error in the bit map or something similar. When the damn thing had been installed, a week ago, it had seemed like part of the miracle. The workmen had finally finished converting the stone-built outhouses in the garden of Honeysuckle Cottage and departed, taking with them their transistor radios, their cement mixers, their tabloid news-papers and their beer bellies. The council had approved the work and, without the least hint of a smile, assured her that the cheque would shortly be in the mail. The interior fittings had been installed and such stock as had already arrived was tastefully set out. Stripped beams abounded, old pine shelving adorned every wall and there was enough wicker basketry to inspire even the most lethargic occupational therapy class.

Trestle tables down the middle of the floor and various woven rugs of vaguely ethnic design lent a delightfully rural yet nonetheless completely businesslike air to the place, or so Natasha kept pointing out.

The computer was supposed to add the final touch. And so it probably would, once they had worked out how to operate it. Hmm. Easier said than done. Cassie picked up the telephone and dialled the number of a large computer centre in Oxford. Having explained her problem, the response was reassuring.

'One of our trained and qualified personnel would be delighted to assist,' said the voice at the other end of the line.

'I'd need to be shown the most basic—'

'Don't worry, madam. We're very used to it.'

'Wonderful!' It was only then that Cassie thought to ask how much this service would cost.

'The basic fee for a half-day's instruction would be somewhere in the region of two hundred and fifty pounds, madam. Given the complexity of the technology, and a not unreasonable sum, I think you'd agree—'

'I most certainly would not.'

'I'm sorry to hear that, madam.'

'*How* much did you say?'

The voice repeated the sum.

For that kind of money, even Bill Gates would have been delighted. 'I'll think about it, thanks,' Cassie said, and hung up.

Instead, she thought about whether she was charging enough for the private bridge lessons she offered. If expertise cost so much, maybe she ought to hike her prices per hour when the new season started in the autumn.

Through the open door into the garden, she could see the lily pond. Across its surface, the white cat and a supercilious heron eyed each other with mutual distrust. Both were after the same thing: the goldfish which precariously inhabited the pond. The heron's throat undulated; the cat's ears twitched. It was a war of attrition in which the goldfish were bound to lose out. Beyond them, reflected in the water, was the slate slab which Charlie Quartermain had incised for her: a beautifully curving C inside a chiselled heart, and, above it, a stylised swan.

Charlie! If anyone knew the right person to help her gain some technological expertise, it would be Charlie. And if he did not himself know, he would have a mate who did. It would be a simple matter to call him, but she hesitated nonetheless. Asking Charlie for help would involve being nice to him, and being nice to Charlie was apt to give him ideas. Wrong ones. No, she would exhaust all other avenues open to her before she involved Charlie. The trouble was, she didn't know of any. At least none, judging by the exchange she had just enjoyed with the computer shop, which wouldn't bankrupt the fledgling business before it had even been christened.

More important, right now, than a bankrupt business, was the possibility of a bankrupt Cassandra. She'd thrown up the day job because she wanted to be free. Her own mistress. Answerable only to herself. It was a question of independence, of self-respect. She had been allowed precious little of either at the Vicarage. The idea was fine, and worked as long as the cheques came in. When they didn't, the air seemed colder. And despite the recent heat wave, it had taken on a distinct chill in the past few weeks. Most of the chill emerged from brown envelopes. There'd been far too many of them lately, all containing bills. All nagging, all demanding money she hadn't got. The trouble with freelancing was that there was nothing to fall back on, no salary cheque at the end of the month, however incompetent the level of your work.

SUSAN MOODY

The bridge sundries business was an attempt to rectify the uncertainty. There was no question that the chanciness of daily living had changed her. Once, the ferocity of her desire for independence had led her to refuse even the smallest help. Now, she was unashamed about accepting favours. The rent-free cottage, for instance. The fact that Natasha and Chris had put up the money for the business stock. Her willingness to let other people pick up the bill for lunch or drinks. She'd pay them back when she could; that was one promise she'd made herself. But for the moment, it was a matter of getting by the best she could. And clinging on to as much of her self-respect as she could salvage.

She looked up as Natasha, friend and business partner – once the business existed – came, in her pelvic-thrusting ex-model's lope, across from the cottage.

'Ah!' she exclaimed, in her deep Russian voice, snuffing the air like a cat scenting salmon. 'The sweet smell of success.'

'Is that what it is?' To Cassie the place still stank of the Mountain Herbs cleaner she'd earlier sprayed about to hide the odour left by the rotting corpse of a starling which someone – almost certainly the white cat – had deposited on a pile of linen tablecloths exquisitely appliquéed with bridge motifs.

'Oh, Cassie.' Natasha gazed round the showroom with satisfaction. 'I just know we're going to be really big.'

'Some of us are already as big as we want to be, thank you very much,' Cassie said glumly. 'If not considerably bigger.'

Natasha punched the air like a boxer. 'We're on a roll. I can feel it. We're going to win. And do you know why?'

'Why we are going to win, Natasha?'

'Because we're hungry, that's why. We are *starving*.'

'Tell me about it,' said Cassie. 'Do you want to hear what I tried to eat for breakfast this morning?'

'No.'

'Wheat germ. And olive oil. Have you ever wondered what large amounts of olive oil can do to a healthy system?'

'Never. Not once.'

'I'd tell you, but you wouldn't enjoy it. Not this early in the morning.'

'Honestly, Cass. Why can't you get it into your head that just because you don't look like a matchstick man in a Lowry painting, you're not in some way inferior?'

'Perhaps it has something to do with being forced to grow up with three midgets. Or confronting one's image unexpectedly in the mirror, as I did this morning.' God, what a nightmare *that* had been: belly like a barrel, boobs down to her ankles. What the hell would she look like at forty?

'You are a beautiful woman, and the sooner you accept it, the better it will be for all of us, especially you.'

'Do you take cheques or shall I pay by credit card?'

'Oh, Cassandra, Cassandra,' said Natasha. 'Why do you refuse to take yourself seriously?'

She turned to the new equipment which had been set up in the little office adjoining the showroom, and began to stroke the handsome dove-grey computer. 'Talking of beauty: how's this little baby doing? According to Chris, it'll halve the amount of work we have to do. It's real cutting-edge technology.'

'What does that mean, exactly?'

'Um . . .'

'I read somewhere that by the time you'd got things like this out of their boxes, they were already obsolete,' continued Cassie. 'I hope we haven't paid out good money for something that's fit only for the technological scrap heap.'

'Scrap heap?' Natasha, who remembered reading something very similar, gave a laugh which lacked sang-froid. 'I think that's a slight exaggeration.'

'I was hoping it was a wildly over-the-top one.'

'When it comes to computers, Chris knows what he's talking about,' Natasha said, protective, as always, of her husband.

'In that case, why did he decide to leg it for the States the minute all this stuff arrived? Especially—'

'You know as well as I do that he's been booked to conduct this course in Florida for months.'

'—when he knew how difficult we'd find it to cope on our own.'

'He said we are both intelligent women. He said the best thing for us would be to bootstrap it. Like throwing someone in at the deep end and letting them sink or swim.'

'That's what they used to do to witches.'

'He said that if we just followed the manuals, we wouldn't have any problem at all.'

'Yeah, yeah.'

♥ 3 ♥

Lift your eyes above ground level and Oxford could still pass
for medieval. Frontages of mellow stone, ancient doorways
and carved windows, statues and spires lent the city an indefin-
able and illusory sense of grace. Down on the streets, it was
different. The place was more like a speedway track, especially here outside St John's, with the traffic pounding down
the Woodstock and Banbury Roads from North Oxford to
conjoin in St Giles. Drawing in a lungful of carbon monoxide,
Cassie made a dash for one of the central islands in the middle
of the wide thoroughfare. She was only halfway there when a
belligerent taxi driver screeched to a juddering halt on the toe
of her shoe in an emergency stop worthy of Nigel Mansell.
Momentarily, terror drained her body of feeling before she
turned a look of outraged hatred at the driver.

'Dickhead!' she screamed, above the roar of combustion
engines.

He inched aggressively forward, the heavy black bonnet of
his vehicle nudging her skirt. 'Who're you calling dickhead?'
he demanded, raising an offensive finger.

'Give you one guess.'

'Takes one to know one.'

'Hey, that's really good.'

31

Before he could come up with something even wittier, she had slipped behind him and edged between a temporarily halted bus which exhaled a thick cloud of diesel fumes, and a small car containing a large number of young women with enough collective hair to fill a duvet. This time she made it to the other side, where she leaned for a moment against the scabby bark of a plane tree to catch her breath. There was sweat on her forehead. The broad reach of St Giles buzzed with late-summer pedestrians: tourists, for the most part, with a sprinkling of earnest graduate students and resident young from former colonies taking an hour or two off from their temporary jobs in the hamburger and sandwich joints which liberally studded the city centre. Summer dresses fluttered under the plane trees, tanned flesh paraded. The hell with skin cancer: minimal clothing was the rig of the day.

She watched an elderly woman with a white stick negotiating her slow way across the road, cars and vans unwillingly pulling up to let her pass. She thought it might be a good idea to get one for herself. Especially when the old woman straightened up as soon as she had reached the safety of the pavement in front of Regent's Park college, telescoped her white stick and shoved it into her shoulderbag. Catching Cassie's eye, she grinned.

'Desperate situations call for desperate measures,' she said, before heading briskly for Somerville where, Cassie reflected, she almost certainly had to take a tutorial on the later Romantic poets.

A shabby man was heading towards Cassie, calling her by name. He wore a stained V-necked sweater and unseasonal corduroy trousers, his only concession to the heat being his open-necked shirt, beneath which he clearly wore a vest.

'Oh, hi,' Cassie said. Though American tourists frequently

pressed coins into his hand, taking him for a passing indigent or a piece of local colour, Professor Richardson was in fact one of the senior members of the university. Cassie occasionally played bridge with him and his aged aunt, who lived in Frith.

'Are you well?' Richardson asked.

'Very. Though whether I'll still be after a day breathing in the city air is a moot point.'

'Frightful, isn't it? One of my colleagues has been studying the pollution levels here and maintains that they're fast approaching those of Mexico City,' said the professor.

A young man in ripped jeans and a T-shirt emblazoned with the first line of the Bill of Rights in pseudo-copperplate approached. 'Ah, Richardson,' he said. 'Just the fellow. That paper of yours published in the *Proceedings of the Leipzig Symposium*. How did you obtain your data? It directly contradicts my own research.'

The professor looked gloomy. 'Isn't it a bit early in the day for this sort of thing?' he asked. 'By the way, do you know Cassandra Swann?'

The younger man fingered the gold studs attached to his left ear. 'Not yet.' Smiling at Cassie, he waited for his own name to be produced. When it became clear that Richardson had forgotten it, he added: 'Ian Butler. Medievalist. Christ Church. How do you do?'

'On the other hand,' Richardson said, looking brighter, 'we could pop into the pub and discuss the matter you raised. What do you think?'

'Excellent idea.' Butler looked at Cassie. 'Join us?'

'I'd love to, but I'm meeting someone for tea.'

'Another time, then.'

'Yes.' Cassie managed to choke off the word "please" before it emerged from her throat. Was it because she was in

33

her thirties that she found herself so susceptible to young men? Was she going to become one of those knowing older women who take lads in hand and show them the sexual ropes? She sincerely hoped so.

She ploughed on. Oxford wasn't the way it used to be when Betjeman and Waugh were up, that was for sure. Nor as it was in the heady days of her godfather's youth, as he was much too fond of pointing out. On the other hand, tea at the Randolph hadn't changed much since her own adolescence. Scones. Clotted cream and raspberry jam. A pastry, probably. There were few eternal verities left these days, but tea at the Randolph must surely be one of them. She ran lightly up the hotel's shallow steps and made her way to the lounge where she settled into the bosomy embrace of a velveteen-covered sofa and ordered the cream tea for two. Her godfather arrived five minutes later.

'I'm so glad you didn't wait for me,' he said tartly.

'Desperation drove me to discourtesy, Robin. I skipped breakfast *and* lunch for this.'

'I hope that's not my scone you're devouring.'

'Oops,' said Cassie.

'You mean it *is*?'

'We'll order some more.'

Cassie kissed his smoothly-shaven cheek as he sat down beside her. If you wanted eternal verities, Robin Plunkett, well-known novelist, ex-pat and godfather, was probably as close as a human being could get. In all the years Cassie had known him, he had scarcely changed. He still wore the wasp-waisted suits his tailor had designed for him, years ago, upon the occasion of his going up to Oxford. The curly hair remained as elegantly silver, the Floris cologne as discreet, the tie was the usual shantung silk. Today it was peacock green, though he possessed an extensive wardrobe of similar ties in equally brilliant colours. 'How was your afternoon?'

Robin's shoulders rippled in an exaggerated shudder. 'Don't remind me,' he said. 'Oxford's become more like an SAS assault course than a centre of learning. When I wasn't being hounded by importunate beggars – many of them, I suspect, undergraduates, or possibly even Fellows – I was being hassled by tourists wanting directions to Oxford College or narrowly escaping being mown down by lunatics.' He raised his eyes to the ceiling and shook his head.

'It's not like it was in the heady days of your youth, I bet,' Cassie said sympathetically.

'My God, no. When I was an undergraduate, there weren't any . . .' he began, then stopped. He eyed her coldly. 'Why do I have the impression that, as usual, you're being irreverent, Cassandra?'

'I can't imagine.' She sighed appreciatively as the waitress placed a plate on the low table in front of them. 'I love scones, don't you?'

'I thought you were on a diet.'

'I am.' Cassie dolloped clotted cream onto the side of her teaplate.

'Which is it this time?' said Robin nastily. 'The See How Much Jam You Can Crowd onto a Single Scone diet? The Pig Out on Clotted Cream diet?'

'Actually, it's the Once In A While A Girl Deserves a Break diet,' said Cassie. 'Especially formulated for self-employed bridge teachers who've lived off packets of pink powder for the past month.'

'You look good on it, I must say.'

Cassie flicked at the crumbs which clung to the side of her mouth. 'You too,' she said. 'Really well.'

'Well? *Moi*? You must need glasses.'

'But you do.'

'Don't toy with me, Cassandra. *All* my friends, without exception, tell me I've never looked more like a harried kipper in my entire life than I do at the moment.'

'They sound like really warm human beings.'

'Which leads me on to something I've been meaning to discuss with you. As you cannot fail to be aware, your best interests are, and always have been, my primary concern.'

Cassie cupped a hand round her ear. 'Is that the sound of expediency I hear, or just a car honking outside?'

Robin sighed in exaggerated fashion. 'If you wish to fling my generosity back in my face, that's your affair.'

'Which particular generosity are we talking about?'

'The latest in a long line of them.'

'And I don't have to tell you how grateful I am, and how much I appreciate everything you've done for me.'

'As you say, you don't have to.' Robin managed to sound both caustic and pathetic. 'But occasionally it would be quite pleasant if you did.'

'Dearest Robin. You are the sweetest, kindest . . . if it hadn't been for you, I probably wouldn't have survived the Vicarage years, you know that.'

It was true. The years of living with her cousins, after the death of her parents and grandmother, had been an emotional obstacle course which Cassie was still trying to complete. Without Robin's kindness . . . it was he who had insisted that she go to a good boarding school, which removed her for two-thirds of the year from the rigours of the Vicarage. It was he who had persuaded her to go and live in Honeysuckle Cottage, although she would never have chosen to move to the country. But after sharing a flat for far too long with Primula and Hyacinth, her odious twin cousins, teaching biology in a girls' school, eating the twins' idea of good nourishing food, she had been only too pleased to accept Robin's offer.

'It's my health,' he had said one evening, having taken her out for dinner at La Caprice. He raised an effetely pale wrist to his forehead.

'I've always understood it to be rude.'

'Once maybe, but alas, no longer. You see before you the mere ruins of the man I used to be. If I am to survive another year, I must have Mediterranean skies, heather-clad hills, dance and Provençal song and sunburnt mirth.'

'The doctor's prescribed this, has he?'

'More or less.'

'Does it come on the National Health or do you have private insurance?'

'Flora.' Robin raised his voice. 'And the country-green.'

'*Flora*? Don't tell me you've turned.'

'I speak metaphorically,' Robin had said hastily. 'Anyway, I've decided to move more or less permanently to France. O for a beaker full of the warm south,' he added.

'You just want to get pissed in the sunshine instead of the rain.'

'Coarsely but correctly put, Cassandra. I therefore wondered if you would like to take over my country cottage.'

'That tumbledown cowshed, do you mean?'

'I mean my delightful rural retreat set among the unspoilt Cotswold scenery, a haven of peace and tranquillity surrounded by all that's best of the English countryside.'

Cassie had opened her mouth to reply but, before she could do so, Robin had fixed her with an Ancient Mariner stare and continued. 'And before you come out with one of your cynical remarks, Cassandra, let me add that not only would there be no rent, it would also provide you with a home entirely free of twins.'

Magic words. She hadn't hesitated. 'I'll take it.'

Stopping only to purchase a pair of green wellies and a waxed jacket, Cassie had moved in as soon as she had served out her notice at the girls' school. Only occasionally did she regret the move, usually when the mud was particularly persistent, or when receiving telephone calls late at night from psychopaths, which made her uneasily aware of her isolation. She was a townie, born and brought up in a pub off the Holloway Road, yet that first morning after she moved into the cottage, she had to admit to a sense of something which it took her a while to recognise as peace. Later she had discovered that there were rats in the thatch, cowpats in the lane, spiders in the bath and slugs in the kitchen, but compromises having been made, pellets laid, nests destroyed (by someone else), she and the country had eventually established a working relationship.

Now pouring tea in the Randolph, she said carefully: 'I hope there's nothing wrong. You're not over here, for – for tests or anything, are you?'

'Nothing like that. I'm here to see my publishers about the next book, and visit the few people left in this world who matter to me. Like you.'

She squeezed his hand. How old was he now? It was not something she had ever considered. 'Robin,' she said. 'You're a star.'

'No, no.' Robin held up an unconvincing hand. 'I'm just a foolish old man still carrying the memory of your dear mother in my heart and with more money than I know what to do with.'

'Far be it from me to argue with you.'

'It's never stopped you before.' After a pause, which Cassie did not fill, Robin's mouth turned down. He said, piteously: 'Do you really think I'm old?'

'Of course I don't. You know as well as I do that you make Peter Pan look like an advanced case of senile dementia.'

Somewhere, bells sounded. Robin glanced at his watch. 'Oh, my Lord. I shall have to run. I'm supposed to be meeting someone at 5.15.'

The bill paid, the two of them headed towards the panelled passage which led to the hotel's reception area. 'It's been lovely to see you again, my dear,' Robin said. 'I'll ring you this evening. You can tell me what you've decided about house-sitting for me in France.'

'Yes.' Cassie stared at the dark-haired woman who sat reading a letter in the corner of one of the chintz-covered couches. Slithery plastic shopping bags from some of Oxford's more expensive boutiques sagged against the edge of the seating: visible was a fold of flowered dress, a pair of pretty sandals, a straw hat. Another bag held half a dozen books from Dillons: on the top lay *Sophie's World*, which Cassie had been meaning to buy herself. She crossed the room and looked down. 'Naomi?' she asked uncertainly.

The woman looked up. Seeing Cassie, her eyes filled with what seemed very like panic. She crushed the letter and thrust it into her pocket before pushing herself to the front of the sofa and pressing her hands down on the cushions, as though preparing to rise. Her face was unhealthily sallow and the skin beneath her eyes was the colour of coffee. Instead of responding to Cassie's greeting, she raised a hand to her face and stared warily about, like someone hoping very much not to be caught in such downmarket company.

'Are you all right?' Cassie asked, guiltily conscious of the fact that she had only visited Naomi once since she had returned home from the hospital nearly four weeks earlier.

Naomi shrank back into her corner. 'Fine, thank you.'

'How are you feeling?'

'Feeling?'

'After the operation, I mean.'

'Fine, thank you. Really well.'

She didn't look it. Cassie noted the plastic bags beside Naomi's chair. 'Come over to shop?' she asked idiotically.

'Something like that.'

She so clearly did not wish to get involved in a conversation that Cassie tried no further. 'Well, it's nice to see you looking so much better,' she said, and followed Robin out of the doors into Beaumont Street. Across the road, the Ashmolean was shrouded in plastic sheets and scaffolding. It could have been an artistic happening by Christo but was more likely to be builders. Standing on the pavement, she frowned. 'That was rather odd.'

'A friend of yours?' he said.

'More or less.' She took her godfather by the sleeve. 'It wasn't just my imagination, was it? She definitely wasn't thrilled to see me.'

'That's certainly the message I got.'

'I wonder why.'

'As I see it, there are two possibilities. Either she mistook you for an offensive body odour, or she's meeting a lover. I'd incline to the latter. You can usually tell. That shifty air is a dead giveaway.'

'A lover?' The possibility hadn't occurred to Cassie. But it seemed obvious now that Robin had pointed it out.

'I take it she's married.'

'Yes. But she's not the sort I'd have expected to go in for extra-curricular activities.'

40

'Is there a sort?'

'Perhaps not. But you know what I mean.'

As they turned to walk towards Worcester College, Cassie distinctly heard a laugh of the rafter-ringing variety. A familiar laugh. A boisterous laugh. One which could only have emanated from the barrel chest of Charlie Quartermain, master mason, human buffalo. Which meant he was uncomfortably close at hand. But where? Discreetly she looked back. Oh God, there he was, standing by the Martyrs' Memorial, in the act of flinging his arm around the grubby woollen shoulders of Professor Richardson. The professor staggered slightly and clutched at Charlie's arm for support. What on earth could two such different men possibly have in common? Perhaps Charlie had been in the pub when Richardson went in with Ian Butler, and had latched on to him in that endearing way of his. Telling tired anecdotes, making appalling jokes, laughing at them uproariously himself because no one else did.

Robin had stopped. 'Oh look,' he said, following her gaze. 'There's Polly Richardson. I believe we're both dining at the same High Table this evening. Who's he talking to.' He waved, then peered more closely. 'Isn't that your friend, Cassandra? Charlie Something? That rather nice fellow who—'

'Polly?' said Cassie quickly, hoping to deflect him. 'Yes, I've played bridge with him and his aunt several times.'

'No, the other one.'

Cassie tried to steer Robin onwards, but he had already attracted Richardson's attention and, in so doing, Charlie's. If there was one thing she was not ready to face this afternoon – or any other – it was Charlie Quartermain. 'Look,' she said. 'I really must get back. At this time of the day, the rush hour traffic starts building up and I've got masses of work to do. The new computer and I aren't on speaking terms yet.'

'Ah. Good thinking.'

'I'll be all right, if you want to go and join them.'

'Are you sure? In that case, I will. I haven't seen Polly for ages and I don't expect we'll get much chance to exchange news this evening.'

Kissingly, they brushed cheeks. Cassie gave her godfather an extra hard hug. 'Even if I don't always show it, you know how much I love you,' she said.

'Yes, my dear. I do.' He touched her face. 'Aren't you going to wait for your friend?'

'I don't think so. Once he starts talking it's difficult to stop him and I haven't got time to hang about.'

'Pity,' said Robin. 'I've always found him rather amusing.'

'On the single occasion you met him?'

'Single? Quite the contrary. Or didn't you know that—' But who or what Charlie Quartermain was this time Cassie did not find out, as a lorry paused beside them, engine throbbing. Behind her, a mighty bellow clove the petrol-fumed air. 'Cassie. Hey, Cassie. Hang about, darlin'. Got something to tell you.'

God, what a racket. His lungs must be the size of an aeroplane hangar. As Robin walked back towards the Martyrs' Memorial, she pretended not to hear Charlie's call. Plunging into the maelstrom of traffic like a traveller into hostile territory, she was immediately separated from him, first by a motorcyclist in futuristic garb and then by a bus. But as she hurried towards the spot where she had parked her car, it was not of Charlie she was thinking.

She could not rid herself of the remembrance of Naomi's face and her expression, not so much of surprise or even dismay, but of guilt.

♠ 4 ♠

Some kind of fracas was taking place in the lane. Cassie leaned out of her bedroom window and listened with some interest to the discussion between the driver of a large green van and a farmer standing with arms spread in front of a herd of cows. How Horatius kept the bridge. It was easy to pick up the gist of the conversation since, for the most part, it was conducted in hostile shouts. The driver had no intention of backing down the lane towards the road in order to allow the cows to pass; the farmer, a testy soul, was equally resolute in his determination to remain where he was until there was room for the cows to proceed. The cows swung their udders and chewed in a wet-lipped way.

Cassie's enjoyment of the scene was abruptly halted when she realised that in all probability the van contained a delivery of supplies for the bridge sundries business. If so, the delay in milking was down to her. There was no end to the indignities which a choleric farmer could inflict on his neighbours if he wished. She pulled on some clothes. Anxiety led her to give an extra hard yank to her belt so that it did up two holes tighter than last time she had worn it. The fact gave her no satisfaction. Scarcely able to breathe, she raced outside. A couple of cows were advancing up the short rutted entrance-way to her

shed, pausing to crunch down a clump of desiccated foxgloves
on their way. One had just lowered its head to a bush of
moulting roses which were clearly feeling the heat. She
whacked it on the nose as she went by.

'What seems to be the trouble?' she asked authoritatively,
though it was fairly obvious.

'Got a delivery to make,' the van driver said.

'And I've got cows to milk.'

'Name of . . .' The driver reached inside his cab and pulled
out a clipboard.

'Swann?' asked Cassie.

'No.'

'Sinclair? Natasha Sinclair?'

'Don't think so, luv.' He stared at her with what seemed
like an appreciative smile and she sucked in her gut even
more. It might not be PC, but you had to take it when you
found it, after all, and appreciation of one's personal charms
wasn't that frequent a commodity in these troubled times.
'Did you know there was a spider on your – um – shirt?' he
continued. 'A big one. Looks like one of them black widows,
actually.'

'Black widow?' she said, trying not to panic, remembering James Bond's reaction when he'd found one in his bed,
or was that a scorpion, not that it mattered one way or the
other since a bite from either would be equally lethal. 'But
they're poisonous!'

'I know.' The driver nodded. 'Ever see that James Bond
movie, the one where he—'

'Yes.' Through the open window of her bedroom she could
hear the telephone ringing.

'What about my cows?' said the farmer belligerently.

'Kurtz,' the delivery man said. 'Ivy Cottage.'

44

'That's back there.' The farmer jerked a thumb over his shoulder.

If the delivery was for Kathryn, it wasn't Cassie's responsibility. 'I'll leave you two to sort it out,' she said, and ran back to the house. Breathing heavily, she was in time to pick up the phone before it stopped ringing.

'Cassandra?'

'Yes,' she gasped, tugging at her belt with her other hand. She's always thought that breathing involved pulling air in through the mouth and directing it to the lungs via the throat. So how come having a constriction around the middle made it so difficult to inhale?

'John Harris here. I'm ringing from the Caledonia Hotel in Edinburgh.'

'In Scotland?' Stupid question, but she was trying to work out in advance why he was ringing her.

'Yes. I was hoping you'd do me a favour.'

A favour. Of course. She should have guessed. 'What is it?'

'I've been trying to get hold of my wife for the past couple of days, but she never seems to be home. I've left messages on the machine, but she hasn't rung me back. As you know, she's not in terrifically good physical shape, so I wouldn't have thought she'd be gallivanting about, not for this long, anyway.'

'Maybe she's taken advantage of your being away to go and stay with her parents.'

'Oh no. No question of that. None at all. She never sees them.' It sounded like yet another dysfunctional family. Perhaps that was the only kind there was. 'So I was wondering,' Harris continued, 'whether it would be a dreadful imposition to ask you to pop over and check that she's OK.'

It would, as it happened. And popping was hardly the word to use. The Harrises lived a good half-hour's drive away from

Honeysuckle Cottage and she already had three classes to give that afternoon, all in different parts of the county. On top of that, she had very much been hoping to get in an hour's lying in the garden before she set off. Surely there must be someone closer that John could ask. Closer emotionally, as well as geographically. 'Isn't there anyone else who could go?' she asked. 'It's a frightfully busy time for me.'

'The thing is, Naomi doesn't have many friends, for one reason and another, but—'

Like her sharp tongue, Cassie thought. Her air of imminent bad temper. Her inability to smile. Her paranoid sense of privacy.

'—but since you've been so kind, visiting her and so on, I thought you might not mind too much . . .'

Cassie didn't answer.

'I realise it's a lot to ask. I wouldn't bother you except I'm getting really worried that she might have fallen. Or even . . .' He broke off.

Alarmed, Cassie said: 'Even what?'

'Well, she was terribly depressed before I left. As you can imagine. The operation and everything. It was just unfortunate timing that the company's sales conference was timed for this week, when she's still recovering. I tried to get out of it, but with things the way they are, well, I really had no option but to be here. Can't afford to look slack.'

'What are you saying, John: that you think she might have—'

'—done something stupid,' Harris said. 'Yes, that's what I'm afraid of.'

'Wouldn't it be better to call the local police, in that case?'

'That seems a bit over the top, when she might only have been in the garden or something.'

46

'For two days?'

'Maybe I just keep missing her . . .' His tone made it clear that he did not believe this for a moment.

'OK, I'll go,' said Cassie. She knew she sounded grudging, but he couldn't have everything.

'That's wonderful. Look, just in case there's some difficulty about getting into the house, you'll find a spare key behind the little summerhouse, under the third rock down from the house. You can't miss it.'

Which meant that she almost certainly could.

'And I'll give you the number for disabling the burglar alarm,' John said. 'Has to be done within thirty seconds of entering the house or you'll have the local constabulary trying to feel your collar before you can say "break in".' Cassie would have liked to join in the laughter this occasioned him but somehow she didn't find it all that hilarious. She took down the combination and also the telephone number of his hotel in Edinburgh, promising to call him as soon as she could.

'I'm terribly grateful,' he said, several times. 'And awfully sorry to disturb you. I'm sure you've got better things to do.'

She didn't deny it. After all, anything she might have to do – and the hour in the garden would certainly include pouring herself a glass of white wine and reading Tim Gardiner's latest crime novel – was going to be better than creeping through the country roads behind a horsebox or a refrigerated lorry on its way to deliver lettuce to one of the local supermarkets.

In the lane, some sort of compromise had been reached. The farmer had opened the gate which led into the field opposite Honeysuckle Cottage and the cows were filing into it, looking about them, and moaning gently as their swollen udders knocked against their legs. The van driver had climbed back into his vehicle and was waiting for them to disperse. Cassie had a feeling that by the time he had delivered whatever package it was for Kathryn, the cows would be out in the lane again, meandering slowly towards their destination, with the driver seething behind them.

She tried calling Naomi's number. Perhaps John Harris had simply been unfortunate in missing his wife when he telephoned. There was no answer. After five rings, the answering machine kicked in. 'Hi, Naomi,' Cassie said, awkward as always when conversing with a plastic box, 'It's Cassie Swann. I'm going to drive out and see if you're all right, later this afternoon. If you come home before then, do give me a ring.'

By five o'clock, Cassie was feeling frazzled after three sessions of teaching bridge. The OAPs, thrilled to pieces to be old in the late 1990s rather than the 1930s, were always a delight to teach; the members of the other two groups had been either argumentative or stupid or, in several cases, both. The heat of the morning had given way to sweaty sub-tropical temperatures, although the sun was now hidden by cloud. The thought of driving to Naomi's house definitely did not appeal, but since she had promised John to do so, she would have to go. Part of her reluctance stemmed from the fact that the car had recently developed a plasticky rattle which emerged from the heating vents, as far as she could judge, whenever she turned a corner. Whether it was serious or simply a dead leaf which had got inside the works, she had no idea, though she had lifted the bonnet on a couple of occasions and stared blankly at the contents. All that mattered was whether it needing fixing or not, and, if it did, how much it was likely to cost. On her car radio, someone was insisting that big girls don't cry. 'Oh, believe me, they do,' Cassie said aloud, crashing her gears,

48

wondering how much that had taken off the value of the car. 'And here's one of 'em about to burst into tears right now.'

The only positive note lay in the fact that to drive to Naomi's house from Market Broughton would take her so near to her own home that she might as well stop there on the off-chance that Naomi had returned her message.

But she had not. Lifting the phone, Cassie wearily dialled the Harris's number again, just in case Naomi was at home but hadn't bothered to call her. This time, to her delight, the phone was lifted.

'Naomi!' she said. 'Cassie here. Thank goodness you're all right. Did you manage to get in touch with John yet? He's been trying to reach you.'

Naomi did not answer.

'Naomi?' Cassie said.

More silence. Then the phone was replaced. It was a probably a wrong number, but nonetheless, in the sweaty place at the top of Cassie's buttocks a shiver started and began looking for a spine to run up. She pressed the Redial button and saw Naomi's number appear in the display panel. So it had not been a wrong number. Quickly she cut the connection before the telephone could ring again at the other end. Was that creepy, or was she simply being melodramatic? The desire not to drive over to the Harris house had developed into a compelling urge. She dialled Kathryn Kurtz in Ivy Cottage to ask if she would come along on the ride, but there was no reply.

Darn it. Should she go over anyway? It was clear that, whatever Naomi was doing, at least she was alive. But she knew in her heart that she had no choice. It wasn't until she was negotiating the narrow lanes at the end of a convoy of cars held up by a caravan that Cassie admitted to herself that she was beginning to wonder what exactly she would find when she got to Bridge End. (Bridge End . . . was that a good name for their fledgling company, or did it have too apocalyptic a ring about it?) Naomi at the wrong end of an overdose was one thought which had occurred to her. Or swinging from a rope in the garage. Or lying with slit wrists in a bath full of blood.

The house, when she drove through the open gate and pulled up on the gravel drive, seemed as immaculate as on the previous occasions Cassie had been here. The Harrises had moved here not long ago from an attractive but poky cottage full of inglenooks and beams; Bridge End represented a considerable step up the housing ladder. The grass was a brilliant green and had recently been mown; clearly, no one here had heard that there was a ban on the use of hosepipes and sprinklers. Beside one of the rose beds stood a trug half-full of dead heads; she lifted it and saw that the grass beneath it was as green as the rest, indicating that it could not have stood there for very long. A spade was stuck in the soil of a bed in which flowering shrubs fountained gracefully over the edges of the lawn, filling the air with glorious scent. Shell-pink roses clambered over pergolas and ancient stone walls. A branch of the river ran along the bottom of the garden, edged thickly with yellow and purple flags. Rural peace. Rural beauty. Hard to imagine anyone staying depressed for long in such surroundings. But if a baby was what you wanted, buds and blossom were probably no substitute. All that fecundity might even make things worse.

The only indication of anything untoward was the two deep gouges in the gravel drive, as though someone had turned in a hurry and driven off fast, and an earthenware pot of geraniums lying on its side. She rang the front-door bell and stepped back to look up at the upper windows. There was no movement, no curtain twitching, nothing to indicate that anyone was at home.

50

She rang again, tried the handle and found the door locked, then peered in through the windows at the elegantly beamed drawing room. All seemed in order. The chintzes and silver, the glass and antique furniture were arranged as they had been whenever Cassie came here to play bridge.

She walked under a trelliswork arch towards the side door which led into the kitchen. That too was locked when she turned the handle. She trod the ankle-deep lawn to the summer-house, which was covered in rambles of honeysuckle and late-flowering clematis. Behind it, empty flowerpots were neatly stacked, together with a number of granite rocks. The third down from the house . . . She squeezed into the narrow space between it and the hedge, and turned over the rock. As Harris had said, there was a key there.

She let herself into the kitchen as noisily as she could. After all, if Naomi *was* at home, and had simply decided not to answer the door, she might be frightened stiff at the sound of someone entering the house. 'Naomi!' she shouted, but there was no reply. She stood for a moment. Other people's houses were always alien, however intimately known they were, however familiar the objects contained therein. It was the smells, Cassie decided, looking round her. Naomi's kitchen smelled of sink-cleaner and oranges and coffee, with an over-lay of furniture polish coming in through the hatch to the dining room. There was no indication, however, that anyone had eaten or drunk anything recently. The only sign of human occupation was a faint insinuation of cigarette smoke. Cassie stared into the slate-ledged larder, opened the dishwasher – it was empty – and then the refrigerator. Yoghurt, recently purchased, a punnet of strawberries, butter on a green dish, free-range eggs, sauces, jams, lite mayonnaise, some ham in an unopened plastic pack, a similar packet of smoked trout.

She pulled open the drawers, the top one holding cutlery, the ones below crammed with neatly rolled pieces of string, rolls of garbage bags, sandwich bags, tidy piles of folded plastic bags, including a couple of the ones Cassie had noticed beside Naomi's seat at the Randolph.

In the drawing room there were flowers arranged like something from one of the more classy magazines, several of which lay tidily arranged on the coffee table, alongside a pile of brand new hardcover books, a luxury which Cassie defined as the difference between rich and poor. The mushroom-coloured carpeting had so recently been hoovered that the lines from the machine's wheels were still visible, though there was a stain by one of the linen-covered couches, where something had been spilled and then inadequately wiped up. Blood, was it, or coffee? She did not investigate. There was no dust on the furniture. The glass front of the drinks cabinet gleamed. Depressed she might have been, but Naomi had still kept her house neat. When Cassie was feeling despondent, housework was always the first thing to go. Often it didn't even wait for despondency, it just went.

'Naomi,' she called again. 'Anyone there?'

Again, there was no answer.

Feeling unaccountably nervous, she pulled at the bolts on the front door, turned the various keys, unhooked the chain then flung the door wide. At least she'd be able to get out in a hurry, if necessary. She did not want to think further about why she might need to, reminding herself that, less than an hour earlier, Naomi must have been here, since she had lifted the telephone in answer to Cassie's call.

Or had she?

But if it had not been her, who else could it have been? An intruder? There was no sign of any break-in. Silver still stood on the sideboard in the dining room and on various surfaces in the other downstairs rooms; drawers were firmly shut. The television sat in a corner, and in the little room which John had clearly been using as a study, there was an up-to-date computer and a new-looking laser printer. These were the things that a burglar went for, but they had not been touched. And in any case, why should a burglar, interrupted by the telephone, bother to lift the receiver?

It occurred to her that Naomi, hearing her voice, had simply locked the house and left. Understandable. Cassie often had days when she didn't want to see anyone. There had been occasions when she had stood in the little passage between kitchen and sitting room, waiting for a caller to leave; one ignominious time when she had spent twenty minutes squatting under the table by the window, while the people outside peered in and told each other that they were sure she must be around since her car was there. There were moments when the last thing you wanted to be was sociable.

Feeling more cheerful, Cassie mounted the stairs. Here, too, all was in order. Beds made, bathrooms cleaned, signs of recent vacuuming. She lifted the lid of the dirty-linen basket which stood behind the door of the main bathroom, but it was empty except for underwear which unmistakably belonged to John, unless his wife had a penchant for size 42 scarlet boxer shorts with hedgehogs scattered across them. Snooping into someone else's life was not something she went in for very often, but while she was here, it seemed worth checking out the drawers in the bedroom. She started with the ones in Naomi's dressing-table and found them shame-makingly tidy, compared to the disorder of her own drawers. Sweaters, neatly folded. T-shirts, lurex leggings for aerobics or step classes. Cotton underwear, clean but used, each bra folded together with each boring pair of knickers. Talk about organised. But there was nothing to indicate whether Naomi was at home or had gone away. And, if the latter, nothing to give any clue at all as to where she might have gone. Cassie opened the built-in wardrobes, swishing a hand along the neat lines of blouses, skirts, dresses, suits. Filled bags contained evening wear; shoe-treed footwear was ranged tidily underneath.

Sweating with horror at the thought of what Naomi would have to say if she returned home to find Cassie up to the wrists in her underwear, Cassie pulled out some of the drawers in the tallboy. Lots of scarves, every one of them expensively tasteful. Packets of new tights. Bathing suits, both one-piece and bikini. A hair dryer. And, surprisingly, a number of other items of underwear, rather different from the first lot Cassie had found. Some of them were so new that the labels were still attached, all of them were cobwebby, diaphanous, flimsy. Which revealed nothing about Naomi herself except that she was well-off. And occasionally liked a change from her every-day undies. But who didn't?

Cassie looked around. Could she bear to open the drawers in the tables on either side of the bed? There was something deeply horrible about probing into such privacies – and the chances that Naomi had written a helpful memo to herself about where she was going or what she planned to do, and then shoved it into the bedside table were less than zero. Suppose she found evidence of John's and Naomi's sex lives? Condoms she could cope with, though given Naomi's longing for a child, that was unlikely. But spiky attachments for the male member? Rubber knickers? Vibrators? Snaps of either of them in weird positions or with a third or fourth party? And in the latter case, what if it was someone she knew? Someone she played bridge with, even? How could she ever sit across the baize cloth from them again without feeling deeply uneasy?

She marched across the thick pink carpet and snapped open the first drawer. Creams, mostly. Hand and body and eye and throat. Make-up remover. Cotton balls. Something medical in a tube. Half a bottle of pills dispensed by the chemist in Bellington. And, pushed against the back of the drawer, a photograph of a baby. Judging by the slit eyes and buttoned-up mouth, a brand new one. Wrapped in something white. A baby much pored-over, if the worn appearance of the photograph was anything to go by. Sad Naomi.

Cassie went round to the other side of the bed, John's side. Cotton buds, here. A gadget which might be used for the removal of blackheads. A paperback from the States called *How to Get Up and Going When You're Really Down and Out*. A folder of postcards of the kind sold in Port Said by Arab vendors: blondes, mostly, in the most outspoken of poses, often with added attractions like bananas or ice cream cones. Cassie could just imagine John in the pub: 'Local views, old man, and I'm not talking pyramids here, know what I mean?' But perhaps she was being sexist and this was Naomi's side of the bed, after all.

And the Pope's a protestant, right?

She gave one last look around. Apart from the evidence of the lifted telephone receiver, there was nothing to indicate that Naomi was at home. Or had been for a while. Equally, there was nothing to indicate that she was not. A quick look into the other upstairs rooms, including under the beds, a whip round the bathrooms to check there was nobody neck-deep in bloody water, and she was coming down the stairs, only too glad to have discharged whatever duty might have been involved.

The front door was still open. And standing in the hall was a young woman. At a first glance, Cassie put her around eighteen or nineteen. She had bleach-white hair cut punkily short. 501s. Caterpillars. A battered leather jacket. She looked up at Cassie and ran towards the bottom step, flinging out her arms.

'Mother!' she cried. 'At last!'

♣ 5 ♣

'It's so weird.' The girl stirred sugar into the mug of instant coffee which Cassie had, unwillingly, made in Naomi's pristine kitchen. She had been crying. Little balls of peach-coloured Kleenex lay on the table beside the mug. 'We made the arrangement on the telephone only a couple of days ago. I was to come here at six o'clock and have a drink, maybe have dinner, we'd get to know each other. She was – she was going to tell me everything.' She began to cry again. 'Why isn't she here? Do you think she can't bear to meet me after all?'

That's certainly how it looked. But Cassie did not feel she should say so. The fact that this girl – Lucy Benson – was (or claimed to be) the daughter Naomi had given up for adoption more than twenty years ago was shock enough. 'I'm sure there's some rational explanation,' she said, racking her brains for one.

'I can't tell you what it meant to me,' Lucy said. 'I've known for years, ever since I was a child, that I was adopted. Sometimes it was the only thing that . . .' She plucked at the gold chain round her neck. 'I mean, if I'd ever thought that I was related to . . .'

'To whom?'

Lucy didn't answer directly. She said: 'For quite a while, I'd really needed to know who my real parents – my biological parents – were, and why they gave me up for adoption and – and stuff like that, but I didn't want to upset my parents – the people who'd brought me up, that is. Her, at least. I wasn't particularly bothered about *him*. So I let it ride until I finished university. When you realise that you're finally about to get out there into the big wide world, you start to, you know, wonder about who and what you are.'

Cassie nodded encouragingly. Personally, she was still wondering.

'But I just faffed about, really. I suppose I was a bit afraid of what I might find. And then, out of the blue, just as I'd got in touch with one of the adoption societies to find out how I was supposed to get started doing something about it, my birth mother got in touch. Naomi. Just a few weeks ago.'

A few weeks? About the same time she must have reconciled herself to her drastic operation. Was Lucy the precipitating factor in her decision to go ahead with it?

'I see,' Cassie said. Although she was ready to be wary of this complete stranger, the more she looked at the girl, the more she could see the likeness to Naomi, despite the dyed hair, the unlined face, the mode of speech. She wondered whether, in the course of their telephone conversation, Naomi had spoken of her operation.

'It was such a coincidence,' Lucy continued. 'Don't you think so? Both of us, at the same time, deciding that after all this time, we really had to seek each other out? Though she did tell me she'd started looking for me some time back.' She scrubbed at her pinkened eyes. 'I just can't tell you what it meant, hearing her voice on the phone. She sounded really nice. Exactly what I would have wanted my mother to sound like. I was so excited about meeting her. So excited.' She got up and walked restlessly around the kitchen, as though the excitement needed the release of movement.

'I'm surprised she didn't want to meet you on neutral territory,' Cassie said.

The girl swung round. 'How do you mean, neutral?'

'Somewhere impersonal. In a restaurant or something.'

'You think she would have been ashamed of me?'

'Of course not. It's just, the first time . . .' Cassie shrugged. 'I'd have thought somewhere without significance to either of you would have—'

'But why?'

'Good question. I don't really know. I must be thinking of people who meet through dating agencies. Neutral ground gives you a chance to get away.'

'Dating agencies? What're you on about? Why should she want to get away from me? I'm her daughter.'

'Of course,' Cassie said. 'By the way, does John Harris know about any of this?'

'Jo . . .? Oh, her husband, you mean.' Lucy paused and thought it over. 'I don't think so.'

'I'm going to have to call him when I get home and say that there's still no sign of Naomi. Should I tell him about you?'

Again Lucy considered the question before answering. 'Perhaps it'd be better not to. My mother might prefer to be the one to tell him.' Her eyes lit up and she rested her hand on her hip, looking almost flirtatious. 'Could I ask you a favour?'

'Go ahead.'

'I'd love to see over the house. See where she lives. *How* she lives. Would you come round with me, just to, like, chaperone me? See that I don't nick her jewellery or knock over the Ming vase or something?'

'I don't know.' Cassie felt the same reluctance as she had

earlier. What would Naomi feel about it? 'Mightn't she want to show you herself?'

'But if she's not here . . . oh *please*,' Lucy said. 'I've waited so long for this. And it's not my fault if she's not here. Besides, you know as well as I do that if she was, she'd be delighted to.'

'I'm sure she would. But it's quite different having me do it. Besides, I'm not really a close friend of – of your mother's. I don't know the house at all.'

'You were upstairs when I arrived.'

'I know. But I'd been asked to check whether Naomi was here somewhere, maybe ill or having had an accident.' Cassie was certainly not going to disclose the darker thoughts which had crossed both her mind and Harris's. It occurred to her that she should have looked in the garage to see whether Naomi's car had gone.

'*Please*,' said Lucy.

It was difficult to refuse. Cassie tried to put herself in the girl's place. All keyed up to meet her real mother for the first time, arriving at the house to find what she assumes is the right woman, only to be told that not only is it someone else entirely, but the real – the *birth* – mother isn't even there. 'All right. But if Naomi shows up, you're to take the blame.'

'I promise.' Lucy tugged at Cassie's arm as though she were a five-year-old. 'Come *on*.'

Cassie, feeling presumptuous, led the way into the comfortable drawing room. She stood awkwardly while Lucy exclaimed, touching pieces of furniture with the tips of her fingers, picking up objects and holding them for a moment before carefully setting them back down in their place. 'Look at this!' she exclaimed, holding up a crystal egg against the window so that the early evening sun dazzled through it. 'It's all so lovely. Where I grew up wasn't like this at all. I mean, it was OK, but not . . . *rich*.'

Lucy's confiding air was beguiling: Cassie wondered how she would feel if such a young woman had walked into her own life and claimed, even demanded, kinship. She would like to have explored Lucy's background further, discovered more about her, but it would not be fair to take those confidences away from Naomi, wherever she was. 'Really?' she said, deliberately sounding as if she were not interested. 'Look, let's move on, shall we?'

They went into the dining room, the little utility room where Naomi did the laundry and kept flower vases and wellington boots, the small parlour where the monthly foursome played bridge. They climbed stairs and peered into the bedrooms. Lucy seemed overwhelmed. She stood beside the dressing table, fondling a cut-glass bottle half full of *Opium*. 'It's all so . . .' She looked round. 'Isn't it?'

'It certainly is.'

'Pristine – that's the word I'm looking for.'

Or unlived in. Depending on your point of view. Going round the house again, Cassie was gripped by a feeling of loss. This was a lovely house, yes. But it lacked animation. It could have been a picture in a Design for Today manual. There was no sense of people living here, piloting their way through the eddies and shoals of family interaction. If there had been storms, they were tight-lipped and contained, not full-blooded rows ending in passionate reconciliations. If there was appetite, it was dainty, not Rabelaisian. She tried to imagine Charlie Quartermain in these untouched rooms.

They returned finally to the kitchen. Cassie coughed, said: 'Look, I don't want to sound ungracious or anything, and I'm so very sorry that Naomi wasn't here, but I think I ought to leave the house the way I found it.'

'You want me to go.' Lucy's smile warmed her grey eyes. It emphasised even further her likeness to Naomi, despite the fact that Naomi seldom smiled. 'Of course. I absolutely understand.' Her face sagged. 'Do you think it's worth waiting for her any longer? I can sit in my car outside . . .'

Cassie said sympathetically: 'It's gone half past seven. And you arranged to meet her at six. Either some emergency's come up or she's decided she just can't face you after all this time. Perhaps she feels ashamed of letting you go. Or shy. Or something.'

But she knew it could not be an emergency. Naomi would have left a note for Lucy, knowing she was on her way here. Or even telephoned to cancel the appointment.

Tears began to spill again down Lucy's face. She stared wordlessly at Cassie. 'Why should she be ashamed? We already talked about it on the phone. She just doesn't want me in her life, that's what it is. She's taken a dislike to me. She hates me.'

'Now then.' Cassie caught the girl's arm as she swung towards the door. 'Whatever else is true, that is not. She wouldn't have looked for you in the first place, would she? And how could she hate you when she doesn't know you?'

'Once she'd contacted me she obviously decided she didn't like me.'

'Over the phone?'

'Why not?'

Cassie had no knowledge of boys but, from her time as a biology teacher in a girls' school, recognised what she was up against. 'Aren't you being a little melodramatic?'

'It's perfectly possible,' Lucy said, pouting. 'She obviously loathed the sound of me.'

'If she'd taken against you, she wouldn't have arranged for you to come here, would she?'

'She might just have been curious.'

'There has to be a reason why she's not here, and I'm sure that she'll get in touch with you the very minute she can. Now come on. I'll buy you a drink at the local pub, if you like, before we go our separate ways.'

'Cool.' Lucy brightened again. 'And you can tell me all about my mother. It'd be interesting to hear an outsider's opinion.'

'Yes.'

Or, much more likely, no. As Cassie drove to the pub, Lucy following in an old blue VW, she revised and edited her views on Naomi in order to present an acceptable version to Lucy. They found a table outside, overlooking fields which sloped away to the Chilterns, and Cassie talked warmly of Naomi's skills as a homemaker, her kindness to the nervous newcomer at their regular bridge four, her elegance, the generosity she had displayed a couple of years ago by inviting Cassie to stay free of charge at her house in Tuscany.

'Gosh,' Lucy said. 'What's it like?'

'I didn't go,' said Cassie. 'I didn't go because something else came up. But I was very grateful for the offer.'

The list of Naomi's qualities seemed meagre indeed, but Lucy appeared to be satisfied. 'I'd love to go to Italy,' she said. 'I wonder if she'd let me stay there.'

'I'm sure she would.'

'I'm due some time off at work,' explained Lucy. 'Once you get stuck into a job, it's so much more difficult to take time off.'

'What do you do, exactly?'

'I'm a drop-out made good. I did a year of maths at Leeds

University and then decided I wasn't cut out for the scholastic route so I applied to join an accountancy firm on a sort of apprentice scheme.'

'Which one?'

'Bancroft & Unwin.'

'I've heard of them.'

'I should think you have. They're one of the top London firms, with branches all over the southeast of England and offices in Hong Kong, New York, Rio – you name it.' Lucy laughed self-deprecatingly. 'Accountancy sounds dull, doesn't it? But it suits me. I've done really well in the four years I've been there.'

'Four years?' Cassie said, astonished. 'How old are you, exactly?'

'Nearly twenty-three.'

Which brought up a question which had been bothering Cassie. Did she really seem old enough to be the mother of a nearly twenty-three-year old? Don't ask: the look of stunned amazement on Lucy's face as Cassie introduced herself and explained that she was not Naomi Harris was probably answer enough. 'You don't look it,' she said.

'I know. I wear specs at work, just to add a bit of gravitas. Believe me, in a power suit and horn rims, I look much more elderly than I do today.'

'And you like the job?'

'Love it. I like to feel safe and you can't get much safer than my job, it seems to me.'

As she spoke, an image of dank wells flashed into Cassie's mind. To a casual glance, Lucy seemed like any young woman of her age – or did she? Having had to opportunity to study her a bit more closely, Cassie could see that there was something unformed about her, something embryonic, as though she had not yet fully embraced adulthood. And at the same time, it was clear that dark events crawled and slithered like worms behind the public façade she presented to the world. To know that you are adopted must be very unsettling, however well the matter is handled. Although Lucy was doing her best to maintain a bright sociability, Cassie could see that underneath the girl was distressed and nervous.

On impulse, she said: 'Look. I'm sure your mother will sort everything out with you as soon as she gets back home. Meantime, if you need anything, do get in touch.' She handed Lucy one of her business cards.

'Thank you.' Lucy read the printed rectangle with absorbed care. 'Thank you very much indeed.'

She didn't notice him until she was driving towards the exit from the parking lot behind the pub. He was standing on the far side of a white car – was it the same Peugeot? She couldn't be sure – so that only his head and shoulders were visible. Almost as if, this time, he were trying to conceal himself. How long had he been there? He must have followed them from Naomi's house – he must have. Which meant he had been waiting somewhere along the road for her to drive past, and then fallen in behind her. Oh God. What did he want? Why was he doing this? If Lucy had not been with her, she thought she might have pulled up and jumped out to challenge him. As it was, she didn't want to involve this vulnerable creature in her troubles. She looked across at the girl, who was tugging at her seat-belt, and then put her foot down hard on the accelerator. Too hard. It was only by wrenching at the steering wheel that she avoided hitting another car turning slowly in off the road.

John Harris was not in his room at the Hotel Caledonia the first time Cassie called, nor the second. It was nearly midnight when she finally reached him, by which time she was pretty fed up. It must have been audible in her voice because, as soon as he heard who it was, he started apologising.

'Sorry. Hope you haven't been trying me for ages. Some of my colleagues insisted that I join them for dinner. It was difficult to get away.'

'I went over to your house, as requested,' Cassie said stiffly. 'Naomi wasn't there.'

'Not there?' he echoed.

'Not her, nor her car.'

'Where on earth can she be?'

'I think you ought to telephone the police,' Cassie said sharply. 'Register her as a missing person.'

'That sounds a bit drastic. It's probably just bad timing. She's out when I call, she's in when I can't get to the phone – that sort of thing.'

'I think it's more than that. When I was there this afternoon, someone arrived who had a specific appointment to meet her at your house.'

'Who was it?'

'I don't know,' Cassie lied. She was not about to give away Naomi's secrets. 'The point is, the appointment was set up by Naomi only a couple of days before, but she wasn't there. And while I can believe that you might just keep missing her at home, I can't believe she would have gone out after arranging to meet someone.'

'I suppose she could just have taken off,' Harris said. 'She's been so depressed recently. Maybe she thought the hell with it, and went away somewhere for a few days, to be on her own.'

'Maybe she did. But I don't think she'd do so without at least having the courtesy to cancel this particular engagement.'

'If she's in the middle of some kind of mini-breakdown,

maybe she wouldn't have bothered.'

'I don't believe that. I really think you should contact the police.'

'And you don't know who it was, the person who'd come to see Naomi?'

'Absolutely no idea.' The only way to make a lie believable was to stick with it. 'I didn't ask.'

'I'll ring home now,' said Harris.

'I already did, before I telephoned you. There was still no answer.'

'I'll try again early in the morning.'

'And if there's no reply, you'll call the police?'

Harris sounded extremely reluctant. 'I really don't want to. It seems so over the top.'

'But you must be fairly worried about it yourself, or you wouldn't have asked me to drive over to the house to check things out.'

'I know, but—'

'You thought she might have slit her wrists or something, didn't you?'

'It had occurred to me. The depression and everything.'

'She doesn't appear to have done that. At least, not at home,' Cassie said brutally, and heard his sharp intake of breath. 'But suppose she's had an accident and is lying somewhere injured. Or the stress of the situation has made her lose her memory and she's wandering about not knowing where she is. These things do happen. The sooner the police are involved, the better for everyone.'

'All right. If she doesn't answer the phone in the morning, I'll call them. But they'll probably think I'm wasting their time.'

'I'm absolutely sure they won't.'

'Cassandra, would you mind awfully if I gave them your name as a contact? I'm supposed to be here until the end of the week, though obviously if anything . . . dreadful happened, I'd come back immediately.'

'I suppose so. But I have to say I'm not particularly keen.'

'I really appreciate it.'

Cassie, disgruntled, did not answer.

♦ 6 ♦

Over the next couple of days, Cassie continued to ring the Bridge End number. Waiting for a reply which never came, she had plenty of time to wonder why she was doing this, and how it was she'd allowed herself to get involved when she scarcely knew either of the Harrises, and didn't much like what little she did know. If she hadn't felt sorry for Naomi, knowing she had few friends, and gone to visit her in hospital, it would not have occurred to John Harris to call her in the first place, nor would she be wasting so much of her time on what appeared an increasingly fruitless exercise. It seemed obvious that Naomi had gone away somewhere and, in the confusion of the moment, had simply forgotten to let Lucy know. By now, the two women had probably been in touch and fixed up another appointment. And she herself was worrying needlessly.

She told herself that in future, any good she did, she would, as commanded in the Bible, do by stealth. Or not at all. As it was, she was now embroiled in someone else's domestic drama. Just what she wanted, when she already had a couple of perfectly good ones of her own to deal with.

Like, for instance, the reluctant Walsh. Detective Sergeant Paul Walsh, her policeman lover. The man with the beautiful mouth and the dark fleck in one of his hazel eyes. He'd gone back to his estranged wife once already, then said it wasn't working and that he wanted to come back to Cassie. Had even spoken of them having children together. Or, to be fair, she, in a moment of insanity, had spoken of it and he had not demurred. He had not been round to see her for weeks. So had he returned to his wife a second time, or what? On again, off again, like a bloody lighthouse, she thought crabbily, getting ready for bed. And what about Tim Gardiner, writer of indifferent detective fiction and all round cutie-pie? He hadn't called her for ages. Well, for at least a week. Maybe even ten days.

Why should she care what either of them felt about her?

Well, she did, that's all. The reason why was completely immaterial.

And there was her other drama. The stalker. If that's what he was. Thinking about him, she sympathised a little more with Harris's disinclination to involve the police in Naomi's absence from home. Suppose she told Paul Walsh – were she ever to speak to him again which, from where she was standing, seemed extremely unlikely – that a man was following her: he would demand specifics, time and date and number of occasions the subject was sighted, and when she'd supplied all that, he'd probably say that her imagination was in overdrive. She could hear him now:

'The man has a perfect right to walk the same streets as you do, Cassie. Shop in the same supermarket. Pay a visit to the same hospital. You've no real proof that he's following you at all.'

No real proof, agreed. Just a gut feeling. And if she insisted that she knew he was out to get her, that people didn't follow you in their cars or wait across the road when you went to pick up the Sunday papers, Walsh would shrug. He would say that until the man actually did something – uttered threats or attacked her – the police weren't able to act. Which was bloody marvellous when you thought about it. There was nothing they could do to stop him killing her, merely conduct a murder hunt when he did.

But he couldn't be planning to kill her, which was the ultimate nightmare. Because if he was, he'd have done it by now. Wouldn't he? Unless sadism came into it. First the thrill of the chase and the excitement of knowing that the victim was growing increasingly terrorised. Then the inexorable closing in, the final ambush, and then, at last, the move in for the kill. It was grotesque. But what other explanation was there? Or was he merely trying to scare her off? And if so, off *what*, exactly? It was all more than enough to keep her occupied, without the added hassle of Naomi's whereabouts.

The temperature continued to climb. With the passing days, the countryside grew more veldt-like. The radio reported further hosepipe bans, and spoke with gravity of the increasing risk of fire. As well as her private lessons, Cassie was preoccupied with the charity bridge tournament she was organising in the village hall at Moreton Lacey, in aid of the Bosnian refugees.

Because of the heat, she found it difficult to sleep at night. Waking from sweaty dozes, she worried about Naomi. Where she might be, who she might be with, what exactly was troubling her, other than simple post-operative trauma. The revelation that she had a daughter was startling enough. How long had Naomi been searching for her? Years? Or only from the moment they told her she must give up her long struggle to become pregnant?

Presumably Lucy had been born at a time when mothers who produced children out of wedlock were still condemned and their children discriminated against for faults which were not their own. Despite the current government's attempts to curry favour with the electorate by blaming all society's ills on young unmarried mothers, these were, at least on that score, more enlightened, more compassionate times. Who had the child's father been, and had Naomi kept in touch with him? It was easy to imagine Naomi's own doubts and fears about meeting Lucy for the first time; however much she had longed for a child – and that longing must later have been exacerbated a thousand times by the cruel knowledge that she had had one and had given it away – it was bound to be an awkward encounter, given the circumstances. Yet she had been more than ready to see Lucy, had invited her to her home, had obviously been prepared to welcome her. So what sudden panic had caused her to drive off without a word, either to Lucy or even to her husband, for she must have known John would have tried to get in touch with her while he was away.

On the third night after Harris's call, Cassie could not sleep at all. Her mind kept dwelling on details of her visit to Bridge End. The unmarked grass beneath the trug of dead rose heads, the racks of dresses, the boxer shorts in the dirty linen basket, the air in the rooms which, though stuffy, was not stale. Someone had been there until very recently and the logical inference was that it was Naomi herself. Cassie had never undergone an operation of any kind, beyond the removal of a wisdom tooth, so she had no means of guessing how she would feel under the stress of post-operative trauma. She had read many times that it could lead to depression, that it took time to recover emotionally, as well as physically, from major surgery. And a hysterectomy would have deeper psychological implications for a woman than, say, having an appendix out, or repairing a hernia. Particularly a woman who desired children.

But Naomi had found her lost child. She had something to live for after all. It did not seem reasonable to assume that she had driven off just before that child arrived for their first meeting in twenty something years.

And if it were not, then something must have happened. Cassie sat up in bed and reached for the switch of the lamp. Sweat prickled along her thighs and under her arms. Certainty swelled, as hard and smooth as an egg. Though seldom given to hunches or intuitions, she knew that something *bad* must have happened. She bit her lips, staring at the faint stir of the curtains in the breeze from the open window. Impossible to sleep. Impossible to read, even. Her skin vibrated with tension.

Mother. Daughter. Her own mother, Sarah, had died when Cassie was six. She had no complete remembrance of her, no scenes to replay, only fragments stored at the back of her mind. Bric-à-brac memories. A hand holding hers as they crossed a road. Floury fingers in a bowl the colour of envelopes. A voice, forgotten for the most part but returning sometimes at the edge of sleep or wakening: *They're changing guard at Buckingham Palace*. Bare brown feet on the Margate sands. A particular perfume.

It must have been the same for Naomi. Recollection distilled into nothing more than a baby's featherthin eyebrows, the roundness of a newborn head, the weight of vulnerability briefly in her arms. A creased photograph in a bedside drawer. And then, the voice on the telephone, her daughter, an adult now, all the years between gone, irrecoverable. Cassie stirred restlessly under the sheet. If Lucy had conveyed over the phone any of the undertones which Cassie had picked up, then Naomi must have felt culpable. Perhaps, as the time fixed for the meeting drew closer and closer, she had felt unable to take on the burden. Had gone outside and driven away, rather than come face to face with the daughter she did not know, rather than load herself down with blame.

Cassie could see her now, groomed and elegant – because she would certainly have wanted to look her best, would have wanted her daughter to be proud of this new-found mother – pacing the drawing room, thin hands clasping and unclasping, unable to keep still, glancing at the brass carriage clock, then at her watch. And then, at the last possible moment, realising this wouldn't work, that she could not assume the responsibility for Lucy's griefs. Walking out, closing and locking the front door behind her. Opening the garage door, backing onto the gravel drive, getting out to shut the garage before turning in a swirl of gravel, knocking over the pot of geraniums as she went, then heading down the lane to the main road. After that, where? Would she just drive, waiting for Lucy to give up waiting for her and go away? Would she head for some quiet hotel in Bibury or Burford? Or would she make for the city, for Oxford, where she could lose herself among the bookshops and quadrangles, the crowds and the traffic, until it was safe to come home again?

No. Cassie shook her head. It couldn't be that simple. If Naomi had been overcome by panic, she would not have wasted time in reclosing the garage doors. She would simply have taken off, it didn't matter where. Therefore she had to have left Bridge End in more leisurely, more calculated a fashion. Cassie tried to remember if there had been any indication of suitcases being packed. Discarded clothes-hangers lying on the bed, or shoes lined up to be taken along and then, because there was no room, left behind? Was there an absence of toothbrushes in the bathroom, spaces on the dressing table where a scent bottle might have stood? No sign of hasty departure had imprinted itself on her memory: the bedrooms had all looked neat, dusted, the drawers fully closed, the coverlets unrumpled by the weight of luggage.

She creaked downstairs to the kitchen and made herself a pot of tea. It was five-thirty in the morning, and the sky was lightening, the edge of the sun already incandescent behind the hedge at the end of the garden. From the kitchen window she could see the white cat lurking under the apple tree, on the lookout for unsuspecting early birds to start smugly catching worms. She was not going to go back to sleep now, so she might as well put the time to good use by getting in some technological practice. Carrying her mug, she opened the back door and walked across the dry grass to the headquarters of Bridge'n'Things. Or whatever. With most of their stock already delivered, it was becoming increasingly necessary that she and Natasha settle on a name for their company. Without a name, it could hardly be said to *be* a company. She unlocked the wooden door, admiring the solid look of it, the black metal keyplate, the handle shaped like an ancient British torc. The healthy scent of raffia matting met her nostrils as she walked in, and the smell of newness. On the desk in the office, the computer squatted beneath its plastic cover like a malevolent budgerigar.

The next time she checked her watch it was nearly twenty to nine. She'd been sitting there for almost three hours and could feel the stiffness in her thighs. She'd learned something. The mouse no longer felt alien under her fingers. She was growing more adept with the command keys. Even so, if it came to a knock-down drag-out between her and the computer, the machine was still going to win without even breaking into a sweat. Two hundred and fifty pounds for half a day's tuition was beginning to sound like a steal. Stretching, she switched

75

off and walked into brilliant sunshine. Although the outhouse conversion, built of thick stone, was cool, out in the garden it was already glutinously hot. Her conviction that something had happened to Naomi seemed ludicrous in the harsh summer light. She went upstairs and ran a bath, took off the T-shirt which substituted for a dressing gown and weighed herself.

Jesus! She stepped off the scales and then stepped on again. How was it possible that, after so much deprivation, her weight had not dropped by so much as a milligram? Sometimes she wondered if the water supply was deliberately being contaminated with calories. That was it: she would never eat again. In the bath she sang hymns to keep up her spirits. *Ye holy angels bright*. She liked the ones which sounded like songs. *Morning Has Broken*. Launching into *Guide Me, O Thou Great Redeemer*, she came to an abrupt halt. Bad mistake. With each *bread of heaven*, her stomach rumbled like a distant train.

In the bedroom, the telephone started ringing. Sloshing across the carpet, she picked up the receiver to hear Tim Gardiner's voice.

'Cassandra. Sorry to call so early . . .'

'That's all right: I was up anyway.' A small pool of bathwater gathered at her feet.

'. . . I wondered if you were free at lunchtime today.'

'What exactly did you have in mind?'

There was a pause. Then Gardiner said, cautiously: 'Lunch, of course. Why, what else might be on offer?'

'Nothing at all,' Cassie said. 'But just before you rang, I'd decided never to eat again.'

'That could be life-threatening.'

'I guess for you I might make an exception.'

'I'm flattered.'

'What time?'

76

'Midday? I'll come to your place, yes?'

'Lovely.'

Something to look forward to, after so many hours of worrying about the Stalker and the whereabouts of Naomi Harris.

She spent the morning organising her appointments. Next term, she had agreed to teach one session a week to the boys at St Christopher's, the prep school on the other side of Moreton Lacey. There were her usual evening classes, the Intermediate class augmented now by graduates from last year's Beginners. And she wanted to think very carefully about the plan put to her by Robin, the idea that she would use his house in France to hold a very upmarket Bridge Week – or even Fortnight. Intensive coaching from an expert, wonderful food, as much wine as the punters could handle, swimming pool, sun. 'What more could they want?' he had demanded.

'Sex?'

'You'll have to organise that yourself,' he'd said. 'I can't do everything.'

At precisely midday, there was a knock at the front door. Tim Gardiner stood outside, striped shirt tucked into chinos, brown eyes, as usual, lugubrious.

As they drove away from the cottage he said hollowly: 'Did you see the reviews last Sunday?'

'Reviews? Oh, of your latest book. No, I'm afraid I didn't.'

'One of the bastards said he thought it was "utterly unconvincing".'

Cassie rather agreed. 'Bad publicity is supposed to be better than no publicity, isn't it?'

'Halitosis is better than no breath at all. Doesn't mean it's much fun.'

SUSAN MOODY

By now, she was used to his gloomy ways. In spite of them, she liked him. His voice, his looks, the fact that he and she seemed to function on the same wavelength. So different from Quartermain. So far in their short relationship, he had done nothing at all to suggest that he was attracted to her. That didn't worry her. Were he to make a move, she thought her response would be positive.

He came back to the cottage for coffee, and outlined the plot of his next book. It was difficult for her to follow it clearly since he assumed that she was as well acquainted with the ongoing characters as he was, this assumption being based on the fact that he had presented her with signed copies of his entire oeuvre – ten books. The trouble was, she did not really like the way he wrote and, in addition, found his serial heroine a pain in the butt. She tried to look intelligent, though what she really wanted to do was curl up on her bed and catch some sleep to make up for what she had missed the previous night.

Just after he had left, the telephone rang. This time it was John Harris. Hearing his voice, she clenched shut her kindness glands. No way was she going to drive over to Bridge End again. Or anywhere else, for that matter. Not in this heat. Not on those roads.

'It's about Naomi,' he said, his voice scarcely audible.

'I can't hear you.'

He cleared his throat. 'Naomi. They've found her.'

'Oh, my God.' It sounded ominous. 'Where is she?'

'In Wales. They called me out of a meeting. She's – they found her – she was in the . . .'

They were cut off. In the what, for the love of Mike? Was this simply a blip in the phone system or had something so dreadful occurred that he had put down the receiver, unable to continue? Before she could give much thought to either

78

hypothesis, someone began knocking at the front door. She took the phone off the hook; if Harris rang back, she wanted to be free to talk to him.

The grey-suited man on the doorstep was familiar. 'It's Miss – um – Swann, isn't it?' he said.

'Inspector Mantripp.' There was an ache of apprehension inside her chest: her blood seemed hotter than was quite bearable, as though she had stepped under a shower of scalding water. Something *bad* . . . There was a woman officer with him, blonde, sensible-featured. 'You'd better come in.'

She stood aside and they walked past her down the stone-flagged hall towards the sitting room. In passing, the woman's dark skirt brushed against an unpleasant pot of fern which had been a gift from her cousin Rose. Half the fronds fell off and lay on the stone flags in mute admonishment.

'This is Detective Sergeant Valerie Lund,' Mantripp said, as they all stopped in the middle of the sitting room. Cassie nodded at the woman officer.

'You won't know what this is about,' Mantripp continued portentously. 'We were given your name by—'

'It's to do with Naomi Harris, isn't it?' Cassie sat down on the sofa. 'What's happened? Is she . . . dead?' As she spoke, she realised that subconsciously, this was what she had been waiting – and dreading – to hear.

Mantripp's face took on a suspicious expression. He fingered the knot of his tie, a mock club affair fashioned from a slippery man-made fibre. 'How would you know that?' he barked. 'We've released no details.'

'Then give me some.' Cassie felt immensely weary. Whatever he was going to say, she knew she would never be ready to hear it.

'Shall I make some tea, dear?' DS Lund said. Her air was

that of a grandmother, although she was some ten years younger than Cassie.

'Just say whatever it is you've come to tell me, for God's sake.'

Mantripp smoothed down the hair which sprang from his scalp like a crop of withered mustard and cress. He coughed. 'We were telephoned the other day by a Mr John Harris,' he said. 'Reporting a missing person. A Mrs Naomi Harris. His wife.'

'Figures,' Cassie said impatiently. If she'd ever met a man two coupons short of a pop-up toaster, Mantripp was it. How he'd ever risen to the level of Detective Inspector defied comprehension.

'You were acquainted with this Mrs Naomi Harris, I believe.'

'That's right.'

'A blonde lady, was she? What you might call on the plump side? Aged somewhere in her fifties?'

Relief began to seep into Cassie's foreboding. 'Nothing like that. You've got the wrong person. Naomi's thin and dark. She takes a lot of care of herself. And she's only in her early forties.'

'Oh dear,' Mantripp said. He shook his head. 'I'm sorry to hear that.'

'Why?'

'Because the lady you've just described—'

Behind him, the DS was frowning. It was obvious that this was not how she would have conducted the conversation. Now she broke in. 'We've had a report from Aberystwyth,' she said quickly. 'A fatal joyriding incident. A chase down the M40 at over a hundred miles per hour. There's a body. From your description . . . it sounds very much as though Mrs Harris might be involved.'

'Thank you, Val.' Mantripp seemed to put on weight in front of Cassie's very eyes. 'Exactly what I was about to say.' He took a blue plastic pen from his breast pocket and began clicking the ballpoint in and out.

Cassie stared at them both in disbelief. Naomi involved in joyriding? Stealing a car to go speeding down the motorways at 100 mph? And the body: who did that belong to? Had Naomi run someone down? She thought of the aborted call from John Harris. *They've found her* . . . What exactly did it mean?

Mantripp opened his mouth again, but Val forestalled him. 'Woman's touch, sir,' she remarked firmly. 'If you don't mind.' To Cassie, she said: 'It seems Mrs Harris's car was left in the station car park at Aberystwyth. Keys still in the ignition. An open invitation to steal it. And that's exactly what the little blighters did. Went haring out of the station, at God knows how many miles an hour. Nearly knocked down a woman waiting for a bus. Crashed into the side of some parked cars. Someone took down the number and reported it to the local coppers, who went after it. Ended up with a high-speed chase, the car went off the road on a bend, two of the kids dead, two others seriously injured. The local coppers took it in and . . . and . . .' She faltered, looked at Mantripp apologetically. She swallowed.

'This was yesterday morning,' Mantripp said. Click, click. 'The car stood in the police pound until today, when some bright spark thought to take a closer look at it. Popped the boot open and found . . .' He too came to a stop.

'Naomi,' Cassie said faintly. 'Is that what you're trying to say?'

'It turned out to be Mrs Harris's car, yes,' Mantripp said. 'And Mrs Harris herself was . . .'

The DS stood up and came to sit beside Cassie. 'She was in

the boot,' she said hoarsely. 'She'd been there for . . . for quite
some time . . . a few days at least . . . in this heat.'

'Dead, you mean?'

'It appears that she took her own life.'

Dear God. Cassie closed her eyes. 'How?'

'Pills. She apparently left a note for her husband. It was
quite peaceful, I should think.'

Cassie thought of Lucy's distress. 'When was this?'

'Um . . . hard to be specific, dear. Not given the conditions
prevailing. The heat and so on.' DS Lund looked over at
Mantripp and added, in an embarrassed mutter: 'Tissue
degeneration.'

Which was something Cassie was not prepared to consider.
'What was she doing in Aberystwyth?'

'Didn't want to be found too soon,' Mantripp said, clicking
his pen. The words *Bellington Bowling Club* ran in white
letters down its length.

'If it was suicide,' Val put in.

'Hence climbing into the boot,' continued Mantripp, moving his eyebrows into admonitory mode. 'In case anyone went
looking for her. Or gave notice that she'd disappeared – which,
of course, her husband did. People don't give a second glance
at a car in a car park. The attendant had taken note, of course,
but she'd paid for long-term parking, stuck the ticket on the
windscreen. No reason for him to suspect anything.'

'I don't know what to say. It's just too terrible. Pills, you
said?'

'A bottle of them. She'd thought it all out beforehand, that
much was obvious.'

'*If* it's a genuine suicide,' said Val Lund.

Mantripp ignored the DS's interruption. 'She'd got a pillow,
a big bottle of water to wash them down with, half a pint of

Johnny Black, a note saying she couldn't face life any longer. They always say that.' He clicked the pen one last time and then replaced it in his pocket.

'She'd just had invasive surgery,' Cassie said faintly. 'A hysterectomy, a few weeks ago. She was extremely depressed about it all.'

'No wonder.' Val patted Cassie's hand. 'She was young for that. Bound to be upset. Any children?'

'No. At least . . .' It was too complicated to explain. 'No.'

'Anyway,' said Mantripp. 'They ran the plates through the DVLC at Swansea and came up with her name. Called us, as the local police. We already had her on our files as reported missing, plus your name. Which is why we're here now.'

'You've informed Mr Harris, of course.' Superfluous question. Of course they had, which was why he'd rung her.

'He's on his way home right now.'

'I can't understand why she'd drive all the way to Wales, though. Why not – if she was going to – do it at home? Her husband was away. She'd have been alone.' Except of course, there was Lucy's visit. And she might have guessed that John would contact someone if the telephone went unanswered for too long.

'Neighbours,' said Mantripp vaguely. 'People dropping by. Wanting to read the electricity meter. Or the gas. You never know. It wasn't just a cry for help – she was obviously determined to go through with it.'

'I feel really bad about this,' Cassie said. 'Really dreadful.'

'It wasn't your fault,' soothed the DS. 'I'm sure that as a friend, you did everything you could.'

'But I didn't,' said Cassie. Tears came into her eyes. 'That's precisely what I didn't do.'

'You shouldn't blame yourself.'

'She must have been so terribly unhappy.' The words choked Cassie. She wished she had liked Naomi more. Perhaps if she had, none of this would have happened. It was not her responsibility and yet she felt accountable. Someone was going to have to tell Lucy, too. The girl had never even met Naomi, and now she never would. The cruelty of it made the tears finally fall.

Dimly she heard Mantripp say: 'Better have that tea now, Val.' And was aware of the DS getting up and banging about in the kitchen for a while before reappearing carrying a tray with three filled mugs on it.

'I've sugared it,' she said, handing Cassie one of them. 'Go on, dear, do you good. By the way, did you realise your receiver was off the hook? I put it back, hope that was all right.'

Cassie loathed sweet tea. Nonetheless she sipped at it, not wanting to be impolite. Horrible. She gulped quickly and set it down half-empty. 'When does Mr Harris get back?' she asked.

'We've asked him to contact us as soon as he reaches his home.'

'He'll probably be in touch with you too, dear,' said the DS. 'Seeing as you've been involved.'

'Yes. I expect he will. And the bod – Mrs Harris, where is she?'

'Still in Wales. He'll have to identify her for them there before it can be brought back here.'

Oh, John, Cassie thought. Please please don't ask me to come with you. *Please*. She stood up. 'Is there anything else I can tell you?'

'You've already confirmed that Mrs Harris was depressed,' said Mantripp.

'Definitely.'

'Did she ever talk to you about taking her own life?'

'No. But we weren't exactly on those kinds of terms.'

'Right.' Mantripp, too, rose to his feet. 'Then I don't think there's much else at the moment.'

The two officers headed for the front door. DS Lund turned on the doorstep and said softly: 'I'm sorry, dear. The news must have come as a bit of a shock for you.'

'Yes,' Cassie said. 'Even though I was half expecting something like this, it has.'

As she shut the door behind them, the phone began once more to shrill. She knew it would be John Harris.

♥ 7 ♥

Turning her car into Back Lane, she saw a brand new, top of the range BMW outside her house. Because it completely blocked the roadway, she was forced to park behind it, which she did with a certain amount of irritation. She walked up the drive towards her shed-cum-garage, and round the back of the cottage, but there was no sign of anyone around. Standing beside the back door, however, was a bottle of claret which she could tell just from looking at it was expensive, and four dozen creamy-yellow roses wrapped in silver paper. That clinched it. It had to be Charlie. A dozen roses might have indicated Paul Walsh; four dozen was a sure sign of the kind of excess to which Quartermain was so prone. Where was he? Possessed of a considerable amount of bulk, he was not the sort who might inadvertently be concealed by the pear tree halfway down the garden. And then, as she pondered the question of his whereabouts, a mighty laugh split the country quiet. Even softened by a distance of three hundred yards or so, it was still loud enough to cause panic among the flock of starlings in the field over the hedge so that they thrummed into the air, squawking, their spotted feathers glistening like the bodies of weightlifters as they turned under the sun before resuming their original position.

Charlie was down at Ivy Cottage with Kathryn. Charlie would unquestionably call in to see her before driving away in his fancy car – partly because he would be unable to move it until she had moved hers. So she might as well forestall him by walking down to Kathryn's place. At the same time, she could ask him if he knew anyone who might be able to tutor her in the intricacies of the computer. He always knew someone.

She found them in the garden, enjoying the end of the afternoon sunshine. They were laughing, both of them, Kathryn with her Disney-cute face screwed up like a crumpled paper sack, Charlie with head thrown back and tonsils exposed, as indeed was the fact that he had failed to pay regular visits to the dentist as a child. At the sight of the two of them so comfortable together, Cassie was aware of her face wrinkling like a dried apricot. She felt left out. Cross and edgy.

Before she could offer herself the slightest of theories as to why this might be so, Charlie caught sight of her and had lumbered to his feet. 'Ullo, darlin',' he roared. He took her arm and led her tenderly towards the garden bench on which he had been sitting, though she tried to shake him off.

'Oh, Charlie,' Kathryn said, still laughing at his last sally, wiping her eyes with the back of her hand. 'You're a real hoot, you know that?'

'Yer,' said Charlie. 'Go down a treat at the Ferret & Filofax, I do.'

His hand was still on Cassie's arm and she removed it with a greater show of fastidiousness than was necessary.

'Uh-oh,' Kathryn said, raising her eyebrows. 'Did a black cloud just cross the sun or what? Suddenly I'm shivering.' She and Charlie started giggling like a pair of kindergartners.

'How droll,' said Cassie.

'What's up, girl?' Charlie said.

'Nothing, Charles, is up.' This did not seem the time or place to inform them that she had just returned from Bellington, where she had been, at John Harris's request, arranging the details of Naomi's cremation, set for later in the week, if the police were ready to release the body by then.

'Here, have a glass of this plonk and you'll feel better,' he said. His wink was grotesque. 'Trust Dr Quartermain.'

'Thank you.' Cassie felt as sour as milk left out in the sun. She sipped in ladylike fashion at the wine and was astonished at how good it was.

'Plonk? Oh, sure.' Kathryn displayed a bucktoothed grin. 'It's only a 1983 St Emilion.'

'They'd run out of the new stuff,' Quartermain said.

'Why exactly are you here, Charlie?' The question sounded so ungracious that Cassie immediately felt ashamed. She added hastily: 'I mean, did you come for something special or—'

'You could say that.' Quartermain leered repulsively. 'Only she wasn't at home, was she? So I decided I'd have to make do with something a bit less special and came down here. No offence, darlin',' he said to Kathryn.

'None taken, Charlie, I promise.'

Cassie breathed heavily. 'Are you two pissed?'

'He's thinking of buying property round here,' Kathryn said. 'Go on, Charlie, tell her.'

'Right. Got me eye on the Old Dower House at Frith,' said Charlie.

'Frith?' screeched Cassie.

'Yer.'

'You're thinking of *buying* it?'

'That's the general idea. I made them an offer which they thought they could refuse, until I stuck the dead horse in their bed, and now they've accepted it.'

'But Frith's only—' Cassie broke off. She'd been going to say that Frith was less than a mile away from Honeysuckle Cottage. She was going to say that he had no right to invade her territory, that she didn't want him practically camped on her doorstep, that she hated the idea of running into him as she shopped in the supermarket or dropped into the pub for a drink.

Quartermain moving to Frith: did this constitute invasion of privacy? Or even sexual harassment? Was he about to take on the role of the local squire, dressing in loud tweeds, carrying a shooting stick and patronising the locals? What a prospect. With an effort, she choked down her resentment. 'Why,' she said, trying to smile, 'would you want to move out here?'

He gave her a look shrewd enough to make it clear that he knew what she had been thinking. 'Believe me, darlin', it's not because I fancy playing the Lord of the Manor. As you've probably noticed, I'm essentially a man of the people, fashioned from common clay.' He sucked horribly on a hollow tooth. 'And there's plenty'll tell you my clay is particularly common.'

'Nonsense, Charlie,' said Kathryn. She looked at Cassie. 'Anyway, that's not the real reason he's moving out this way.'

'What is?'

'Well . . .' Charlie moved his massive shoulders in a shrug, '. . . for starters, the area appeals. Nice neighbours, know what I mean?'

All too clearly. Spots of rust appeared on the iron in Cassie's soul. It was going to be at least as bad as she feared. She'd never be able to get away from him. Incubus . . . the word floated into her head. Or albatross, hanging round her neck and her life, never to be shaken off.

'On top of that, it's a nice bit of property,' explained Charlie.

'Be a good investment, according to my accountant. They're flogging off some cottages with it. I thought I could do 'em up and let 'em out for a socking great rent to visiting Yanks or some of them brainboxes from the University wanting temporary accommodation, like young Kath here.'

'The Old Dower House?' Cassie said. 'Isn't that the beautiful Queen Anne house on the edge of the town?'

''S right, girl.'

Charlie, living in that house? She knew it by sight: as well as having sale boards outside, it had been featured in local papers for some months, and she'd even seen an advertisement in the Property for Sale pages of *Country Life*, last time she was at the hairdressers. If she remembered rightly, the asking price had been something unbelievable in the region of—

'He's rich.' Kathryn, who possessed the American unabashedness about money, had been following her train of thought.

'Dunno about that,' said Charlie, trying to organise his large features into modesty.

'Oh, you *are*.' Kathryn glanced at Cassie with the triumph of a marriage broker about to clinch a match with the country's most eligible bachelor. 'Very rich.'

'Let's just say I can afford to buy wine with corks in.' Charlie glanced without surprise at his empty glass. 'Not bad tipple, eh? Shall we finish it up?'

'You bet.' Kathryn held her glass under the neck of the bottle.

'Not for me, thanks.' Try as she might, Cassie could not prevent herself from sounding at her most repressive. She felt like the Wicked Fairy, determined to wreck the festivities. 'I don't want to break things up but I'm afraid some of us have to work for a living. Charles, your car is blocking the lane and

I'm blocking you. Perhaps you'd just knock at the door when you're ready to leave, so we can rearrange the cars.'

'Hang about, girl.' Charlie dashed the contents of his glass down his throat and rose to his feet. 'I'll walk down the lane with you.'

'How sweet,' said Kathryn, disingenuously and laughed when Cassie scowled.

'Are those beautiful roses from you?' Cassie said, as they left.

'That's right, darlin'.'

'Thank you very much. And for the bottle of wine.'

'Thought you might want to celebrate having the place to yourself again,' Charlie said. 'Them workmen've been hanging round the place for months.'

'Yes.' She was surprised that he should have remembered.

'Peace at last, eh?'

'More or less.' She had a sudden urge to unburden herself. To throw herself on his broad chest and let him take over responsibility for her worries. The way Gran used to. And before her, Dad. Handsome Harry Swann. Charlie'd see the Stalker off, for a start. Confronted by Quartermain's bulk, he'd head for the hills on the first train out of town. And Naomi. If she told him how guilty she felt about Naomi's death, Charlie would comfort her, she knew. Tell her what she had repeatedly tried to tell herself: that it was not her fault. But if she did look to him for emotional aid, she would be committed in some way. And once committed to Charlie, there could be no going back.

She wrenched her face into a frozen smile. Behind his big head lay a panorama of sheep-dotted slopes, full-leafed woods and calm sky. A square church tower of pale stone lurked among the distant trees. Despite the drought, Queen Anne's Lace thronged the ditches on either side of the lane and elder bushes hung over the mossy stones of the walls. The cuckoo was still burping. Beautiful.

Every prospect pleases and only Charlie's vile . . but that was unfair. He was not vile at all. He was kind and generous. He was highly successful, both professionally and – not that it mattered a damn – financially. As an expert stonemason, specialising in restoration work, he was sought after by half the churches and cathedrals in Europe. He adored – or professed to adore – Cassandra Swann. Why could she not be sweeter to him than she was? Why was she always filled with resentment when she heard his voice? Why did he bring out her worst side, the Vicarage side, the side moulded by Aunt Polly?

Fear was the key. Deep in the recesses of a heart which she suspected was much less stony than she would like, she was terrified that one day she was going to wake up and find herself locked into a nightmare. Charlie's shaggy head would be lying on the pillow beside hers. His giant dressing gown would be hanging on the back of her bedroom door. His toothbrush – assuming he used one – would be standing next to hers in the mug on the bathroom shelf. If she was feeling really depressed, this nightmare extended to a vision of herself finding that there was a gold ring on her wedding finger. A ring with a message carved inside. *To my darling wife, Cassandra, from your devoted husband, Charlie Q*. Something like that. Or possibly even schmaltzier: *To my Smoochikins from her devoted Chazzwazz*. That sort of thing.

Panic washed through the lower half of her stomach. 'Charlie,' she said quickly, before it could completely engulf her. 'I know you've got a lot of contacts in different fields.'

'What you after, girl?'

'A computer whizz-kid. Someone who's got time to help me get to grips with the Apple Mac we've just installed in the office but who won't charge the earth.'

'I know just the bloke.'

'Really?'

'Gotta mate with a computer whizz-kid shop.' He grinned lopsidedly as, despite herself, she laughed. ''Ere, that must be a first.'

'What must?'

'You laughing at one of my jokes.'

She did not look at him. 'Do you think your friend'd have time to fit me in?'

'You betcha, baby.'

'What does he do? Who is he?'

Charlie smirked. 'Who d'you think? Me, of course.'

'You?' Cassie attempted to hide her dismay.

'They don't call me MacQuartermain for nothing.'

Why hadn't it occurred to her that, among his other gifts, Charlie would be a technological expert? 'Charlie,' she began. 'I really don't think . . .' She felt like someone knocking a kid's ice-cream cone into the sandpit. But it was best to be cruel to be kind, right? To wield the surgeon's knife.

'Wouldn't charge you a penny, either,' he said, oblivious to her inner struggle. 'All I'd want in exchange for one-on-one tutoring would be a touch of the old TLC now and then. Bit of a snog, maybe a quick feel, hand up your—'

'Stop right there,' she snapped. The surgeon's knife suddenly seemed a pleasure to wield. 'I thought I'd made it clear long ago that I would rather eat rat-poison sandwiches than—'

'Whatever you say, girl.' His big face was suddenly serious.

She stopped, white dust settling on her feet from the dry lane. 'Look, Charlie, I've never pretended, have I? Never tried to show you my good side? Never given you the slightest encouragement?'

'Not once.'

'So why do you persist in – you know – *courting* me?'

'Love is blind.'

'Then get yourself a guide-dog, Charlie.'

'I'm not worried about it . . .'

'You bloody well ought to be.'

'. . . because I know it'll happen one day.'

'What will?'

'You and me. Playing hide the salami.' He grinned again and stuck out a blobby tongue which he waggled lasciviously about.

'For God's sake,' she shrilled. 'Can't you get it into your head that it won't? Never. Ever. *Ever*.'

'Might as well give in now, darlin',' he said as she marched towards her car and wrenched open the door. 'You're only delaying the inevitable.'

'Absolutely no way,' she shouted fiercely, as she turned the key in the ignition and slammed the car into gear. 'No. *No!*'

So why, as Quartermain backed his car further along the lane until she had room to turn into the grassy patch in front of her shed, as she got out and locked the car doors, as she went round to the back door and unlocked it and carried in the wine and roses, as she cut two inches off their stems before dumping them in a vase up to their necks in water and poured herself a large neat whisky, did she feel so terrible? Why did she dread that he might be right?

By the time she had swallowed the whisky she was feeling more secure. So Quartermain was a doubt-free zone. And he might be able to manipulate her – OK: *was* able to manipulate her – over some things. But nobody got manipulated into marriage. You'd have to be a mindless idiot to find yourself walking down the aisle towards a groom you couldn't stand. Wouldn't you? Even if the doormat was ankle deep in bills and the car was a write-off, the bailiffs were moving in and the bank was foreclosing, nobody could be that desperate.

Christ, how she hoped she was right.

When the telephone rang, she picked it up gingerly, half-expecting to hear Charlie raucously suggesting that he come round and give her a lesson on the computer.

It was Lucy. Griefstricken. Sobbing. Howling, open-mouthed, down the phone. Her pain was so palpably desperate that tears came into Cassie's own eyes. 'Don't,' she said. 'Oh Lucy . . .'

'I . . . I . . .' Lucy choked. 'I read about it. She's . . . Oh, *God* . . .'

'You could come here,' said Cassie. Then stopped short. What was she saying? She *never* invited people to stay: her solitude was too precious. She swallowed. 'Come and stay with me for a while, if you'd like.'

A pause. Gulping. Sniffs. 'Can I? You really mean it?'

'Of course.'

'Only for a couple of days. I've taken a b-bit of time off work but I have to be back next M-monday.'

'As long as you want.'

'I won't . . . won't be much of . . . of a guest.'

'That's all right. I'm a pretty lousy hostess.'

'I'll drive up. Shouldn't take me . . .' Her voice wavered into a wail.

'Whenever you get here.' Cassie gave her brisk directions, knowing from her teaching days that briskness in the face of grief arouses the dislike of the griever to such an extent that it temporarily dams the tears.

As soon as she had finished with Lucy, she called Paul Walsh. He did not sound pleased to hear from her, but by now she had learned that he did not like mixing business with pleasure. Though whether she constituted pleasure seemed, at the moment, to be a moot point.

'It's about this . . . alleged suicide,' she said, speaking briskly so that he would know she wasn't about to burst into recrimination. 'Mrs Naomi Harris?'

'What about her?' he said, voice guarded.

'What's the official verdict, if you can tell me? I mean, *is* it suicide?'

'Why do you want to know?'

'Paul, honestly . . .' She tried to keep exasperation out of it. In Tim Gardiner's books, when Pandora Quest (oh, please . . .), his sleuthette, rang up her policeman lover, he was (in her own phrase), always there for her, giving out the privileged information without a qualm, dishing the dirt. Just as well because, without his help, she'd never solve the murders. But when Cassandra Swann, concerned citizen, rang up the man who was in love with her (or had been, once) for data to which she ought, simply as a member of the public, to have access, he acted like she had an Irish accent and wanted a detailed schedule of the heir to the throne's travel plans.

'Well, why?'

'Because she was a friend of mine. Because her husband gave my name to the police when he first reported her missing. Because I have a grieving relative of hers to cope with. What does it matter why? Isn't it enough that I bloody well want to know?'

'Keep your hair on,' Walsh said coldly.

'So?'

'At the present moment, we're keeping an open mind.'

'In other words, you're not convinced it was suicide.'

'In other words, we haven't yet reached a conclusion either way.'

'When will a conclusion be reached?'

'When the investigations are complete.'

'According to Mantripp, it was open and shut.'

'Mantripp is a wanker.'

'An opinion not based, I hope, on personal observation.'

He didn't answer.

Pain filled her. Recognition of love gone cold. Longing for it not to be so. 'Paul . . .'

'I'm sorry I haven't been in touch,' he said rapidly. 'I'll come by and see you very soon. I . . . I miss you, Cassie.'

'And I you, Paul.'

The ache in her chest did not subside. She carried it with her about the house as she dealt with domestic mundanities. Laundry. Loo clean. Hoover. She even sprayed the mirrors in the bedrooms and rubbed them back to brightness with paper towels. Anything rather than acknowledge what she should have accepted weeks ago. Her love affair with Paul Walsh was almost certainly toast.

'Suicide.' Lucy said. Every now and then, she gave a shuddering sob, but at least the tears had stopped falling. She had wept on first arriving at Honeysuckle Cottage, moving into Cassie's arms so naturally that Cassie had found herself patting and soothing as though she were calming her own child, instead of a grown woman. Now, she set her jaw and repeated the words. 'I've got to face the fact that rather than meet me, her own daughter, she killed herself.'

'Nonsense.' They were seated on either side of the kitchen table, eating the lasagne that Cassie had prepared and drinking Charlie's bottle of wine. It was much too good for such a dish, but Cassie knew that he wouldn't mind. 'There's no reason why it has anything at all to do with you. You have absolutely no way of knowing what the pressures on her might have been.'

'She didn't seem to be stressed when we arranged my visit.'

'You're old enough to know that people fake it all the time. We all pretend to be something we're not: richer, nicer, healthier, happier.'

'If she didn't want to see me, why didn't she say so?'

'I'm sure she wanted to see you.'

'Then why kill herself?'

'*If* that's what she did.'

'How do you mean?'

'They aren't entirely convinced about it, apparently.'

'You mean . . . they think – the police – that it was *murder*? Not suicide?'

'They haven't drawn a definite conclusion.'

Dabbing at her eyes, Lucy sat up straight, her mouth grim. 'If it turns out to be murder, I know who did it.'

'Do you?'

'Him, of course. Her husband.'

'We still don't know exactly how she died.'

'If they decide she was killed, we've got to see that man is brought to justice.'

'They'll deal with all that. They always look at the husband first.'

'But suppose they don't?'

'We'll handle that problem when we come to it. *If* we come to it.'

'When will they make up their minds, do you think?' said Lucy. 'It's best to be prepared. We shan't want to lose any time.'

Wineglass in hand, Cassie leaned back in her chair, shaking her head. 'Lucy, I can understand why you don't want to accept that your mother committed suicide. But aren't you a trifle ready to condemn what might be an innocent man?' She could not forget how reluctant John Harris had been to contact the police about his missing wife, and the way he kept on stressing how depressed Naomi was. Had he been preparing her to confirm it if the police should start asking awkward questions?

'*If* he's innocent. She told me, when we were talking over the phone, that he was trying to kill her.'

'She said the same thing to me, once. I put it down to the fact that she was still pumped full of drugs and painkillers. Did she explain why she thought John wanted her out of the way?'

'Oh yes. She was very clear about it. It's to do with money. First of all, she was planning to change her will.'

'How on earth do you know that?'

'She told me.'

'Change it from what to what?'

'It was one of those everything-left-to-the-surviving-partner-until-death things. What do they call it – a life interest?'

'Where does it go after that?'

'Dunno. But when I came back into her life, she said she was going to leave half of everything to me. I don't know if she managed to change it before . . . before . . . I hope not, because I don't want her money. But if she told her husband about it, he wouldn't have been thrilled, would he?'

'I was under the impression that he didn't know about you.'

'Perhaps he doesn't. Or perhaps that's part of his plan, to pretend that he didn't know of my moth— of Naomi's intentions.' Lucy wadded tissues into her eyesockets again. 'But I bet he was doing everything in his power to stop her. She's the rich one, you see. She inherited stuff from her grandmother. His business has been going down the tubes for quite a while, and with the recession lasting so long, he hasn't been able to dig himself out. Plus the fact that the house is in her name, not his.'

'I don't believe this.' Nonetheless, Cassie remembered that John himself had told her about the house. Remembered, too, his anger as he said that Naomi was all right, not a care in the world. 'Anyway, he was miles away, up in Edinburgh when it happened. As near as they can establish.'

'That's what he says.'

'He was at a meeting. There'll be people who can vouch for him. Hotel staff. His colleagues. Other people.'

'Alibis can be broken.'

'Oh, Lucy.' Cassie took the girl's hand. 'You've got to accept the fact that, in all probability, she killed herself in a fit of a depression.'

'I don't want to.'

'You may have to, Lucy.'

Lucy began to weep again. 'We had so many things planned. She'd always wanted to see the Grand Canyon and the Australian outback, Ayers Rock and stuff like that. We were going to go right round the world, see India and Africa, visit Europe. I was telling her all about India because I spent four months there in my gap year, between leaving school and going to Leeds.' She looked at Cassie shyly. 'We had lots of telephone conversations, you see. Trying to build a relationship before we actually met. It was her idea. I wanted to rush in, see what she looked like and what sort of a person she was. But she thought it would be better to take it slowly. I realised she was right. We got on so well, laughed at the same things, liked the same things, had the same kind of viewpoint. It was . . . it was really wonderful. Except that we didn't know that bastard was going to murder her before we actually got together.'

Cassie could only guess at the strength of the girl's desire to believe that Naomi had not killed herself. But whatever she said, the police weren't idiots. Technology was the name of the game these days, and if there were suspicious circumstances, they were likely to be alert to them. Whatever Lucy chose to think, it was much more than probable that Naomi had killed herself. Lucy just did not want to accept it.

Would I? thought Cassie. If the situations were reversed, wouldn't I want to postulate almost any theory I could dream up, however improbable, rather than come to terms with the fact that the mother I'd searched for over the years hadn't changed, that the woman who hadn't wanted me as a baby still didn't want me now I was grown up?

Briefly, she wondered if the phone calls between the two of them had ever taken place. Or if they had, whether Lucy had imbued them with what she wanted to hear rather than what was really being said. Was it believable that Naomi was going to travel to India with this new-found daughter of hers? At some point in their lives, all children indulge in fantasies about their parents: these aren't my real mother and father, I'm actually the child of a nobleman/Cabinet Minister/film star who, for reasons of duty/national security/career, is unable to raise me himself but sooner or later will acknowledge my birthright and take me away from all this to the life I was truly born to lead. Funny how nobody ever fantasised that they were the child of an arsonist or a garbage collector. Bankers were OK as fantasy parents; bank clerks were definitely not.

'Or,' said Cassie gently, 'that she would find that for one reason or another, she couldn't go on. Reasons which had absolutely nothing to do with you.'

Tears dropped onto Lucy's clasped hands as she bent her head over her lap. She said nothing.

♠ 8 ♠

The lavender bush whirred and hummed like a clockwork toy as bees clambered among the drying heads. The scent was almost overpoweringly sweet. In the distance, a harvester chugged faintly, bringing in the sheaves. Pears hung plump and golden in the tree at the end of the garden. On the patio, a thrush slammed a snail against the bricks. Swallows zoomed overhead.

Seated on the wooden bench by the pear tree, Cassic heard a powerful motorbike turn into Back Lane to crunch and pop along the gritty unmade road. Outside Honeysuckle Cottage, it roared in a couple of brief and unnecessary revs before shutting down. Footsteps stamped up the path. Someone lifted the brass knocker and let it fall once against its underplate. Cassie groaned. So much for the rural idyll. She heaved out of her deckchair and went reluctantly around the side of the house. 'Yes?'

The person slouched against the door jamb wore gold earrings, leathers and one of those heavily highlighted Lion King hairdos.

'Cassandra Swann?'

'Yes.'

'I'd like to talk to you.'

'What about?'

'Naomi Harris. Would that be OK?'

'Who are you?'

'Let me in and I'll explain.'

He seemed harmless enough. Early thirties, handsome in a florid, TV host way. He had very round eyes and the kind of weatherbeaten complexion usually found on ski-instructors or long-distance yachtsmen. A helmet sat under his arm like a spare head. 'All right,' she grudged. He bent to pick up the briefcase leaning against his long legs and followed her round to the open back door and into the kitchen.

She poured him a coffee and pointed at the chair opposite hers. 'Sit down and tell me what you want.'

'Thanks.' He held the mug in both hands and frowned, considering where best to start. Finding a logical point, he looked up and said: 'First of all, I should introduce myself. I'm Philip Mansfield.' He waited an expectant beat.

'Bells aren't ringing. Should I have heard of you?'

'That depends how much Naomi told you.'

'Well, we weren't exactly bosom bud—'

'She and I met about twelve months ago, playing bridge at a charity tournament in Oxford,' continued Philip. 'We bumped into each other several times after that, mostly playing bridge. I invited her out for dinner one evening. One thing led to another.' He rubbed at the side of his face as though embarrassed.

Why was he telling her all this? 'How do you mean?'

'We got it together. You know. Bonked. Became lovers. Whatever.'

'You and *Naomi*?'

Mansfield bristled defensively. 'What's so surprising?'

'But you must be at least—'

104

'So there's an age gap. What difference does ten years make, once you're past twenty-five?'

'None at all,' Cassie said hastily. 'I just find it difficult to believe that Naomi was involved with someone else.'

And yet . . . even as she spoke, Cassie remembered the neat bedroom drawers, the unspectacular bras and knickers and, unexpected, the cache of expensive froth: silk and lace, designer labels, all new. Wasn't that what women did when they had a love affair? Rushed out and purchased the sexy stuff which husbands didn't warrant, partly because husbands were no longer interested, which was usually the reason for taking a lover in the first place. Nor could she forget her uncomfortable encounter in the Randolph Hotel, and Robin's assertion that Naomi was obviously meeting a lover.

'Why? Her marriage was a sham, had been for years. And she was a very attractive woman.'

If you liked thin and nervy, if you were turned on by worry lines. 'I suppose she was. I always thought of her as very controlled,' Cassie said.

'What's control got to do with it?'

'Love affairs are messy,' said Cassie, thinking of Walsh. Thinking, too, of Tim Gardiner – not that there was anything remotely messy about him. At least, not yet.

'Are they?'

Cassie was surprised that he hadn't already found that out. But perhaps he was still at the age when love was relatively straightforward. It seemed so long ago since she had been twenty-five – twenty-*any*thing – that she could scarcely remember. 'I take it you're not married yourself,' she said.

'I'm not. I've knocked around a bit, had girlfriends and that, but it was never serious. Naomi's the first woman I've ever really fallen for.' He bit down hard on his lip but not before

Cassie had seen it tremble. 'What about yourself? Got a feller, have you?'

The simple truth was that she didn't know whether she had or not. 'Yes, thank you,' she said, primly.

'You know all about it, then. I mean, you read about love. You see it in the movies, hear about it all the time. But you don't have a clue what it means until it happens to you.' Again the shake in the voice, the quivered lip.

'I'm really sorry.'

His eyes watered. 'Not as sorry as I am. She was planning to – we were going to . . .' He breathed in deeply through his nose, trying to force the tears back to where they came from. 'We were going to move in together. I saw her at the beginning of last week and she was going to go home and tell her husband for once and for all that their marriage was over.'

'And instead, she drove to Wales and killed herself.'

'In the paper I read that the official verdict at the inquest was suicide. That's why I came to see you. Because I don't buy it.'

'What do you think I can do about it?'

He gazed at her with eyes that were as clear as a kitten's. 'You were her best friend,' he said.

'That isn't exactly—' began Cassie. Dammit, why did people persist in believing that she and Naomi were close to each other?

Philip wasn't listening. 'She often told me about you—'

'There's nothing to tell. I hardly knew—'

'—and I'm sure you'll be as determined as I am to see that justice is done. Because I know that Naomi Harris did not kill herself. She couldn't have done. She had too much to live for.'

'What happened, then?'

'It's obvious, isn't it? Her husband murdered her.'

Cassie groaned. Another one. 'And made it look like suicide?'

'Spot on.'

'His motive being?'

'To stop her leaving him.'

'Why would he want her to stay if the marriage was over?'

'Money. He didn't have any – whatever he'd had in the first place was gone, and he was heavily committed, even though Naomi contributed to the household expenses. If she kicked him onto the street, he was going to be a bit desperate. Not that she'd have deserted him, or let him starve. She was very loyal. She often used to say that it wasn't that they hated each other, simply that their marriage had sort of fizzled out.'

'If she was going to see he was all right, why would he want to kill the goose which laid the golden eggs?'

'Greed. He wanted the lot, not just whatever she was prepared to give him.'

'But he only gets a life interest, doesn't he? Which means he can't spend it in any meaningful sense of the word. It reverts to someone else once he's dead.'

'Anything's more than he's got at the moment. That's why he's been trying to kill her over the past few months.'

'You mean . . . all those accidents,' said Cassie, her eyes round.

'Except they weren't.' Philip banged his coffee mug down on the table. 'She was getting more and more terrified of him. Especially after he pushed her down the stairs one night. He wanted to make it *look* like an accident, you see. He'd have got away with it easy if he said she'd got up in the night and fallen. No problem. The poor girl'd been on tranks for quite a while. It would have been easy, if she'd died then, or the time he tried to drown her, for him to make people believe that she was a bit woozy or whatever. But unfortunately for him, it wasn't as simple as he'd hoped.'

It sounded to Cassie more like the ravings of an extremely neurotic, not to say depressive, woman, than a true version of events. Yet at the same time, it all hung together in a horribly persuasive fashion. John Harris himself had told her that he had money worries. And there was her own difficulty in believing that Naomi would choose to kill herself just as her lost daughter returned to her. Philip Mansfield's story only added to the conviction that she had not been in the least suicidal – that, on the contrary, she had a whole new life to take up. But whether John Harris was responsible – *if* she should prove to have been murdered – was quite another question.

'What do you want me to do about it?' she said.

'You were good friends.'

'We were *no*—'

'I thought you might know something about the last few days of her life which would convince the police to reopen the case. Because I don't believe the verdict.'

'They're not stupid,' Cassie said, as she had already said to Lucy. 'They're not just going to take your word for it. They'd demand compelling evidence to back up your suspicions.'

'That's the point, isn't it? If Harris murdered her, he'd have planned it all down to the very last detail, in order to make it look like suicide.'

'Did you know he was up in Edinburgh when they found her?'

'So he says. Supposed to be at some sales conference, wasn't he?'

'Not supposed to be. He *was*. The police checked it all out.'

Mansfield leaned down and felt around inside the briefcase which stood against the table leg. He pulled out a blue cardboard wallet-file and slapped it down on the table top. Something about his manner reminded her of an attractive bank robber she had met inside the prison a couple of years ago. Was it the earnest expression? The hair? 'It's all in here,' he said, eyes round and marble-shiny. 'The police told us that it was difficult to pinpoint precisely when she died because of – because of the weather conditions. I'll just bet that if we looked into it, there'd be periods of time when he can't prove where he was. And anyway, how long does it take to get from Edinburgh to here? He could drive overnight and no one would be the wiser.'

'Naomi's car was found in Wales. Scotland to the Cotswolds to Aberystwyth and then back to Scotland – that's a lot of driving.'

'He could have flown down. He wouldn't need a passport. He could have used a false name. Got her to meet him at Heathrow, driven on from there, killed her and left her in the station car park then got on a train back to London. Then out to Heathrow again and he'd have been back in Edinburgh before anyone even realised he'd gone.'

'How do you think he killed her?'

He set his mouth and stared at the kitchen wall behind Cassie's head. After a moment, he said: 'I think he would have given her something to drink which was already laced with the pills she was supposed to have taken and then, when she was too dopey to resist him or to realise what was happening, somehow persuaded her to take enough more to kill her. Maybe that's when he got her to write the note – do we know what it said?'

What had Mantripp said? 'The police told me. *I can't go on.* Something like that. *I can't face life any more.* We can ask them.'

'Or Harris himself.'

'Would he tell us?'

'If he has no reason to believe that he's a suspect, why wouldn't he? With an official verdict of suicide, he thinks he's perfectly safe. And perhaps he is.' Mansfield unzipped one of the pockets on his leather jumpsuit and took out a pen. 'As you say, we've got absolutely no proof against him. Nothing beyond a gut feeling. But I know we can find it, if we look hard enough.'

'Mmm.' Cassie was less convinced. Quite apart from anything else, Harris was so much the obvious suspect that the police would have gone through his alibi backwards, frontwards and sideways.

'I've already been through the schedules and timetables. It was perfectly possible for him to fly down to Heathrow, get Naomi to meet him, drive with her to Wales and then get back to Edinburgh, all within a half-day.'

'What did he tell Naomi? That his conference finished early?'

'He wouldn't have had to. He's been planning this for a while. He could easily have said he didn't need to stay any longer and was coming home early. Or he . . .' He picked up his coffee mug and swirled the contents around inside it. '. . . I got hold of a copy of the police report.'

'How?'

Mansfield tapped the side of his nose. 'You don't think I'm going to reveal my sources, do you? Did you know there were golf clubs in the back of Naomi's car when they picked it up in Wales?'

'I hadn't heard that.'

'She didn't fucking play golf.' His face registered bleak bereavement. He sighed. 'I rang up all the local golf courses, private and municipal, just to make sure. She wasn't a member of any of them.'

'So?'

'Don't you see? That could have been his excuse.'

'I'm lagging behind here a bit,' Cassie said.

'He rings up from Scotland,' said Philip. 'He says something like: "I say, darling, some of the chaps want to play a round or two tomorrow. Can't imagine why I didn't pack my clubs, place like Scotland, famous courses, hah hah hah. If I popped down on the shuttle, would you meet me, darling?" And of course, she agrees.'

He was never going to be asked to step in for Roger Moore, but he had exactly caught John Harris's intonation and abbreviated manner of speaking. 'Ever met Naomi's husband?' Cassie said.

'No. Why?'

'You sound very like him, that's why.'

'They're all the same, aren't they?' said Mansfield scornfully. 'Clones. Ghastly middle-class twerps from minor public schools. Silly voices, silly faces, I'm-all-right-Jack mentality, brains of a fruit-fly.'

'Some of my best friends are from minor public schools.'

'You know I'm right. See one, you needn't bother to look at the rest.'

'Thanks for the socio-economic rundown. So – where were we?'

'Golf clubs. But it doesn't matter what the excuse was. He arrives down here, she meets him, he gets her to drink something and slips her some knockout drops.'

'Which he just happens to have with him?'

'I told you. He'd been planning this for ages.'

'Wouldn't she have been suspicious if he stopped the car and tried to force her to drink doctored whisky?'

'You've got no imagination, Ms Swann. There are hundreds

111

of ways he could have done it, depending on the time he arrived down here. Stopped at a pub or had a cuppa in a café. Or even asked her to bring a thermos with her. I don't know how he did it, but it wouldn't have been difficult. And when she started getting sleepy, he would have got her to take a whole lot more of the pills.'

'How?'

'Does it matter?' Mansfield was getting increasingly wired. The lower edge of his right eye stuttered. His thick blond eyebrows were pulled together across the bridge of his nose; his teeth were clenched together.

'Yes, of course it does. If you're going to present the police with a serious alternative to suicide, then you've got to have answers – or acceptable hypotheses, at the very least – to any question they come up with. And I should point out that nothing you've said so far, beyond the timetabling, is anything but a guess.'

'OK. He overpowered her, poured pills down her throat, held her nose and added water. Or he reminded her that she was due to take her medication and, when she was woozy enough, did it again. And then again. Or he just fed her more of the doctored drink he'd brought with him until she was docile enough to do as he told her. Thinking about it, the middle one's the best because they would need to find pills in her body when they autopsied her.'

'Boy, you've really gone into this, haven't you?'

'I loved her, Ms Swann,' he said pathetically. 'And he took her away from me. The way I look at it, he's ruined my life. Do you think I'm going to let him get away with that?'

'I'd believe in all this a lot more if you could convince me that John Harris wasn't in Edinburgh at the time he said he was,' she said. 'Especially when the police, who've checked it, think he was. Otherwise, you're just indulging in wishful thinking.'

Manfield's jawline hardened. For a moment he stared at the dregs in his coffee mug. 'I can understand why you're reluctant to face the truth,' he said.

'But the police have decided it was a suicide.'

'They're wrong. That's all I can say. They're completely wrong.'

Cassie did not want to be involved in any of this. Yet Naomi herself seemed to have genuinely believed that her husband was trying to kill her. What's more, if Mansfield was right about the timetables, it was certainly possible to make the journey down from Edinburgh and back in a relatively short time. Reluctant though she was to accept it, murder made a lot more sense than suicide.

Before she could say so, he thrust his face towards her. His mouth was determined. 'Have you ever thought about rotten flesh, Ms Swann? What it looks like? Or smells like?'

'Not very often.'

'I read up on the process of decomposition. I wanted to know what would have happened to Naomi's body. The temperature must have been way over 120° inside that car boot, which would have speeded things up quite a bit. The bacteria would have begun working on her within hours. She'd have gone off quite quickly, the way meat does if you leave it out for too long.'

'I don't want to hear about it.'

'As she decayed, she'd have turned red or green or black. She'd have gradually filled up with bacterial gas, so her body would have been straining against her clothes like a barrage balloon. Her skin would have gone shiny and stretched until it split. The meat would have begun sliding away from the bones, turning to mush. Her eyes would have bulged, and her tongue pushed out between her teeth.' He demonstrated. 'By then her lips would have—'

'I take your point,' she said loudly.

'Blood would have been forced through her nose and ears by the pressure of the gases. The contents of her stomach would have come out of her mouth. She'd have already shit herself when she died, but pressure would have forced more faeces from her anus. There'd have been flies laying eggs on her. In the heat, they'd have turned into maggots very quickly. Great heaving clumps of them, white and shiny, crawling all over her . . .'

'*Stop* it!' Cassie put her hands over her ears but he merely raised his voice.

'. . . Feeding off her flesh. They'd probably have got down to the bone in places, before they found her. She have looked like—'

'Shut up!' shouted Cassie. 'That's enough.'

'And the smell,' he said. 'That terrible, gagging smell of rotten meat. Can you imagine it? I can't. People who've experienced it say it is literally indescribable. How Naomi would have hated anyone to see her like that when she always took such care to look good.'

Cassie stood up. 'I do not need to know this.'

'No,' he said simply. 'Neither did I. The more I heard, the less I wanted to know. The one thing I'm sure of is that she deserved better than that. But then she had a rough deal most of her life. Did you know that she was sexually abused for years by her stepfather?'

'All *right*,' said Cassie. 'I'll help you.'

'Thank you.' Mansfield pushed back his chair. 'I knew you would.'

'If – *if* – you're right, and John Harris *did* murder his wife, how would we set about proving it?'

He moved the wallet file about then squared it between his fingers. 'I've drawn up a plan of action. We know it's feasible for him to have got down here from Scotland and murdered her. Now we've got to check his timetable, his alibi. We've got to see Naomi's solicitor. Take a copy of the so-called suicide note to a handwriting expert, get an opinion on whether she really wrote it.'

'Hard to see how someone, however doped up, would have written a suicide note when she wasn't contemplating suicide. Especially if the person trying to make her write it was some-one she had already accused several times of wanting her dead.'

'It's one of the many things to be looked into. We'll also have to find out if there were any witnesses when the car arrived at Aberystwyth station.'

'Won't the police have already done this?'

'Probably. We'll do it again. See if the facts can support a different conclusion.'

'This is going to cost time and money.'

'No problem. If it means nailing the son of a bitch, I can find both.'

'You're rich and idle, are you?'

'Since I run my own computer business, I can take what time I want.'

'A computer business?'

'Yeah. Near Chipping Camden.'

'Are you talking software, or does that mean you know about computers themselves?'

'Software, mostly, but I could hardly write programmes if I didn't know something about the hardware. Why do you ask?'

Cassie wondered if the look on her face bore any resemblance to that of a nun whose cell has just been visited by an angel. 'Because I've recently got involved with a new machine and so far, friendly is not how I'd describe the relationship between us.'

'What make?'

When she told him, he shrugged. 'Simple. You shouldn't have any problem.'

'I bet that's what Orpheus said when people asked him how to play the lute.'

'I'll have a look at it for you. But first . . .' He tapped the blue file. 'I want to get on with this. Seeing the solicitors seems to be something you could do.'

Bribery. Pure and simple. 'Who were her solicitors?' Cassie asked.

'Symons, Ambler. Based in Oxford, but covering the whole of the Cotswolds.'

'I know them. I sometimes play bridge with one of the partners – Graham Blacklaws. He works at the Market Broughton branch.'

'Great. That's where Naomi went.'

'Even if Graham's the one who handled her affairs, it's not going to help much. He can't break the client-confidentiality code.'

'But all we need is a nod and wink, isn't it? You could ask him whether Naomi recently came to see him about changing her will. We're all going to know the contents of her will very shortly, anyway, so it won't be giving much away for him to tell you that much.'

'I hope you're right.'

'While you do that, I check out the Scotland end.'

'The police believed John Harris when he said he was there

116

all week. Won't they have looked into it? They always suspect the husband in these cases.'

'The police!' Mansfield said, his voice heavy with contempt. 'You can't trust them further than you can throw them. And everybody knows they're all bent as paperclips.'

'*I* don't know that.'

'That's because you're not black or a lesbian or some other disadvantaged minority.'

'I'm a woman. That's pretty disadvantaged.'

'But you're also posh.'

'I grew up in a pub off the Holloway Road in London.'

'In their eyes you're posh. You've got the right accent. You're OK. If you want to know what the filth are really like, you should be out on the streets. You'd soon lose this image of kindly PC Plod, the universal friend.'

'You don't look like someone who spends much time on the streets.'

'Not now, maybe. But I've slept rough. And I've got friends who still do. The legacy of Thatcher's Britain.'

'You sound quite middle-class to me,' Cassie said mildly.

'That doesn't mean I'm safe. The middle classes are beleaguered these days, just like everybody else. Even that murdering sod, John Harris – the recession's certainly hit him. Not that I feel the slightest sympathy for him, don't get me wrong.'

'You don't know for sure that he killed Naomi. Or even that she was murdered.'

He ignored the statement. Getting gracefully to his feet, he pushed back his heavy hair. 'Well, now we've got things sorted, why don't you show me your computer?'

♣ 9 ♣

Whichever way you cut it, Graham Blacklaws was a nerd.
There was no denying the fact, even if anyone cared enough to
try. He stood hesitating in the doorway of the pub restaurant,
his gold-rimmed glasses catching the light, nerdishness writ
large in every angle of his body. Navy-blue suit, striped shirt
with stiff detachable collar, rosebud in his lapel: you'd have
picked him out as a solicitor without even hesitating. And a
bachelor. Almost certainly a virgin.

Although Cassie had played bridge with him from time to
time, she knew him mainly because he had carried out various
pieces of legal work for Robin connected with the conversion
of the outhouses at Honeysuckle Cottage into business
premises. Graham, thirty-five next birthday, worried about
losing his hair and still lived with his mother, Bitsy. There is a
school of theory which states that a never-married man over
thirty who lives with his mother must be gay. Whatever
Graham's sexual orientation, nobody knew what it was. Least
of all Graham.

The time was one-fifteen. Cassie wondered where he had
been yesterday: she knew his routine seldom varied, that at
precisely twelve-fifty-five he opened the door of his office
(*rattle, squeak*) and walked past his assistant's desk,

('*Lunchtime, Anthea . . .*') down the creaking stairs (*thump, thump, plod*) to the ground floor, out into Market Square and across it to push open (*fumble, shove*) the restaurant door of the Two Magpies ('*Mmm: something smells good today*'). She knew this because Anthea had been in the same Weight Watchers group as Cassie. Anthea had spoken compellingly of her desire to scream on occasion.

Catching sight of her across a room which possessed all the charm of a bowling alley, he blinked and waved. 'Cassie! What a surprise to see you here. Mind if I join you?'

'I was just leaving.' Cassie bustled a bit, to indicate imminent departure.

'You've got time for another coffee, haven't you?' His voice trilled richly. For a number of years he had been a stalwart of the tenor section of the Bellington Choral Society.

She made a show of being reluctant. 'I shouldn't really . . .'

This was the second day in a row that she had showed up here at lunchtime in the hope of accidentally running into him. Not exactly an ordeal. The Two Magpies might be short on atmosphere but it was extremely long on grub. Yesterday she had forced herself to get through freshly-baked walnut bread, poached salmon with home-made hollandaise sauce and tiny new potatoes, and strawberries in a chocolate basket. Today it was a pigeon-breast salad in a hazelnut-oil-and-raspberry-vinegar dressing, garnished with Stilton and avocado, followed by a ravishing crème brulée.

Graham removed his jacket and hung it carefully on the back of his chair, pulling at the sleeves to eliminate the risk of wrinkles, making sure the lapels lay flat. According to Anthea, he had six suits, practically identical, and wore them in precise rotation, except on Saturdays, when he went really crazy and decanted his long legs into jeans. He brushed at the seat of the chair opposite Cassie before sitting down at the table. Picking up the knife set alongside the place mat, he squinted along it, picked up the fork and examined the tines. Then he leaned forward. 'Long time no see,' he said, always one for an original turn of phrase. 'How's it all going? Is the bridge business doing well?'

'Not bad. And yourself?'

'Good. Excellent. I'm taking the solo tenor in *Messiah* this Christmas.'

'Taking him where?'

'Singing it, Cassandra. So all my free time's going on that.'

'I'll have to come and hear it,' said Cassie insincerely. If I'm really desperate. 'How's your mother?'

'In Egypt.'

'Ah.' Cassie was not going to ask what Bitsy Blacklaws was doing in Egypt in case he started telling her. But enough with the small talk: it was time to go in for the kill. 'Yes,' she said. 'Everything's fine. Except, of course, for this dreadful news about Naomi Harris.' She saw Blacklaws stiffen. 'Perhaps you haven't heard about that,' she added. Disingenuous or what?

'Of course I have. Quite apart from anything else she was . . . What's your interest, anyway, if it's not a rude question?' Graham held his wineglass up to the light and checked it for smears and fingerprints.

'She was kind of a friend. We played bridge together quite a bit. I've had to spend a lot of time helping out her husband since it happened. He seems completely devastated by it all.'

'Not surprising,' commented the solicitor. He paused then said, in a voice rounded by drama: 'She was one of my clients, did you know that?'

Cassie, who did, having telephoned Anthea the previous

day, widened her eyes and Ooh!ed her mouth. 'No! How extraordinary!'

'Small world, isn't it?'

'Oh Graham: in that case, you must know *all* about it.'

Graham looked gratified. Queen for a day – or possibly for life. 'I don't know about *all*.' He swelled with self-importance. 'Certainly a little more than the general public.'

His droning delivery never failed to activate Cassie's yawn-producing mechanism. She swallowed one now. 'Well, of *course*,' she said. 'Privileged information and so on.' The waitress appeared and Cassie continued to act spellbound while Graham gave his order.

He coughed in an irritatingly pompous manner. 'I suppose I may be privy to one or two details not generally known,' he continued, having waited until the waitress went off to get him a glass of wine.

'Like what, Graham?'

'Like, for instance . . .' He looked cautiously round. 'This is strictly for your ears only, by the way.'

'Abso*lute*ly.'

'Something rather odd. At least I thought it was.'

'What? Not dirty work at the crossroads.'

'Not really. Just one of those slightly funny things.' He stopped, bit his lip, drew back. Said ponderously, with every intention of being contradicted: 'I shouldn't really be telling you this . . .'

'Oh Graham, you can't stop now.'

His order arrived. He looked it over carefully before cutting into a slice of pigeon breast with the punctiliousness of a watchmaker and stowing it away in his mouth. He chewed thoughtfully. 'The food here's really excellent.'

'So I've always heard. That's why I'm here. I was on my

way to . . . um . . . see someone and made a special detour.'
Cassie was deliberately vague.

'Anyway.' Blacklaws took a fastidious sip of wine and
patted his lips with the stiff linen napkin. 'Naomi rang me
about a week before all this blew up, made an appointment to
see me for the following week.'

'What's "slightly funny" about that?'

'Nothing, really. Except . . .' Once more he gave her the
theatrical pause, looked around and lowered his voice. 'This is
absolutely in the strictest confidence, you understand?'

Cassie pretended alarm. 'I wouldn't want to be party to
anything . . .'

Worried that he was about to lose his audience, Graham put
down his fork and placed his hand on her arm. 'No, no. The
poor woman's dead. Can't alter anything now – though I
would ask you to keep what I'm about to tell you under your
hat.'

'Oh Graham! It sounds terrifyingly mysterious.' Keeping up
the girlish twitter was proving more of a strain than Cassie had
expected. Such unaccustomed exercise made her realise just
how hard the bimbettes and trophy wives must work for their
diamond bracelets and third homes on Mustique.

'The thing is . . .' He leaned even further forwards.

'*What?* Honestly, I can't stand the tension.'

'. . . she said that she wanted to draw up a new will.'

'Golly. Did she say in what way?'

'We didn't go into great detail, naturally. Not over the
phone. But I gathered that she had a new legatee in mind.'

'The local dogs' home, do you mean? Or the donkey farm
out near Larton Easewood?'

He pursed his small mouth. 'You're being facetious. Wills
are not laughing matters, Cassandra.'

'I know that, Gray. So, come on, tell me. Who was she going to leave it all to?'

'She didn't say. Well, naturally, she wouldn't. Not on the telephone.'

Cassie pretended not to find this of particular interest. 'I still don't see that it's "slightly funny". People are always changing their wills, aren't they?'

'Not that often, actually. No, the *funny* thing was that it was only a few days later that she must have killed herself. Before she could get in to see me.' He pushed his glasses up against the bridge of his nose, remembered his calling. 'Not, of course, that such a dreadful occurrence could remotely be called funny.'

'Of course not.' Cassie stared at him as though she didn't quite get it. 'You're not suggesting there's anything strange about the verdict, are you? You're not trying to suggest that someone maybe killed her and then faked it to look like suicide, are you?'

'God, no,' Blacklaws said hastily, foreseeing a multiplicity of possible legal complications. 'I just thought it strange that if she was going to take an overdose, she didn't wait until she'd dealt with whatever changes to her will she had in mind. Especially when she'd been quite insistent about it on the phone – she wanted to come in immediately but I didn't have a single spare window that week.'

'So now we'll never know who might have got the money.'

'I suppose not.' His upper cheekbones flushed slightly. Lavishly he buttered a chunk of bread and fed it into his mouth.

She wondered if he knew a little more than he said. She decided not to push it for the moment. 'Is there lots of it?'

'Of what?'

'Money.'

'A fair old bit.'

'And who gets it?'

He frowned, opened his mouth to utter some portentous crap.

'Come on, Gray,' Cassie said. 'If it's not in the public domain today, it will be tomorrow, or the next day. Anyway, I happen to know that the husband has first whack.'

'How do you—'

'So it's lucky for him that she never got round to changing things, isn't it?'

The hair on the crown of his head stiffened with horror. 'What you're implying could be construed as libellous, you know.'

'Did you tell the police about this meeting she'd set up? And the reason for it?'

He looked guilty. 'Actually no, I didn't. It seemed rather melodramatic and unnecessary. After all, they appear to be perfectly satisfied with the conclusions they've come to.'

Cassie nodded thoughtfully. 'As you say, it probably doesn't mean a thing.'

Except that it confirmed the fact that Naomi had been about to leave a large chunk, if not all, of her money to someone other than John Harris, thus adding an ounce or two more weight to Mansfield's theory that Naomi had been murdered by her husband in order to get him out of the financial swamp into which he seemed to be sinking. 'You're absolutely sure that she didn't come in and change her will before she died?'

Blacklaws stared at her oddly. 'Of course I'm sure. What are you trying to suggest: that she sneaked in while my back was turned and got one of the other partners to draw up a new settlement?'

'No. Just wanted to hear you confirm it.' Cassie felt a

profound sense of relief. Even to herself, she hardly liked to admit that there had been moments when she wondered whether Lucy could be taken at face value. After all, she only had the girl's word that she was who she said she was. Had Graham admitted that the will had, in fact, been changed in Lucy's favour, Cassie might have felt obliged to look a lot more closely at her. As it was, her lack of motive only added further conviction to the grief which so obviously consumed her.

Cassie looked at her watch and pushed back her chair. 'I must dash.'

'I'll send you a notification of the dates of the *Messiah* performances.'

'Thanks.'

'Why don't we have a drink together sometime? Or even . . .' he gulped, '. . . meet for dinner?'

'Wonderful,' enthused Cassie. 'Ring me some time.'

If he rang, she would not be free. Anthea, rotund in a crimson Lycra leotard and red and white striped top, had already expanded several times on his meanness. If she was going to pay for herself, then Cassie would prefer to choose her own company. She wondered if he'd still remind her of the *Messiah* when he realised she hadn't paid for her lunch.

Stepping from the Restaurant into the Lounge Bar, she walked towards the door leading to Market Square. Halfway across the room, she stopped. He was there. The man who had been following her. Sitting on an oak settle set beneath one of the leaded windows. An empty glass with a curl of lemon peel in it stood on the table in front of him. He was gazing at her, a half-smile on his face. Willing her to notice him.

Ignore him, screamed her wiser self. *Take no notice. It won't help to—* She marched over and planted herself in front of his table. 'What do you want?' she snarled.

He roused himself as though from a reverie. 'I beg your pardon?'

'Why are you following me?'

'Foll – I'm sorry, I don't understand.'

'I think you do.'

He looked helplessly round at the few people in the bar, as though they might be able to tell him whether she was simply some harmless local eccentric or a dangerously unbalanced sociopath. 'I'm sorry . . .' He shrugged. 'I really can't help you.' He had a pleasantly cultured voice with a faint regional accent which she could not quite identify. Somewhere north of the Cotswolds, she thought. In socio-economic terms she would not have said he was working-class. A copy of the *Independent* lay on the long flat cushion beside him. His clothes were nondescript: he wore a blue check shirt open at the neck, no rings. He had thin fair hair turning to grey. His teeth were good.

She put both hands flat on the table and thrust her face aggressively into his. 'We both know what you're up to,' she said quietly. 'If I see you again, I'll call the police.'

'And what do you think they'll do, Ms Swann? Arrest me for buying a packet of frozen peas? For changing my library book? For visiting a friend in the hospital?'

'How do you know my name?'

'I've made it my business to find out.'

'Why?'

'I think you can guess,' he said.

'I haven't the slightest idea what you're talking about.'

'Oh, really?' His eyes were blue and clear, the skin beneath them flat and curiously youthful. 'On the contrary, I think you have a very definite idea.'

'Give me your version of it, then.'

'You're trying to take something of mine, and I'm not going to let you,' he said.

'How can I take something of yours when I don't even know who you are?'

'Think about it,' he said brusquely. He picked up his newspaper. 'Now, Ms Swann. If you don't go away, I'm going to tell the nice lady behind the bar that you're making a nuisance of yourself.' He smiled briefly and began to read the front page.

Cassie continued to the door. Once in her car, she rested her head on the steering wheel, breathing deeply to calm herself. She was shaking, rage mixed with alarm. Although his tone had remained moderate throughout their short exchange, there was an air of quiet malignance about him which had reached out and grabbed her. She had sensed something implacable in him, something merciless. For the first time in her life, she thought that she might have come face to face with deliberate focused evil. While teaching inside the Bellington County Gaol, she had encountered a number of vicious men, had even been menaced by one of them. Steve's brand of savagery, however, though terrifying, was indiscriminate and uncontrolled; that did not make it any easier to cope with but his lack of direction made it likely that he would eventually end up behind bars again. There was no such looseness about the man in the pub.

The blaring sun was still high in the sky when she reached home. There was no sign of Lucy, but a note was propped up against a vase full of grasses and buttercups, saying that she would be back around six that evening. Guiltily, mindful of the drought, Cassie watered the pots and tubs and trickled water into the lily pond, watched by the farm cat who clearly thought the refill was for its benefit rather than that of the gasping goldfish.

Nausea swirled like fog at the pit of her stomach. She poured a stiff glass of whisky and sat in a deckchair beside the pond, trying to read. That man would stop at nothing to prevent her from having whatever it was he thought she was trying to take from him. Nothing whatsoever. Her breathing shuddered in and out of her lungs. What *did* he think she wanted? How could she persuade him that he was mistaken? How had he found out her name?

She heard footsteps at the side of the house and leaped to her feet. If it was him . . . but it was Charlie Quartermain, monstrous in a cerise shirt of vaguely Caribbean design, a Panama hat with an MCC band round it shading his face.

'Charlie,' she said, meaning it. 'How wonderful to see you.'

'Never thought I'd hear you say that.'

'Would you like a drink? Whisky, gin, wine?'

'Whatever you're having.'

'There's whisky on the kitchen table. I'll go and fix you something.'

He came closer and looked down at her. 'What's up, darlin'?'

'Up?'

'I was in Bellington when you drove past like a bat out of hell, face white as a sheet. Thought I'd better come and check up on you, and here you are, looking like a flying fuck in a thunderstorm.'

There was something subtly wrong about his phraseology but for the moment relief at the sight of his concerned expression was all that mattered.

'Oh, Charlie,' she said.

'Tell me, girl.'

'It's . . .'

When he opened his arms, she stepped into them without a thought for the consequences. When she had blurted out against his big chest the reason for her terrors, he pushed her gently back into her deckchair. 'Wait there,' he said. In a few moments he was back again with a glass containing at least a quarter of a bottle of neat whisky.

'Take me through that again,' he said, and she did so.

'And this all started about six weeks ago?' he asked, when she had finished.

'As far as I can remember.'

'So what did you do? What changed? What did you start doing that you weren't doing before? Or stop that you had been doing?'

'Absolutely nothing that I can think of. I've been over and over it.'

'He definitely said that you were trying to steal something which belonged to him?'

'He said: "You're trying to take something of mine, and I'm not going to let you." And when I said I couldn't be because I didn't even know who he was, he said: "Think about it" and then told me to go away.'

'Hmmm.'

'It doesn't sound like much. It was the way he said it that was so terrifying.'

'There's one thing,' said Charlie. 'While you've still got whatever the hell it is he wants, he's not going to hurt you. So what he's doing at the moment – the following you and so on – is only psychological warfare. Window dressing. You can ignore it. What we've got to watch out for is the moment when he thinks he can get whatever it is back again.'

'I don't want it, for God's sake,' cried Cassie. 'If I knew what it was, he could have it back at once.'

'He only said you were *trying* to get it, not that you'd actually got it. Which sounds as if he hasn't got it either. Whatever it is.'

Cassie looked at the honeycoloured stone of the out-houses. 'You don't suppose—' She cut herself short. 'But that's ridiculous.'

'What is?'

'The only new thing in my life in the past few weeks is the bridge business. You don't think he's the Mr Big of the bridge world, do you, worried that I'm going to steal away all his customers?'

'It's worth looking into.' Charlie sucked at the dregs of his glass and got to his feet. 'All right if I get another of those?'

'Of course.'

From the kitchen, he called: 'What would you do if that's all it was: he doesn't like the competition?'

'I don't know. I'd have to talk to Natasha first, but it sounds like a matter for the police.'

'Trouble is, he hasn't uttered threats, nothing that you could usefully use. And if it came to a fight, it would only ever be your word against his.' He came back outside and started to deposit his generous weight in the deckchair which Cassie had unfolded for him, then decided not to, making do with the wooden bench from under the apple tree instead.

'Charlie, you don't really think it could be something as simple as that, do you?'

'Could be. This recession's hanging about long after its sell-by date. When times are hard, people can get pretty desperate. Perhaps he's got a lot of capital tied up in card tables and scoring sheets and that. But it would be easy to find out if he owns a rival company: there can't be that many of them around.'

'Not more than half a dozen, when we did our research,' said Cassie.

'Leave the list with me. I'll get someone on to it.'

'If he is in the bridge business himself, it would certainly explain how he got my name. We wrote to people, you see, saying that we were trying to fill a niche in the market.'

'Bridging the gap, eh?' Charlie moved his huge head from side to side and sucked at his teeth. 'Very naive. Bad business practice. Why warn the opposition of your plans? It only gives them time to regroup.'

'We were trying to be courteous. But if it *is* what you're suggesting, why is he only going after me? Why not Natasha too?'

'For the simple reason, darlin', that he's checked you both out. And while your friend, Mrs Sinclair, has a husband to keep an eye on her, you, for whatever reason, choose to live alone. Anyone would see you as a soft target. And in any case, your headquarters are here – all the stock and so on.' A laugh rumbled in his big belly. 'Wrote to your rivals, did you? Told them in advance what you were planning? Dear, oh dear.'

'That's what these computer firms do. Microsoft and so on. They give masses of warning when they're about to bring out a new piece of software.'

'That's slightly different. For one thing, it's a rapidly expanding, not to say unlimited market.' He reached out and placed his hand on her knee. 'Let's face it, girl. No one's going to get rich flogging packs of cards to blue rinses.'

'Charlie, how can you be so prejudiced? Bridge isn't a game played exclusively by the old or the rich or the middle classes. Look at you, for a start.'

Launching into her spiel about the way bridge transcended all classifications of race, creed, age and income, Cassie was aware only of relief. Not only might they have discovered what exactly was driving the man who was terrorising her, but even if they hadn't, irrational though it might be to think so, with Charlie Quartermain on her side, everything was bound to turn out all right.

◆ 10 ◆

This morning there were sixteen Active Retireds waiting for her at the Bellington Leisure Centre, permed heads and neat white moustaches turned expectantly towards the door, eager to get on with it. Tough assignment. Every one of them would be on the ball, punctual, practised, pumped to the eyeballs with vim and vitamins. Cassie parked behind the ugly building, all glass and coloured plastic panels designed to indicate a strenuous well-being but demonstrating only a frightening impoverishment of the spirit. The tarmac glittered in the sunlight like a diamond field as she crunched across fragments of glass from the windows of cars which had been broken into. Giant rounded letters in silver and blue spray paint, outlined in black, sprawled crazily across the back wall. OZ. BUZ. KEZ. The alphabet on speed. Graffiti artists always seemed to favour the ultimate letter. A yellow trapeziform dumpster leaked KFC cartons and black plastic sacks. Two empty wine bottles lay at the foot of a concrete lamp-standard, like tidily placed shoes. If there was a white Peugeot anywhere around, she couldn't see it.

Philip Mansfield was meeting her for lunch. To exchange Progress Reports. He had been impatient when she explained that she didn't have one. Had pointed out that grass must not be

135

allowed to grow under their feet. That time was of the essence. That they bloody well had to go for it. 'For Naomi's sake,' he had added.

Following her class, she arrived early enough at the Black Swan Hotel to sneak a reviving whisky in the Lounge Bar before he showed up. Those Active Retireds really took it out of a person. So much damn energy. She saw him before he saw her. Today, he wore skin-tight jeans and a leather belt with a massive buckle of beaten silver. Not so much a fashion statement as a fashion manifesto. His short sleeves demonstrated his muscular development to advantage. He seemed an unlikely type to be a computer expert. Weren't they supposed to wear bottle-bottom glasses and have green teeth?

The hotel dining room was sombred by black beams and fake panelling stained to match. As they were shown to their table, Mansfield had to bend in order not to knock his head against the low ceiling.

'Guess what,' he said, as soon as they had sat down.

'I give up.'

'I spoke to a friend who knows someone who works in the research department of Masters & McKinney.'

'Who're they?'

'The advertising company where John Harris is a director.'

'I thought he owned his own business.'

'Not so.'

'But wasn't his motivation for killing Naomi – if he did – supposed to be that he was facing bankruptcy or something similar?'

'Dunno about that,' Mansfield said impatiently. 'But get this: it turns out that delegates who attended the conference in Edinburgh had two free afternoons slotted into the timetable.

Give them a chance to soak up the local culture or whatever. And one of them was followed by a free evening when they could do what they wanted. So it'd be simple as buggery to get down here, do the biz with Naomi and be back in Edinburgh again, without anyone even knowing he'd gone.'

There was a lull while they ordered, though Cassie was already uneasy, guessing what part he had assigned her. 'What do you want me to do about it?'

'Go over there tomorrow and pump him. Find out what he did on his free afternoons.'

'Wouldn't it be easier to ask the police?'

'They're not likely to tell you.'

'I know one who might. Anyway, I thought you had a copy of their report.'

'I do, but not that bit of it.' The innocent round eyes stared at her until she looked away. How could she possibly doubt him?

'Why would Harris tell me what he was doing?' she asked.

'He's not going to tell you the truth, which is that he was down here murdering Naomi, is he? So he's going to tell you some porky or other which we can then check out.'

Around them was the murmur of Cotswold voices, rounded and soft as bee-hum. Women, mostly, with plump faces and contented mouths, in country-town clothes, plus a scattering of professionals in suits. Against such a backdrop, murder seemed preposterous.

'That's already been done by the police. I'm not going to Bridge End until I've spoken to them.'

'Do you want the guy who killed Naomi brought to justice or don't you?' Mansfield said loudly, drawing stares from the comfortable foursome at the next table.

'Yes,' Cassie said. 'Of course I do. If there is one.'

'You don't seem committed,' Mansfield said.

'That's probably because I'm not.'

'It's exactly your sort who let Hitler gain power. Or Ceaucescu. Saw the injustice taking place right under their nose but did nothing about it until it was too late.'

'Thank you.'

'I don't mean that,' Mansfield corrected hastily. 'And it may even be that she *did* kill herself. I just need to know that I did everything I could for her. It's all I've got left.' Again, the stricken look crossed his face. 'Anyway, I'm flying up to Edinburgh this afternoon. I'll ring you from there – if you're still interested.'

'I've already said I'd help,' said Cassie. 'And I will.'

Back at home, she dialled Walsh's number. 'Hi,' she said, when he answered, trying to keep the Hi neutral, trying to keep any overtones of reproach out of it.

'Cassie.' Behind him, she could hear a track from *Making Movies*. 'How are you?'

'Fine. I wondered whether you'd like to drop by for a drink this evening.'

'This evening?'

'Yes.'

'Um. Yeah. That'd be good.'

So eager. 'Six?' said Cassie.

'Fine. Won't be able to stay all that long, though.'

'It'll be good just to see you.' She was sweating with mortification when she put down the telephone. But it would be easier if she could get the information she needed directly from him, rather than attempting to squeeze something out of John Harris. Who, if he was as guilty as Philip Mansfield believed, was absolutely certain to drop incriminating evidence leading to the hangman's noose – or life imprison-ment – right in her lap. Dream on.

She sat in the garden, scanning an advance copy of Tim Gardiner's latest crime novel, *Die Me A River*. In this one, Pandora Quest took up cudgels with the National Rivers Authority on behalf of the son of a pensioner who had suffered fits after drinking water from the tap and subsequently died. The book was earnest, dedicated to the principle of the lone fighter taking on the evils of society. Gardiner had obviously done a lot of research into the organisation and regulation of our water supplies and had no intention of wasting any of it. As always, Cassie was irritated by what she perceived as a grow-ing trend among contemporary writers of crime novels to polemicise, when all that was required of them was intelligent entertainment.

Attention wandered. Having Walsh round might also lead to a showdown in which she would discover once and for all where she stood. Had it been him playing Dire Straits, or his wife? Or another woman altogether? She tried to concen-trate on Pandora Quest's problems with blue-green algae and contaminated reservoirs, plus the evil folk at the Water Board. It was difficult. Actually, it was impossible. Suspend-ing disbelief was one thing; totally obliterating it was quite another. And there was the matter of the Black Swan's excellent home-made cherry pie and the effect it was having on her attention span.

She was dozing gently when a voice called: 'Cassie? Are you there?'

God. It couldn't be six o'clock already, could it? And she'd meant to wash her hair . . . but it was Lucy. Her hair was red today. Not auburn but a glowing crimson, through which her scalp gleamed. A stud was set into the side of her delicate nose.

Her skirt almost but not quite skimmed her crotch; on the end
of her skinny legs, Doc Martens made her feet seem as big as
mail order catalogues.

'Did I wake you?' she asked.

'I was just doing my eyelid exercises,' said Cassie.

'Gotta keep in shape.' Lucy laughed. 'Don't get up. I'll
make us some tea, shall I?'

'You seem cheerful.' At the same time, there were mussel-
coloured shadows under her eyes. The microscopic skirt and
workman's boots only emphasised her slightness.

'I suppose I am. I've felt completely paralysed ever since
that day I first met you, when I arrived at the house and found
my mother had gone. Now that it's been officially decided that
it was suicide, I feel I can face up to things and start getting on
with the rest of my life.'

'But I thought you were convinced she'd been murdered.'

'Not so much convinced as ready to look at alternatives. But
there's no point wishing for the moon,' said Lucy. 'Naomi's
gone. For a while there, I had these dreams of how it was going to
be, the two of us, but that's all they were. Too much sewage's
gone under too many bridges. It was stupid to hope that I could
go back and relive my childhood, make it all come right.'

'You're in philosophical mode, I see.'

'I'm an adult, and I ought to know you can't change the past.
I just have to make the best of what I've got.'

'Very wise.' And very matter-of-fact. Almost too much so.
Lucy's defence mechanisms at work? They sat over the pot of
tea Lucy brought out on a tray, in a silence broken only by the
sound of the girl's strong white teeth crunching through one
digestive biscuit after another.

'Ever heard of someone called Philip Mansfield,' Cassie
said, after a while.

'The name's vaguely familiar but I haven't a clue why.'

'He was your mother's lover.'

'I didn't know she had one.' Although the news was a surprise, it didn't seem to faze Lucy.

'She was going to leave John Harris for him.'

'Are you serious?'

'As an abscess. He's taking up where you left off.'

Lucy wrinkled her nose. 'How do you mean?'

'He's convinced that your mother was murdered by John Harris.'

'But I thought . . .' Lucy reached for the biscuit tin and then thought better of it, '. . . it *is* suicide, isn't it?'

'According to the police. Not according to the determined Mr Mansfield.'

'Shit.' Closing her eyes, Lucy rested her forehead on her hand. After a moment, she said: 'And bugger. I thought this was all sorted out. I thought I could move on. Can't we let it be?'

'I've no objection. None of it really has anything to do with me. But he's absolutely convinced. And I have to admit that there are one or two dodgy bits which don't add up.'

'Like fucking what?' The girl was angry now. Over her minimal skirt, she was wearing a truncated top which exposed an area of flat brown stomach and the neatest navel Cassie had ever seen.

'Some of the same things you pointed out yourself.' Cassie shrugged, pretending a nonchalance she did not really feel. 'Like her money, for instance. Turns out she'd made an appointment to change her will and then died before she could do so. Like her husband's whereabouts when he was supposed to be in Edinburgh. Like the fact that she really didn't, with both you and this bloke of hers about to change her life, have any reason to kill herself.'

'*Fuck* it!'

'There's no point getting mad at *me*,' said Cassie quietly, aware that she stood on the edge of an emotional minefield. 'I'm the one holding the dummy hand in all this.'

'I'm sorry.' Lucy looked down the length of the garden. 'I just wish it was all settled. You've no idea what it's like, knowing, not knowing, so unrooted, so . . .' She pressed her full lips together for a moment, '. . . hurt.'

The scurry of claws in the cellars. Cruel eyes gleaming in darkness. It was a moment Cassie wanted to seize, on which she wanted to demand enlightenment. She had held this other person in her arms, she had shared her pain, yet she still knew almost nothing about her. So jealous was she of her own privacy that she hesitated to intrude on anyone else's. It was a sensitivity which, she was beginning to see, bordered on indifference. 'Lucy,' she began.

But Lucy was on her feet, staring at her watch. 'The hell with it.' A fine tremble had begun along her jaw. 'I have to go.'

Walsh was, as always, punctual. Cassie had thought the visceral thump of desire was done with but when she opened the door to him, it started up as though nothing had changed . . . *the way we used to be*. Once, he used to walk round to the back door and come in without knocking; this formal entrance was not encouraging. He put his arms round her, nonetheless, and murmured her name. She sank her head against his shoulder and closed her eyes, breathing in his scent . . . *all I do is miss you*.

'It's been a long time,' he said.

'Yes.' And not my fault, she thought.

'Are you hungry?' He held her away from him.

'Not especially.'

'Tired?' he asked softly.

'A bit.'

'You look as if a nap would do you good.'

'I think you're right.' She pressed her hips against him. 'Now that you've brought it up.'

'Paul.'

'What?'

'That suicide. Naomi Harris.'

'What about it?'

'Did you ever suspect the husband?'

'I told you before, darling. We keep all our options open as long as we can.'

'Except he was in Edinburgh at the time she died, wasn't he? Even if they can't pinpoint exactly when that was.'

'Yes.'

'He had some free time during this conference, didn't he? What did he say he was doing?'

'Why on earth do you want to know?'

'I just wondered.' She gave an unrealistic light laugh. 'I've got this friend who writes detective novels and I've been reading some of his books. The plot always seems to twist on unlikely alibis.'

Walsh snorted. 'I don't know why you waste your time on such crap. I've read dozens and none of them's got the faintest resemblance to real life. Especially when the hero's a cop. The thing about police routine is that it's mind-bogglingly boring. They don't make TV series out of the kind of rubbish I spend my time on, believe me.' He laughed, making the bed shake. 'You didn't by any chance watch that bloody awful thing they did last week, did you? The one where the cop's wife was dead but he sat on her tombstone and talked all his cases through with her? Jesus wept. The lads at the nick were falling about.'

The discussion was moving into the realms of small-screen criticism, an area Cassie did not want to explore. 'What I really meant was that he could easily have got down here and back again, if he wanted to.'

'Who? The plonker with the dead wife?'

'John Harris,' Cassie said, trying not to grit her teeth. 'Couldn't he?'

'Why would he have wanted to?'

'If he'd been the one who killed her, I mean.'

Walsh slid his hand over Cassie's naked hip and down between her thighs. 'Mmm,' he said, nibbling at her shoulder. 'I've always said you're the best I've ever had.'

'No, listen,' Cassie said, irritated at being reduced to nothing more than one of several sexual partners. 'Paul . . .'

'Anyway, it was suicide,' he mumbled against her breast.

'There's no possibility it was murder?'

'None at all, sweetheart.'

'How sure are you?'

'As sure as you can be.'

'But suppose it wasn't. Suppose Harris just faked it to look that way.'

'He didn't. Couldn't have. For one thing, he was able to account for enough of his time up there to show that there was no way he could have got down here and back again.'

'So what was he doing on his free afternoons?'

'He went to the National Gallery – still had the ticket stuck down at the bottom of his trouser pocket. Went on a bus tour of the city. In the evening, ate alone in a restaurant, showed us the bill. Visited a friend. Mooched around a bit.'

'So he couldn't account for *all* his time.'

'Enough of it.'

'What was the name of the restaurant?'

'Which one?'

'Where he ate on his free night?'

'The Rivabella, I think.'

'What did he have?'

'Melon and prosciutto,' Walsh said drowsily, pausing between the words to nibble at Cassie's shoulder. 'Lasagne. Green salad. Lemon sorbet.'

'Wine?'

'Yes, as far as I remember. Here.' Paul pushed crossly away from her and sat up, pulling the sheet up to his armpits. 'What the hell *is* this, Cassie? I thought you invited me round for a drink, not a run-down on someone's business lunch. And in any case, what's your interest?'

It didn't take much psychic sensitivity to grasp that the mood had vanished. Cassie hoisted herself up beside him. 'I told you. Naomi Harris was – she was a friend.' She injected a hateful little wobble into her voice. 'I – I can't get it out of my mind, that she was so desperate that she killed herself and I didn't even know. So I suppose I keep looking for alternative theories.'

To her shame, he was sympathetic. 'I know,' he said, taking her hand. 'Violent death's hardly ever acceptable. There's the occasional villain you aren't too sorry to see the back of, but apart from that . . .'

Seizing the advantage, Cassie said: 'I think it would be easier if I knew more of the details. Once I've got it clear in my mind, I can forget about it, sort of. Or, at the very least, stop going over and over it in my head.'

145

He smiled at her. 'That's what I thought. So I brought you the transcript of the inquest.'

It was an odd gift for a lover to bring, yet so exactly what she wanted that her throat thickened with emotion. He must still think of her, then. Enough to know exactly what she was likely to want. She pressed down the guilt of knowing that in fact Naomi was not a close friend, and she was concerned about it mostly because other people had dragged her in. He'd thought about her. That was enough. She opened her mouth to say something along those lines and instead said: 'Are you still screwing your wife?'

Smart move, Cassandra. If there were two things policemen didn't like, one was feisty women and the other was what they perceived as inappropriate language. The police, after all, were the guardians of the nation's morals, bearers of the standard. Or bloody fascists, depending on your point of view. He was out of bed and into his clothes faster than a quick-change artist. The indignation with which he put on his socks made her want to giggle. 'Paul . . .' she said weakly.

He stepped into his blue hipster jockeys and caught a toe against one leg opening. As he went into the quick sideways hop required to maintain his balance, his dick hung over the edge of the elasticised waist, bobbing like a manic glove puppet. The look he threw at her warned her against any reaction but she couldn't help it. 'Oh, Paul!' she said, and burst into peals of laughter.

Someone said – Wilde, wasn't it? – that nothing destroys a love affair faster than misplaced laughter. Boy. Oscar got that one a hundred per cent right.

During the night, rain fell. Cassie woke briefly to hear it tapping gently at the open window panes, and pattering on the parched leaves in the garden. Cool sweet air blew into the room as the curtains parted before the pushing night breeze. One of the gutters must be choked with leaves: water dripped steadily onto the patio below. A comforting sound. The spectre of an England parched into sand dunes and date palms receded. She wished she felt worse about the robust manner with which Walsh had indicated that there was nothing whatsoever left of the feeling which had once existed between them, and that yes, as it happened, Barbara was back, and yes, although it was none of Cassie's damned business, they were sharing a bed and, since she asked, they had made love that very morning. She was struggling too hard to contain the laughter which welled up each time she remembered him hopping across the bedroom floor, to ask him what the hell he was doing, in that case, making love to her, Cassie Swann. But perhaps police-men had more licence to be inappropriate than the sinful citizenry. Or members of the inferior sex. She decided that this was the last time she gave way to the urgings of her hormones. Turning over, she went back to sleep.

When she opened the kitchen door in the morning, the sun was shining once more, edging the damp leaves and grass with diamond brightness. But the air at least smelled fresh, and the few flowers still blooming had an alert look about them. It was a good start to a day which a gut feeling told her was likely to get worse.

She learned little from the inquest transcript which Walsh, despite his fury, had left on the kitchen table. The wording of the suicide note found beside Naomi (*I'm sorry but it's too much, I can't face life any longer*) was not particularly illumi-nating. The pills had been ingested with scotch, but she already knew that. The amount of alcohol in the bloodstream indicated that Naomi had been pretty drunk by the time she lay down in the boot of her car. There was no mention of the golf clubs. Surprisingly, Anne Norrington, who played in a regular bridge foursome with Naomi and Cassie, had apparently been the last person to see her. She gave evidence that she had run into Naomi in Bellington the day after her husband had gone up to Edinburgh, that they had had coffee together and that she had seemed very depressed.

Thinking about the impossibility of John Harris getting down to Bridge End from Edinburgh and back again, if he was visiting the National Gallery and eating dinner in the evening, Cassie walked across the damp ground to the headquarters of – whatever. Bridge'n'Things – oh, please. But something had to give. Natasha was due shortly for a discussion about their much-delayed brochure, the printing of which was being held up because they could not agree on what to call themselves. And as she turned the key in the door, Charlie's resonant voice came back to her. Of course. The ideal name for the business. Bridge the Gap. She took the cover off the computer, logged in, found the Letterhead file she had opened. After two or three hours of one-on-one tutoring from Philip Mansfield, she no longer worried that the machine would blow up if she hit the wrong key, or that her amateur scrabblings might be irrecoverably damaging the hard disk. Confidently, she wrote BRIDGE THE GAP across the top of a document, moved the mouse about, enlarged the letters, boldened them, changed the font. Hey. Impressive, or what? She printed out a page. It looked good.

As if on cue, Natasha showed up.

'Bridge the Gap?' She tossed it about inside her head, her mouth moving as though she were at a wine-tasting. 'I like it,' she said. 'Excellent. Now we can send out the invitations.'

'Which ones would those be?'

'To our opening party, of course.'

'And who are we inviting?'

'Everybody. Everyone you've ever taught, all your current pupils, anyone likely to be one in the future, everyone either of us has ever played bridge with in the past. You do keep a database, don't you?'

'I'm never without one.'

'And I have some good news. That friend of yours, Mainbrace or something, he rang me up recently and when—'

'Quartermain? Why would he ring you up?'

'He said you wanted the list of people we wrote to when we were doing our market research.' Natasha felt in her bag and brought out a piece of folded paper. 'Here. Anyway, when I told him of this party, he begged, absolutely begged, to be allowed to contribute the wine. He is so generous.'

'Isn't he just?' Cassie spoke sourly. It was obvious that Charlie was prepared to pay any price within reason to get inside her underwear. So. Dilemma time once more. On the one hand, this was a gift not to be sneezed at. On the other, yet again good ol' Charlie was stepping into her life, trying to take her over, trying to make her beholden. 'I don't like that idea much,' she said.

'Since when did you start turning down free booze?'

'It's not the booze I object to. It's that particular supplier.'

Natasha lifted her shoulders in a huge continental shrug. 'Unfortunately,' she said, 'I'm extremely busy at the moment.'

'Why is that any more unfortunate today than it was yesterday or last week?'

'Because I need to sit down and give you a lecture.'

'I don't want one, thanks.'

'The man is going to get tired of being forever kicked in the teeth. Frankly, I don't know why he hasn't already. And you'll be the first to cry when he finally marries another woman.'

'You bet I will. With joy.'

'Cassie, Cassie. When will you recognise this man's worth?' Natasha's speech-patterns hardly ever reflected her origins, which were half Sri Lankan and half Russian. Today she managed to sound as though she had just blown in from the Siberian steppes.

'For Christ's sake,' said Cassie. 'I recognise the Archbishop of Canterbury's worth. That doesn't mean I'm in love with him, or want to sleep with him. And call me Cartland if you will, but I've always had this romantic notion that the man you marry has to qualify on both counts.'

'I'm sure he's wonderful in bed.'

'Dr Carey?'

'Charlie.'

'On what do you base that remark?'

'Big men always are.'

'I'm not even going to ask how you know.'

'I wouldn't tell if you did.'

'I've always envied you, 'Tash. Not just because you're beautiful . . .' Natasha had been a legendary model before she threw it all up to get married, '. . . but also because you and Chris are so solid together. So—' Cassie remembered Lucy's word. 'So rooted.'

'You could be too, if you were not so afraid.'

'Afraid? Of what?'

'Everything,' Natasha said. She made some generous Russian arm movements. 'You are afraid of love, of openness, of the opinion of other people. You think you do not love this Mainbrace man, but in your heart, you do. You are frightened that because he is not what you have been brought up to consider a gentleman, you will be demeaning yourself by allowing yourself to love him.' Her big dark eyes flashed Slavically. If Uncle Vanya had come mooning round the corner with a starling in a cage, it wouldn't have been a huge surprise. 'You are my friend, Cassandra, and so I must say this to you: you are a fool. A *fool*.'

'Oh, I get it,' said Cassie. 'They've started rehearsing *Anna Karenina* at the Larton Easewood Playhouse.'

'Alvays you must mock,' said Natasha.

'Knock it off, 'Tash. You know as well as I do that it's pronounced "ways", not "vays".'

'Please, Cassandra. Vun thing I must beg of you,' Natasha said dramatically, her voice deep and tragic, the angst of her suffering people rich at the back of her throat.

'Unto half my kingdom.'

'Do not come veeping to me when you receive an invitation to your Charlie's vedding to another voman.'

'Trust me,' said Cassie.

♥ 11 ♥

Raleigh Grove, Market Broughton, was the first turning off
Columbus Crescent which, in turn, was just after the traffic
lights on Amundsen Way. Cassie parked at the kerb in front
of neat little Number 4, where Anne Norrington lived. The
house was built of red bricks, each one small and perfectly
uniform, without any of the defects which make older buildings so satisfying to the human eye. Such as the Queen Anne
house in Frith which Charlie Quartermain was in the process
of buying. The beauty of its façade lay not simply in the size
and placement of its windows, in the proportions of the door,
in the harmonious relation between height and width, in the
fact that it had been weathered and matured by time, but also
in the irregularities of the materials from which it was
fashioned. It wasn't the builder's fault that Anne's house
looked so new and brash, since it was scarcely five years old,
but someone should be held responsible for the fact that,
even if it lasted for five centuries, it would still look what it had
always been: cheap, speculative building, without character,
without soul.

Cassie drew a fortifying breath into her lungs and got out
of the car. Anne Norrington was something of a challenge.
Although Cassie had played bridge with her once a week for

a number of months, she still did not feel that she knew her. Divorced, two grown children, a former dentist's reception-ist, her ex-husband being the dentist for whom she recepted until he ran off with his dental hygienist: that was the extent of the information filed in Cassie's memory. Was the fault her own, for not caring enough to ask for more, or Anne's, for having so little to give? Anne was a subdued and colour-less woman, with the look of something which has been through the washing machine too many times and is begin-ning to fray at the edges. She had been delighted – too much so – when Cassie had telephoned and asked if she could drop by. Now, as Cassie walked along the neat paved path to the door, she was already waving from the windows of the lounge, obviously on the lookout for what Cassie suspected was a rare visitor.

There was a considerable amount of inane fussing about ("Milk? Sugar? Why don't you sit by the window? Are you warm enough? I can always turn on the gas-fire, it won't take a moment to heat the room . . .") before the two women were sitting opposite each other in a room which smelled of sad sterility, despite bowls of pot pourri and a large bouquet of flowers on the table in the window. The only artefacts with any life to them were the pictures on the wall, a series of charming watercolours of what seemed to be views from the Lake District.

'It's *so* nice to see you,' enthused Anne, faintly flushed, mousy hair curling around her pale face.

'I was going to be over this way, and it suddenly occurred to me that we hadn't met for a while,' said Cassie.

'I know, what with the summer holidays . . .'

'And Naomi being sick for so long . . .'

'. . . and then her dying so suddenly.' Anne's eyes swam

with tears. 'So awful. So tragic. I couldn't – still can't – take it in.'

Cassie hadn't expected to get straight to the point of her visit so soon. Yet, what else would they have talked about? 'I read in the paper that you were the last person to see her, as far as the police could establish.'

'I know. I keep thinking that if only I'd realised how near the brink she was, I might have been able to do something,' fluttered Anne.

'What could you have done? I've felt the same, that we should have been able to help her. But she didn't ask for help, did she?'

'I – I don't think so.'

'What do you mean?'

'She said something odd that day . . . that last morning in Bellington – I ran into her, you see, by the toiletries department in the supermarket – and she suggested we had coffee. I was a bit surprised because, frankly, she's never been all that friendly to me.'

'Nor to anyone else.'

'I didn't have anything much else that needed doing, so I said why not. So we went to that Copper Kettle place on the market square.'

Cassie nodded.

'I don't – didn't even know her all that well. It sounds ridiculous to say so, when the four of us have been playing bridge all these months, but I really didn't. There was always something a bit . . .'

'Offputting?'

'. . . yes, about her. And she's been here, of course, because of taking it in turns to host the bridge game, but she's never suggested getting together before. In fact, I've always thought she was rather stand-offish, as though I wasn't good enough for her.'

Cassie had never heard self-effacing Anne so chatty. She'd probably been dying to talk about all this but didn't know anyone she could tell. 'You told the police that she seemed depressed.'

'Well, she did. She always does – has – didn't she?' said Anne, floundering among the tenses as though she had waded into a pond full of waterweed. 'But she seemed rather excited, as well. Sort of like a child when their birthday's coming up, do you know what I mean? Well, you wouldn't really, would you, not having children, but that's what it was like. And quite honestly, not to speak ill of the dead, but she's got – had – a bit of a sharp tongue on her, so I didn't like to ask her why. She had all this shopping with her, too, and she started showing some of it to me.'

'Shopping?'

'Dresses, and jewellery and so on. Stuff from Body Shop. A pair of leggings which frankly I just couldn't see her in at all – sort of pop art in black and white. Not at all her style. But she was much more human that day – not a bit like her usual self.'

'You didn't say that to the police, did you?'

'No, because I wondered afterwards, if it wasn't just the way the depression took her. You know, up and then down: isn't that what they're like, these manic-depressives? But since then, I've thought about it a lot more and I think she *was* excited about something, but by then the police had investigated and all that, and there didn't seem to be much point in going in and saying so because in the end it wouldn't have altered the verdict, would it? I mean, it *was* suicide, wasn't it?'

'What made you think she might have been asking for help?'

'As I say, it was only afterwards . . . but at one point she asked me what my dearest wish was. If I could have anything at all, what would I want?'

'And what did you say?'

'Nothing. I couldn't really think of anything . . .' Anne twisted the rings on her finger, a platinum engagement ring and matching wedding band. '. . . At least, I could, but I wasn't going to tell Naomi, not when I hardly knew her.' Her gaze dwelt for a moment on the photograph of a bespectacled man in a silver frame. The absconding dentist? Did she still hanker for him to return?

'And presumably she told you what *her* dearest wish was.'

'Not in so many words. She said something like, had I ever thought about how awful it would be to have your dearest wish come true and then realise you didn't want it after all? I didn't have a clue what she meant, of course. And afterwards, I wondered if she needed someone to talk to, if she really *was* asking for help. If something terrible had happened to her that she needed to talk about. So, naturally, I've been thinking that if only I'd encouraged her to carry on, it might have helped her and she wouldn't have . . . done what she did.'

'Did you know that she had a lover?' Cassie figured that it couldn't hurt Naomi now to pass the information on.

'Funny you should say that.' Again Anne fiddled with her rings. 'She didn't look the sort at all, if you know what I mean. But I'd seen her a couple of times in the town with a young man – rather a flashy sort, I thought – lots of hair and a gold chain, that kind of thing . . .'

Cassie nodded. Compared to Anne, almost anyone was going to look flashy. But it certainly sounded like Philip Mansfield.

'. . . And you could tell,' Anne said. 'The way they leaned

towards each other. You can usually tell when two people are – intimate, can't you?'

Which probably provided confirmation of Mansfield's story, in case Cassie had doubted what he had told her about himself and Naomi. 'I've seen him too,' she said. 'She was planning to move in with him.'

'And leave her husband?' Anne's face was almost comically astonished.

'Apparently.'

'But how could she? John Harris is such a *nice* man. But you think she might have been having second thoughts?'

'It's one explanation of what she said to you.'

'The thing is, we weren't particularly friendly. So the fact that she'd say something so, well, personal, to me . . .' Tears welled up again in Anne's eyes. 'Poor thing. She must have been so lonely. Even lonelier than—' She broke off, though it was obvious that she would have completed the sentence with a reference to herself. 'I've just felt dreadfully guilty ever since, for not asking more questions. I expect that's what she wanted, so she could spill it all out.'

'Don't blame yourself, Anne. She wasn't the spilling kind.' Cassie replaced her coffee cup on the low table in front of her. 'Look. Would you have said that she was depressed enough to commit suicide, when you saw her?'

'No. But you can't always tell, can you? Mood swings, and so on.'

'You thought she seemed excited.'

'Yes.'

'As though it was her birthday, you said.'

'She had that sort of anticipation about her, yes. Actually, I remember thinking that she was quite attractive when she smiled. I couldn't ever remember her smiling before.'

'But she smiled that day.' Was that because she was shortly going to meet up with her daughter again after all those years? It seemed an obvious conclusion.

'Quite a lot.' Anne pushed a hand through her hair. 'Oh dear. I should have been more helpful.'

'If it's any consolation, I don't think anything any of us said would have been any help. Whatever happened would have happened.'

'How on earth can you be so sure?' said Anne indignantly. 'You don't know that at all. She offered me the hand of friendship and I – I—'

'You didn't know what to do with it because, coming from Naomi, you didn't recognise it,' said Cassie. 'I wouldn't have done, either. I know this sounds like a bit of sew-it-on-a-sampler philosophy, but she'd erected so many protective barriers around her that none of us would.'

Anne got up and clinked around for a bit with coffee cups and milk jugs. When she sat down again, she said: 'I keep wondering what she thought about while she lay in the boot of that car and slowly died. Did she regret things? Did she wish she hadn't taken those pills and then found she didn't have the strength to climb out and find help? Was she just glad to be leaving everything behind?' She began to sob, one hand pressed to her chest. 'Sorry,' she said. 'But I can't stop thinking about it.'

'You will, though. Soon. I promise. It's just the shock,' Cassie said soothingly.

'It's made me think rather hard about myself,' said Anne. 'I'm a bit the same. I keep myself closed off. I've been thinking how awful it would be if I was found dead, and people said the same things about me that we've been saying about Naomi.' The flush on her face deepened. 'My sons

159

have been telling me for years, ever since their father . . .
they've been saying I ought to get out more, get more
involved in the community. So . . .' She took a deep breath.
'You're so sociable and, well, confident, that this probably
doesn't sound like anything much to you, but yesterday, I
drove over to Bellington and enrolled in an art class at the
Leisure Centre. I used to be quite good, actually, until I got
married.'

'What happened then? You stopped being good?' Cassie
asked, amused by Anne's phraseology.

'I didn't,' Anne said. 'But he . . .' she nodded at the silver-
framed photograph of the dentist, '. . . used to tell me how
useless I was and how I ought to leave such things to people
who knew what they were doing. I kind of lost my confidence.
And ever since he . . . well, I've been living like a nun, and I've
decided I must do more with my life than sit at home, regret-
ting things . . . I would *hate* to die and never have done
anything after the age of forty-two.' She looked again at the
photograph and then, to Cassie's surprise, got up and placed it
face-down on top of the chest. 'I loved him when we got
married,' she said. 'Or I thought I did. But by the time he left, I
didn't. It was just the shock that's made me so hopeless. The
loss of all the things I took for granted. The rejection. She
wasn't even pretty, the woman he went off with. Anyway . . .'

'I'm—'

'You'll wonder why I'm bothering to tell you any of this,
and you'll have to forgive me if I'm boring you—'

'You're not, truly.'

'—but I don't talk to people enough, and I do sort of know
you, don't I?'

'Of course you do,' said Cassie. 'And I think it's very brave
of you to take some positive action like this.' She tried to add

something pious to the effect that Naomi would have been glad to know that her death had galvanised Anne into doing something about her own life, but the words stuck in her throat. The truth was, Naomi wouldn't have given a damn.

'Phil here.' The voice sounded as if it was coming from the bottom of a deep well where they were holding Formula One speed trials.

'Phil?'

'Mansfield. What've you got?'

'One or two things of interest.' Cassie gave him an edited version of what Anne Norrington had told her, emphasising Naomi's anticipation and excitement, and omitting the stuff about the disappointment of dreams coming true. Since leaving Anne's house, it had occurred to her that if her supposition was right, and Naomi had begun to regret the decision to set up with Mansfield, that might give him a motive to kill her himself. Common sense demanded to know why, in that case, he was trying to prove that her suicide was in fact murder. Nonetheless, a niggling worry remained. If he himself was the murderer, he might be worried that the police would eventually discover it, and was therefore concerned to pin it all on John Harris. Just where in all this she had become convinced that Naomi had been killed she would have been unable to say, but by now she was more than willing to go along with Mansfield's theories.

'That's good,' he yelled, while behind him Damon Hill or someone revved ear-splittingly.

'Also,' said Cassie, 'I've had a hunch.'

'A bunch of what?'

'*Hunch*. Where are you, for God's sake?'

'Haven't the foggiest. Somewhere in the middle of

nowhere. I'm on my way back to town after visiting the chap who organised the conference Harris went to. There's nothing but sheep as far as the eye can see.'

Another racing car split the air. 'Bloody noisy sheep they have up there,' Cassie said.

'What?'

'Listen.'

'I'm trying to, but I think there's a fault on your line. I can hardly hear you.'

'I want you to have lunch at a place called the Rivabella.' With some repetition, thanks to the Formula One sheep, Cassie told him what John Harris had eaten the night he was alone for the evening. 'Order the same, will you? And don't lose the bill.'

'Are you going to tell me why?'

'Not yet. What about your sitrep?'

'There's not a lot to report. The organising guy said that they'd wondered where Harris had got to, but that he's always been a bit of a loner – for loner read someone none of the others wanted to pal around with. This guy I've just been with also told me that someone who knows him a bit better than the others hinted that he might have been visiting a prostitute.'

Once, Cassie would have registered disbelief. Now, it seemed no more or less incredible than the possibility of Naomi running off with a guy whose hair could have doubled for Julia Roberts's. Yet only a couple of weeks ago and she would have described the Harrises as Mr and Mrs Dull Provincial.

'Can you check that one out?' she asked.

'I'm going to try. It's something the police seemed to have missed, anyway. Perhaps his colleagues didn't like to bring it up when his wife had just killed herself. Or perhaps it's just a rumour. I'll see what I can do.'

'When are you coming back south?'

'Not until I've done everything I can. You'd better take down the name of my hotel and the phone number. Or perhaps you don't need to: it's the same one Harris stayed in last week. I thought I might get more information if I was on the spot.'

'Good thinking.'

Hanging up the phone, Cassie reminded herself that there was life after Naomi, that there were other matters which had to occupy her attention. Such as business. She walked across to what would shortly become the registered offices of Bridge the Gap and sat down at the desk. The file which Natasha had brought with her the day before contained some letters and a list printed out from Chris's computer. The list contained five names and related addresses. Two were women, one living in Lincoln, the other in Carlisle. One was a couple called MacNamara. The fourth was called Captain Reynard Wolff, at a post office box number in Weybridge. The fifth was called Tony Sutherland.

Four of them had answered the letters sent out by Cassie and Natasha. Both the women explained that they ran their own bridge businesses – one as a part-time tax consultant, the other as an employment agency – and had decided to try and turn their favourite occupation into a money-making concern. So far, the one in Lincoln wrote, she had managed to keep her head above water. The one in Carlisle said she had found the whole thing more hassle than it was worth, even though she had more than covered her expenses, and was winding her stock down; if they liked she would send them a list of stuff she still had and would be happy to come to some arrangement if they were interested. She did not advise taking it up, but offered to do their tax accounts free for one year if they did. The MacNamaras had replied by saying that they were no longer involved in the bridge sundries business as it didn't pay enough, and had recently bought a florist's shop in Dublin in order to be near Mrs MacNamara's elderly parents. Captain Wolff congratulated them on their choice of business and offered them copies of his world bestseller, *Bridge for Profit*, at a handsome discount. All in all, it sounded a rather grim prospect as a money-making concern. Cassie tried to remember why they had been so keen on it, even after receiving these depressing answers to their letters. Natasha's enthusiasm had been one reason. It was hard at this moment to think of others.

The fifth name on the list, Tony Sutherland, had not replied.

His address was just to the south of Oxford, a little village near Abingdon. Cassie had played bridge there on several occasions, once at a charity bridge lunch, and three or four times at the large house which stood on the edge of the village and was owned by a London publisher and his partner. She tried to think back. The first time she had gone as a guest, invited by a woman called Vicky Duggan who had attended one of her Bridge Weekends. The other times she had been partnering a visiting American bookstore owner, who had paid handsomely for the privilege. Could she have met this Tony Sutherland there? Was that why the name seemed faintly familiar? But if he was the man who had been following her, would she not have recognised him? It was perfectly possible that he had not been there, of course; as a matter of urgency, she decided she would drive over to his place tomorrow morning, after Naomi's funeral. Meanwhile, there was a mass of paperwork to complete, now that they finally had a company name. She switched on the computer. She was actually beginning to be fond of it, of the colours and logos, the little messages it sent her from time to time, the impressive number of things Mansfield had shown her that it was capable of doing.

♠ 12 ♠

The morning of Naomi's funeral was one of those glittery, Fabergé-fragile days when, although summer is beginning to give way to autumn, the sky remains blue, the temperature balmy, the light golden between leaves that are just on the edge of turning. As they passed from the church out to the plot behind the building where a grave had been dug, Cassie was able to count the mourners. Considering how inaccessible Naomi had always been, there was a reasonable turnout. A number of her own bridge-playing acquaintances had decided to attend; she wondered how many were motivated by curiosity rather than because they were affected by Naomi's death. A few of John Harris's business colleagues had come down from London; they stood hearty and awkward in good dark suits, displaying solidarity and a barely-concealed desire to glance at their watches. Inspector Mantripp remained stolidly at the back of the small crowd, his hair water-flattened like a small boy's, with DS Valerie Lund at his side. To Cassie's embarrassment, DS Paul Walsh was also with them, hands clasped in front of him, keeping his eyes respectfully cast down. More, she suspected, from a desire not to meet hers than to honour the dead.

John Harris had shrunk in the days since Naomi's death. The

once-prosperous jowls were wattled by weight loss; his lank stripes of hair appeared to have turned grey when only days ago they had been brown. By no means as convinced of his guilt as Philip Mansfield, Cassie was further stricken with doubt as she saw the state to which his wife's death had reduced him. It was difficult to understand how Naomi could have believed he was trying to kill her – today he scarcely seemed capable of raising his voice. Lucy stood separate from everyone else, not looking at the long rectangle cut into the ground. Like all the young girls that summer, she was wearing DMs under a long button-through dress which emphasised the meagreness of her frame, though hers was rather different from the ubiquitous repeat patterns of tiny white flowers on a black or navy background. Cassie had seen the silky material before somewhere: dark cream splashed with crimson rose-buds which more or less matched the current colour of Lucy's hair. Her face was pinched with grief; tears rolled down her white cheeks and darkened the front of her clothes. Close to the police officers, Philip Mansfield, in what looked like an Armani suit, worn over a white T-shirt, kept lifting his sunglasses to dab at his eyes.

She herself was wearing a dark-brown linen suit she had bought in the New Year's sales because she thought it brought out the colour of her eyes but which she now saw made her look like an unwrapped bar of chocolate. She stood beside Harris, both hands clutching at her soft leather bag so that there could be no question of taking his elbow or placing a hand on his sleeve. The only relatives present were John's elderly mother and her even more aged sister. Naomi, it appeared, had none. Or none that cared enough to put in an appearance at her funeral.

Mantripp spoke to her. 'Miss – um – Swann.'

'Good morning, Inspector.'

'A sad occasion.'

'Death out of due season always is.'

'And the circumstances were – um . . .'

'They were, weren't they?'

As they dispersed towards the gate of the churchyard to join the cars left in the lane, Lucy walked unsteadily across the tufted grass and threw her arms around Cassie. 'I feel even more alone now,' she whispered, her lips fluttering like moths against the V of skin between the lapels of Cassie's jacket.

'You will for a while,' Cassie said, as she had to Anne Norrington, whom she could see talking to some of the women from Naomi's various bridge fours. She patted the girl's back with the small meaningless touches of ritualised comfort.

'But you'll be my friend, won't you?' The throat-choking question was that of a sad child.

'Of course I will.'

'I can't even go and say something to her husband,' murmured Lucy. 'I don't think he knew about me, and it wouldn't be fair for me to, if my mother hadn't told him.'

If he murdered her, it was all too likely that he *did* know, but Cassie didn't say so. 'Are you coming back to the house?' she said instead.

'I don't think so. I couldn't really bear it.'

'I shall have to. I promised him I'd help out.'

'That's OK,' Lucy said. She straightened. 'I'll give you a ring sometime, shall I?'

'Please.' Cassie put an arm around her shoulders and the two of them walked together between the gravestones, behind the main body of the mourners. The vicar waited, white cassock billowing slightly as the faint wind caught it. 'So sorry . . . such a dreadful thing . . . miss her . . . poor Naomi . . .' he murmured, seizing the hands of strangers as they passed by.

Waiting to one side while the two elderly ladies, Harris's mother and aunt, negotiated the three steep steps leading down into the lane, Cassie tensed. He was there again. A string of cars was parked close to the churchyard wall. At the further end of the line was a white Peugeot, and, leaning against it, was the stalker. Unmissable. Standing out partly because of his lack of movement, partly because of the intense stare he was directing at her.

He was wearing his sunglasses but when he saw that he had caught her attention, he took them off. The expression on his face was full of malevolence. Scowling, he shook his head in a manner which indicated intimidation rather than denial. Even though there was distance between them, she could feel the negative strength of his personality, as though they were trapped inside a Stephen King movie. At the very least the church spire should have cracked, one of the gargoyled gutter-ends fallen with a crash. Was this Tony Sutherland? If so, she was not about to challenge him. Not here. Not now. She clutched tighter at Lucy's hand as the girl began to sob again, turning into Cassie's shoulder. She was glad about the girl's tears because she did not want Lucy to see him; his focus on herself was impossible to overlook and Lucy would demand to know who he was. Nonetheless, there was a weakness in her knees and the strong desire to sit down somewhere. She was aware of anger, rather than fear. How dare he follow her here, on such an occasion? How *dare* he? Over Lucy's head, she gazed defiantly back at him.

He mouthed something at her. Two words. What was he saying? 'No way,' it looked like. Mouth curving in an exaggerated O, lips coming together for the W before stretching into AY. 'No way.' He continued to shake his head.

Cassie could see Lucy's little car only two down from his Peugeot. She was not going to let the girl walk along the lane alone, not because there was any danger of attack but from an instinctive desire to keep her away from whatever dark impulses ruled this madman.

'I like your dress,' she said, picking a pleat of the skirt between her fingers, hoping to divert Lucy's attention.

'Do you?' Lucy looked down at herself. 'It was a present.'

'It really suits you.'

'She said it would. I wouldn't normally buy this kind of thing for myself.'

'Come back to Bridge End with me,' Cassie urged. 'Please, Lucy.'

'I don't want to.'

'I'll bring you back here afterwards.'

'But Mr Harris will want to know who I am.'

'No, he won't. On occasions like these, people just murmur and move on. All you've got to do is say something polite. What you feel, really. How sorry you are.'

'But I don't think I can face seeing her place again. Knowing that she's gone.'

'Come for my sake,' said Cassie. 'I'd feel better if you were there. I shan't stay long.'

Lucy stared at her. 'You'd really feel better?'

'Honestly.'

'If I came with you?'

'Yes.' Hadn't anyone ever expressed pleasure in the girl's company before? She seemed as screwed up about herself as Cassie was. 'I would.'

'All right.'

They came down the steps to where Cassie's car was parked right behind Harris's. Dry leaves scuttled in the lane as she

169

thrust Lucy into the passenger seat without glancing back and then squeezed herself between the churchyard wall and the door on the driver's side. The lane by now was full of cars pulling out ready to file back to Bridge End. She pushed into the forming queue, waving an apologetic hand at the car behind her. She couldn't see the police officers, but thought they would be unlikely to show up at the house.

When she arrived, John Harris greeted her warmly. 'Thank you *so* much for coming,' he said.

'Are Naomi's parents here?' she asked. 'I ought to go and say something.'

'Her parents?' Harris obviously found her ignorance slightly surprising. 'As a close friend, I'd have thought you knew. Her mother died about twenty years ago. Before I even met Naomi.'

'And her father?'

'I've no idea about the father. Walked out when she was two or three, I seem to recall. She was brought up by her mother and her stepfather, the mother's second husband.'

'What about him, then? Is he here?'

'I think he's dead, too. I don't know, though. Maybe I'm imagining it . . . Naomi never talked about him much.' He smiled at Anne Norrington, who had appeared at his side. 'Anne, dear. How sweet of you to come.'

'You know how pleased I am to help out,' Anne said. She glanced at Cassie. 'Now, John, what shall I do? Give me a job and I'll get on with it.'

'Over here,' Harris said. The grieving air he had worn earlier at the funeral service had vanished. He bustled round, more like a catering manager at a hotel function than a forlorn widower. It was clear that a number of women besides Cassie had been asked to give him a hand with the funeral baked meats. There was something both comic and pathetic about the way they crowded round him: with Naomi gone, he was, of course, both eligible and available. Cassie smiled at Lucinda Powys-Jones, waved to Lottie Haden White and her daughter, nodded at the headmaster of St Christopher's, the nearby prep-school. Mansfield appeared beside her, his weather-beaten complexion blotched with tears. His designer shades did not hide the drawn lines on his face. He looked older and tired.

'I'm surprised to see you here,' Cassie said.

Mansfield picked up her meaning immediately. 'He doesn't know who I am,' he said. 'I told him I was someone who played bridge with her.' He leaned in closer. 'Will you be home this evening?'

'Probably.'

'I'll drop in and see you, if that's OK. Give you a report on what I found out in Edinburgh.' He stared across the room to where John Harris was being flirtatious with a woman whom everybody knew had divorced her husband after finding him in bed with her cleaning lady. 'Look at him. No one would believe we've just buried his wife.'

'There are all sorts of ways of handling grief,' Cassie said, though she found it hard to accept that this was one of them.

'Sure there are.' Mansfield continued to watch Harris. Even with the concealing sunglasses it was possible to detect the hostility in his gaze.

'I'll see you later,' Cassie said, made uncomfortable by the raw edges of his emotion.

'Eightish.' He did not shift his attention from Harris as she moved away.

People were going out through the French windows to walk about on the lawn, admiring the garden. Someone had removed the spade from among the roses and put away the trug. Graham Blacklaws was steering his mother slowly round, stopping to examine the plantings. Bitsy had a glass of clear liquid in her hand. There was no indication here that there had been a nationwide water shortage for weeks. As she watched, Graham reached forward and picked a rosebud which he then stuck into his lapel. What a cheapskate. Cassie couldn't help thinking how much Naomi would have hated such a gathering, how awkward she would have been, how disagreeable she would have looked. Turning, she found herself face to face with a jowly man whom she recollected having seen earlier in the churchyard.

'How do you do?' He held out a hand and shook hers firmly, holding on when she tried to withdraw it. 'Are you a friend of the deceased?'

'Yes. And you?'

'A colleague of John's, actually. A sad business this, don't you think?'

'Very.'

'Depressing too; I only came because one wants to show solidarity on these occasions.' He smiled, showing long dimples. His eyes were a startlingly clear grey, not in the least faded by the passing of time. 'John blames himself, of course. Natural, I suppose, in the circumstances, to wonder what one could have done to prevent it. But she was a difficult woman, I believe. Very difficult.'

'Mmm.' Although privately Cassie agreed, she felt that it was well beyond the bounds of courtesy for him to stand on Naomi's carpets in Naomi's house and say so.

'Still, *nil nisi* and all that.'

'You're a colleague of John Harris's, you said.'

'Yes.'

'Were you at that Edinburgh conference?'

'Of course. Poor fellow got the bad news during a planning meeting. Devastated, really. As one would be.'

'What do you chaps do at business conferences?' asked Cassie. She hoped the question didn't sound too false. 'In your free time, I mean.'

'You know the sort of thing. Sightsee. Shop. A CD for the kids. Cashmere sweater for the wife. That's certainly what John was doing, because he came into the same shop I was in, trying to decide which colour to go for. Long way to come back to exchange it if I got it wrong. I asked his advice, actually. He's good at that. "The green," he said. "Holly looks good in green." Holly's my wife, do you see.'

'Ah. And that was the afternoon of the day when you didn't have to go back for a conference dinner?'

'I believe it was.'

'Did you and John . . .' prompted Cassie.

'What, eat together, do you mean? No, I have family up there. I had to go and eat my way through roast beef and tatties, I'm afraid. And raise a glass or three of the old Glenfiddich, of course, which was no hardship at all.'

'I wonder what John did that evening.'

'Ate with some of the guys from our New York office, as far as I recall. At least, that's what he said he was doing when I asked. Some Italian place, I think he said. He'd been there before, said it was damn good.'

'Oh.' Cassie could not keep the disappointment from her voice. This was what Harris had told the police, according to the statement DC Walsh had provided; this man was confirming it.

His clear gaze rested on her speculatively. 'What's your interest, anyway?'

'No particular reason. It's just these business conferences always sound like such a yawn. I wondered how you passed the time.' Before the man could respond to this piece of artificial disingenuity, a voice beside her said: 'Cassie . . .'

It was Lucy. She stared at John Harris's colleague, who stared back. For a striking second, connection thickened between them, then he put out his hand again. Lucy did not take it. 'I'm ready to leave when you are, Cass,' she said, her gaze still on the man's. With the tip of her finger she delicately touched the stud in her nose.

'And who would you be?' he said.

She turned her back on him without answering the question. 'Let's split, Cassie. Let's move it,' she said rudely, speaking the words over her shoulder. 'Right this minute.' The implication that her desire to leave had been accelerated by meeting the man was too obvious to be ignored.

'It'll take me five minutes or so,' Cassie said, embarrassed by her inexplicably discourteous behaviour. The guy wasn't that likeable, but he'd certainly not done anything to deserve quite such a brush-off.

'I'm outta here. I'll wait in your car.' Lucy walked away from them and stepped out into the garden.

'Your sister?' the man said.

'No.'

'Pretty little thing. Though I can't say I care for the self-mutilation the young go in for these days.'

'How exactly do you mean?'

'Things in their noses, rings through their eyebrows, pierced lips, that sort of thing. She's probably got one through her nipple, too. Or somewhere even more intimate, if we did but know.'

Cassie frowned. 'What?' she said coldly.

'I'd smack her bottom good and hard if she was mine. Up with the skirt, pull down her panties.' He looked at her with pretended contrition. 'Oh dear, you *do* look cross. Just my little joke. I hope I didn't offend you.'

'You did, as it happens. I assume you were trying to.'

'I've got girls of my own, you know. I'm well aware of the naughty things they get up to. Lock up your daughters, eh, Miss Swann?' He grinned, the smile leaving his grey eyes unmoved. She recognised his type. There were a lot of them about. This was a man who disliked women, at the very least despised them; a man who sought at every opportunity to diminish them, in order to hide the fact that he was threatened by them. She felt sorry for his daughters.

Like Lucy, she didn't bother to answer. The unpleasant tone of his remarks was so gratuitous that she could scarcely believe she had heard him right, though she knew she had. She, too, turned and walked away.

Lucy was waiting for her in the car. As Cassie got in and fiddled with ignition keys and clutches, she said: 'What was that all about?'

'What?' said Lucy.

'You know what I mean.'

'I recognised him, that's all.'

'Who is he?'

'I don't mean his name. I've never seen him before. But I know the type. He's an abuser.'

Cassie, moving into the road beyond the broad five-barred gate of Bridge End, pressed her foot slowly down on the brake. She sensed that the lid on Lucy's feelings was about to fly off. 'What did you say?'

'He likes to fuck little girls.'

175

'Lucy! How can you possibly—'

'You can tell. It's the eyes – you can always tell. And the smile.'

Out of the corner of her eye Cassie was aware of movement; turning her head, she saw that Lucy was grinding her teeth together. There was a girl at school who used to do that in the dormitory: it was a strange and lonely sound, speaking of fears unexpressed, of terrors lurking. The girl's hands were twisted together in the lap of her flowery skirt but nonetheless, they trembled.

Cassie speeded up a little. 'I'm not going to take you back to your car,' she said firmly. 'You're coming home with me. It's time we had a talk.'

Lucy nodded. 'All right.'

'From the time I was eight,' Lucy said dully. 'It's all so predictable really. I've read about it so many times and it's always the same. What the bastards say. What they do. The first time was actually on my eighth birthday. I was wearing this pink gauzy dress, my fairy costume which my mother – that's my adoptive mother – had made for the school pageant. She went out after supper, to her flower-arranging class or something. And he followed me into my bedroom and shut the door; he said he was going to give me a special birthday present, and I wasn't to tell Mummy, it was our secret. And then he – he . . .'

'Oh God,' Cassie groaned. The gleaming eyes, the scaly jaws, were brighter now, and closer.

'. . . did it to me.'

Claws scrabbled. Rage, resentment, impotence: 'Eight years old.' Cassie said.

'It hurt like hell. God, how it hurt. I was pushing him off, trying to scream, but he put the pillow over my face. It seemed

176

to go on for hours. I was bleeding, there was blood on the duvet cover. When he'd finished, he didn't look at me. He said that if I told Mummy, she would cry, she'd be so sad she might go away and leave us. He knew that after that, I'd never do a thing which might leave the two of us together.' Tearless sobs shook the girl's thin frame. 'He knew I was frightened of him.'

'Why didn't you tell anyone?'

'Would you have? If you believed him when he said your mother would go away if you did?'

'I don't know. I can't imagine such a thing.'

'When you're eight, you're still buying the shit grownups hand out.'

'Yes.' Cassie could remember that time of total trust. Even though Sarah, her mother, had died, she had been so wrapped round in love by her father and her Gran that she had never doubted that the world was good. Disillusion was still some years away.

'It wasn't every night. I never knew when he'd come creeping, so I was always waiting, sitting up in the dark, wondering when the handle of the door would turn and he'd be there.' Lucy shuddered. 'The smell of him. The slimy feel of his skin. I hated him. I *hated* him. I always will. And when I got older, more able to argue, he told me I owed it to him.'

'How did he work that one out?'

'Because he'd adopted me in the first place. He said I owed him for my food and shelter and education. IOUs all down the line. I was his, bought and paid for.'

'Did you accept that?'

'I had to, at first. I didn't think I had any choice. And when I stopped believing him, started questioning it, he had yet another reason to come on to me. The more I cheeked him, the more he loved it. Gave him the excuse, you see.'

'For what?'

'To come in, pull down the bedclothes, pull down my pyjamas, smack me first before he . . . did it. The special birthday present bit turned into Ooh-what-a-bad-girl-you've-been-I'm-only-doing-this-because-you've-been-so-naughty. All that shit. Someone's got to teach you a lesson. This hurts me more than it hurts you.' Lucy gave a sardonic laugh. 'He was bloody right about that. Sometimes he'd even make me ask him to do it to me. Beg for it. Actually kneel and plead with him to stick his . . . to do it. He said he'd tell my mother what a dirty girl I was if I didn't, and then she'd go away and leave me.'

'Have you ever talked about this to anyone?'

'Who? Who would I talk to?'

'A psychiatrist. A professional of some kind.'

'Nah. I've been down that road. They're all so smug. Getting off on listening to someone else's troubles. Feeling good about the fact that they're OK. Reinforcing their own sense of superiority.'

'We could argue that one, but let's not at the moment. Haven't you even mentioned it to a friend? Someone you've been close to?'

'I did try to talk about it to someone I got involved with at university. Another student. As soon as I started, he was like: you mean your dad fucked you? He was out of there before you could say 'molested'. That's why I dropped out of university, actually. I was terrified he'd spread it round the campus.'

Cassie was tempted to ask whether her adoptive mother knew about the abuse, but was afraid that Lucy might have a problem facing up to the answer. They usually did know, the mothers. Sometimes even aided and abetted, in order to deflect the attentions of their husbands. 'You could do something about it, you know,' she said.

'Like what? Sue him?'

'Yes. Why not?'

'Firstly, because I'd have to see him again. Secondly, what good would it do now? He's not going to do it to anyone else, is he?'

'You don't know that.'

'Unless he's married again and got more little girls to abuse, he's not.'

'Getting him put in jail would be a warning to all the other men in positions of trust.'

'Warnings won't stop them.'

She was probably right. 'Did you talk to Naomi about this?'

'A bit.'

Cassie remembered something Philip Mansfield had told her. That Naomi, too, had been abused. It was something she would have to explore further. 'Have you seen this man since?'

'A couple of times. When my mother was dying, I went back home.'

'What was that like?'

'He didn't try anything on, if that's what you mean. He knew I'd have torn his balls off if he had. He kept telling me how he loved me, how he couldn't bear to let me go, I was all he had left. Or would be, once his wife died. He even had the bloody nerve to try and blame it on her. Not that he ever came out and admitted that there was anything to admit. Said I didn't know what it was like for a man to be married to a frigid wife. I'm like, oh yeah? Whose fault is that, then? He talked about how he's got this high sex-drive and stuff. But that's not what abuse is about, is it? It's a power thing, isn't it? Inadequate people trying to persuade themselves that they're adequate by

179

forcing sex on someone even weaker than they are. God, how I hated him. I couldn't bear to be in the same room as him. I even hid a mug and a plate at the back of the cupboard while I was there so I wouldn't risk using anything *he* might have drunk out of.'

'How long did that last?'

'A few weeks. She had cancer.'

'But he left you alone?'

'Before, yes. After Mum finally – after the funeral, people came back to the house, just like we did this afternoon. Everyone was so sorry for him. They'd always come across as the perfect couple. "At least you've still got Lucy," they all said.' She laughed bitterly. 'I could have told them a thing or two about him, if I'd wanted. When they'd all gone he came and sobbed all over me, fumbled me, pretending he didn't know what he was doing. If he hadn't been so drunk, I think he would have raped me. I'm small, you see, and he's a tall man. Anyway, I pushed him off and he fell on the floor. I kicked him in the balls. I told him that if I ever saw him again, it'd be too soon for me. I spat in his face.' Lucy thrust her trembling hands between her thighs. Her voice rose. 'And all the time, he was smiling that hideous horrible—'

'Ssh,' Cassie said. 'Ssh. You're free from him now.'

'No, I'm not. That's the terrible thing about it. I shall never be free. I'll never get away from him. Every time a boy tries to kiss me, I remember his mouth, every time a man touches my body I remember— Oh *God* . . .' The last word was like a howl from a nightmare. The creatures writhed in the dark place where Lucy lived. She shuddered, holding her head between her hands as though afraid the bones might suddenly explode if she didn't hold them together. 'I can never ever make love with someone. It would be impossible for me. I'll never have any children because I couldn't bear the process of making them. He's completely ruined any chance I ever had of a normal life.'

'You should do something about it, Lucy. It's not too late. Whatever you feel about seeing him again, he mustn't be allowed to get away with all this. He's stolen a lot of your childhood, and – if you let him – of your future.' Cassie wondered if that was why Lucy seemed so young for her age, whether the body was trying to compensate the mind for the things missed and the years lost.

'I do see him,' Lucy said. 'Quite often, actually.' Again her finger touched the silver nose-stud.

'Oh?' Cassie raised her eyebrows. 'I thought you said . . .'

'He follows me. He found out where I was living – I don't know how. When I moved, he found my new address. Wherever I go, he's there. Shops in the same place, turns up in the same pubs. If I go to the cinema, I know that somewhere in the darkness, he's there. When I go to bed, I know he's outside, waiting.'

'What's he waiting for?'

'Me.'

'Why? What does he want?'

'You wouldn't believe how possessive he is. When I was little, people thought it was *so-o-o-o* sweet. "Look, Lucy's Daddy's come to pick her up from school again." "Lucy's Daddy buys all her clothes." What they meant was that Lucy's fucking Daddy wouldn't let her out of his fucking sight.' She gripped her hands together against her thin chest. 'Now he wants me to come home. He caught up with me a few months ago, shoved me up against a wall so I couldn't get away. He said he didn't like living alone, it was my duty to come back, that he'd adopted me, fair and square, and I hadn't paid my debt yet. If I ever could.'

'What did he mean?'

'I think my adoption was one of those "arrangements". Not done though the normal channels? Something my mother said once gave me the impression that they paid for me.'

'Your real mother, you mean?'

'I s'pose.'

'Naomi.'

'Yeah.' Lucy was obviously not happy about the implications. Cassie left it for the moment.

'Do you know anything about your biological father?'

'It was one of the things I wanted to ask Naomi. But I wasn't all that bothered. She wouldn't have been forced to give me up if he wasn't as big a shit as my adopted father, would she?'

'Talking of which, you really ought to contact the police about him. What he's doing, following you, constitutes harassment.'

'Yeah, well. Try proving it. So far, he's done nothing except be in the same places I am.'

This was so exactly what Cassie had felt about her own stalker that she did not press the point. Nor did she tell Lucy about the man following her, in case the girl thought she was trying to put her down by showing that she wasn't the only one with problems.

Lucy closed her eyes and let out a deep sigh. 'I'll never forget the way he smiled,' she said flatly. 'Every time he raped me, he had the same sort of grin on his face as that man at Naomi's funeral. That's how I knew what he was.'

It sounded obsessional. Delusional. Was Lucy so disturbed that she saw her rapist father in every man's face? It seemed obvious to Cassie that she needed professional help. Watching the small, pinched face, she was overcome by a rush of love for this damaged person, and, at the same time, a sense of profound gratitude. Who could bear to bring children into a world where such things could occur? What parent could ever promise that they would always be there to support and comfort? And if such guarantees could not be given, then it was better that the children remain unborn, rather than take the risk. Possibly the same thoughts had occurred to Naomi.

Maybe Philip Mansfield was wrong, after all, and John Harris was entirely innocent. Maybe it was the strain of trying to live with the knowledge that by her actions she had condemned her daughter to such long-term misery, to exactly the same long-term misery as she herself must have experienced, which had pushed Naomi over the brink into suicide.

♣ 13 ♣

Cassie had planned to drive over and check out Tony Sutherland.
She tried to persuade Lucy to accompany her, feeling it was best
not to leave her alone, but Lucy shook her head. 'You're going
towards Oxford,' she said. 'I gotta get back to London.' Her face
was pale, streaked with tears and unhappiness.

'Why?'

'I've got things to do.'

'Do you realise I can't contact you, since I don't know your
address or phone number?'

'Why would you need to?'

The ungracious response didn't worry Cassie. She'd been
pretty ungracious herself in the past. 'Just to keep in touch. To
see how you are, that sort of thing,' she said, keeping it light,
sensing that the girl shied away from intrusion.

'Nah. That's OK. Anyway, I can always contact you.'

'Come on, Lucy, just give me a phone number. I promise not
to keep ringing you up.'

The girl exasperatedly clicked her tongue against her teeth,
but in the end scribbled down a number.

'Will you be all right on your own?'

'I've managed so far, haven't I?' Lucy said, shrugging
dismissively.

'You can stay with me for a while longer if you want.'

'Thanks, but I better not.' She gave Cassie a hug. 'Hey, it was good of you – I really mean it – to listen. To . . . care. But I don't want to rely on anybody but myself. It's best that way, because then you don't get let down.'

'I won't let you down,' protested Cassie, but Lucy's tired smile, far older than her years, said as clearly as words that she didn't believe her.

'You might not be able to help it,' she said. 'You might not even mean to, but sooner or later, everyone always does.'

Driving through the autumn sunshine, Cassie reflected that perhaps her own upbringing had not been as traumatic as she had always considered it. Compared to Lucy's father, Aunt Polly now appeared no more than a frigid snob, rather than the Dragon Lady of Cassie's resentful memories. As for her cousins, the midget twins and their elder sister, for a few moments she saw them in a more kindly light. It was not their fault that Aunt Polly was their mother. And what, after all, had they done to her except be thinner? Could they really help their judgemental attitude to D cups and 38" hips?

All right: 40" hips?

Well, yes. As a matter of fact, they damn well could. Just because the three of them together weighed in at somewhat less than a portable television set didn't make them morally superior. Didn't give them the right to exchange little goblin glances when they thought – or pretended to think – that Cassie wasn't looking. Eating two lettuce leaves and a shred of grated carrot for dinner didn't qualify anyone for sainthood.

On the other hand . . .

She was just beginning to accept what she had denied for years: that she had been damaged by her upbringing, by the loss of her parents, by the contrast between the warmth of family life above the pub off the Holloway Road, and the cold pretensions of the vicarage. But the harm done to her was slight compared to the sabotage Lucy had undergone. She would have to persuade the girl to see someone professional: for all her tough talk, it was obvious that, emotionally, she was very fragile.

Cassie turned off the motorway onto a country road. Sloes and hazelnuts abounded. The blackberries in the hedgerows were huge and luscious: perhaps she should pick a few and make jam or something. Put them up with apples, in preserving jars. Make sloe gin. Be more like the twins; act domestic, for once. It might even be less of a drag than she imagined. Especially the gin bit.

Approaching the village where Sutherland lived, she pushed her other problems to the back of her mind. If he should turn out to be the stalker, what was she going to do about it? She had already approached him in the pub and got precisely nowhere. There was little else she could do except reason with him. Point out that there was room for competition, that she and Natasha were aiming at a slightly different market from himself – though she had no grounds for believing that. She could threaten him with a solicitor's letter. Or mention the police again, with more certainty now that she knew why he was after her. And the fact that he was always where she was might seem more substantive if she could show that he lived some twenty miles away, that it was unreasonable for him always to be so far from home for such mundane activities as shopping or changing a library book.

Yet even as she thought all this, she could hear the generic policeman's voice.

'You say he's always in the public library when you are, madam? Even though he lives twenty miles away? Did it ever occur to you, madam, that he reads a lot, likes to belong to more than one service, it's not against the law, after all? As for the supermarket, maybe he likes the one you use better than the ones nearer his own home. Could be they offer a better bargain in cornflakes or economy packs of detergent, know what I mean?' Then the eyes rolled heavenwards, the sideways look at a colleague, the expression signifying they'd got a right one here. 'In the same pub, madam? There's no law against that, far as I know, not yet, there isn't. They call it the nanny state, don't they, but they haven't started telling us where we can and can't drink, not yet.' And so on and so forth, while she felt more and more of an idiot. No, the police wouldn't be much help at this stage.

Tony Sutherland lived in a nondescript thirties house in a street of similar houses. Bow-fronted and part tile-hung, a strip of stained glass along the upper edge of the windows, rose bushes in the front garden set in a circular flowerbed in the middle of the small lawn. As it happened, Sutherland was not at home. Or if he was, he was not answering his door. Perhaps he knew it was her and wanted to avoid an open confrontation. Next door, a woman was pretending to wield a duster but was, in fact, peering unashamedly between the net curtains of her front room and, on impulse, Cassie stepped up to the creosoted fence between the two properties and raised her eyebrows enquiringly, at the same time jerking her head back at the Sutherland house. The woman lifted a finger, signalling that she was to wait and, after a moment during which Cassie could hear bolts being unbolted and chains rattled, appeared in her porch.

'I'm looking for Mr Sutherland,' Cassie said, walking down the Sutherland path and up the next-door path, squeezing past a J-registered Rover parked on the concrete strips. The garden was almost identical, the major difference being that the rose plot in the middle of the lawn was square instead of round. 'Any idea when he'll be back?'

'What was it in connection with?' the woman asked suspiciously. She was in her early sixties and had a fluffy yellow duster in her hand.

'I believe he runs a small company specialising in the – uh – entertainment business,' Cassie said, wondering whether "entertainment" was the right word for something as sober as a company flogging bridge sundries, conjuring up, as it did, images of long-thighed hoofers and strategic feather boas rather than games of skill. It occurred to her that the zoning laws probably made commercial enterprises illegal in this residential area and this woman looked the sort who'd happily shop her neighbours to the Town Hall planners without even stopping to remove her apron.

Appearances are so often deceptive. 'That's right,' agreed the woman, nodding away. 'Nice little business, so he often told us. Bridge supplies, packs of cards and things like that. They were in it together: she did the secretarial and book-keeping and he was responsible for the sales side, buying the stock and so on. County players, as a matter of fact, the two of them. Champions. I don't play myself.'

'Ah.' Champions? That must be why the name was familiar.

'But with her gone – well, he was telling my hubby and me only last Sunday that he was quite glad to give it up. Got enough with the pension from his company for his own needs, and with his daughter grown and off his hands, well, it was time to give it a rest. And it's not as if he didn't have plenty to occupy him: the Garden Circle – he's the President this year – and the Rotary, and going all over the place with his bridge the way he does.'

'I see.' If Sutherland was the stalker, which seemed unlikely now, it was nothing to do with a desire to force the opposition off his turf.

'I tell him, " Tony", I say, "you ought to slow down a bit, at your age," but he says it's being so active that keeps him young.'

'What sort of age is he?'

'Too old for you, dear,' said the woman as though she suspected Cassie of hoping to make an honest man of her neighbour. 'Younger than me and my hubby, of course. Mid-fifties, maybe.'

The Tony Sutherland this woman was describing didn't sound like her stalker. Even though it was a cliché that the worst crimes were often perpetrated by the mildest and most respectable of people, presidents of garden circles and members of the Rotary Club weren't the sort who went round harassing women, were they? 'Could you describe him for me?'

'Good-looking feller, really,' the woman said. 'Not my cup of tea, but there's plenty who'd say different. Mary had a bit of a time with him when they were younger, that I *do* know for a fact.'

'Blue eyes?'

'Yes. And blond hair – or used to have. Gone grey now, of course.'

'Tall?'

'Taller than my hubby, that much I can tell you, and *he's* five eleven in his stockinged feet.'

'What kind of a car does he drive?'

'Couldn't tell you. I've never been much good on cars. It's something foreign, I do know that. My hubby had words with him about it once. Said we ought to Buy British, support the country and that. Tony came right back at him, said he'd be glad to buy British the minute the British started making cars worth buying.' The woman snickered appreciatively at this retrospective witticism.

'What colour is his car?'

'They give it some fancy name these days, don't they? Oyster or ivory or some such. White's what I call it, but the old ways aren't good enough any more, everything's got to be tarted up nowadays.'

'White.' Like the man who had been following her. Cassie told herself that lots of people drove white cars: she had read somewhere that it was the most popular colour on the road because of its extra visibility during the indeterminate hours between day and night. It did not mean that Sutherland was her stalker. Not necessarily.

The woman leaned against her door jamb. 'What's your interest, anyway?'

'Nothing, really.'

'You're asking a lot of questions about nothing, in that case.'

'I thought he might be someone I used to know, that's all.'

The woman sniffed. 'Don't you know the names of your friends, then?'

'I thought he might be . . .' Oh the hell with it. There was no point making up a story. The woman would undoubtedly be round to describe Cassie in minute detail the minute that Sutherland came home and if he was her stalker, he would know at once who she was. If he wasn't, then it made no difference.

She began to retreat back to her car parked at the kerb. 'Thank you very much,' she said and smiled, and got into her car and drove away.

A J-registered Rover . . . Why hadn't she thought of it before? All she had to do was take down the number of the stalker's car, next time she came across him, and get it identified via the Swansea people – if they gave out that sort of information to the general public. She was not sure that they did. It was a pity she'd alienated Paul Walsh quite so comprehensively. For a few rather delicious moments she played with the notion of getting back together with him. She'd say . . . then he'd say . . . then he would . . . and she would . . . but in her heart she knew this was mere fantasy. She had laughed at him. To a man like DS Walsh, she'd have done better to steal his wallet. At least that wouldn't have made him look a fool. It was probably a measure of their relationship that a misplaced giggle should have dealt it the *coup de grâce*. Not that it wasn't pretty moribund before that. She remembered again how Walsh had hopped across the bedroom floor, and began to laugh but her laughter turned to sudden despair and, never one for the stiff upper lip when histrionic self-indulgence would suffice, she pulled into a lay-by and gave way to a deluge of tears, though not quite sure exactly who she was weeping for. Naomi? Lucy? Or herself?

Face it, Cass, she thought. *There isn't a single person in the entire world who loves you.* There was Charlie Quartermain, of course, but he didn't count. It was obvious that she was doomed to a future of loneliness and aridity. Soon she'd be one of those bearded old bats in dippy-hemmed skirts with their bosoms hanging round their waists. She didn't even have children who'd come and visit her, however grudgingly. Friendless and alone, she would plod out the remainder of her days and be laid to rest at last in a pauper's grave, unmourned and unmissed.

The horror of it dried her tears instantly. She recognised the condition: low blood sugar. The only practical way to get out of her current spiral of despair was to consume a stack of useless calories. Preferably in the form of some utterly sinful cake full of cream and marzipan and nuts. If the worst came to the worst, a chocolate bar would do. Starting up the engine, she continued driving towards Market Broughton. There had once been a tea shop specialising in floral tablecloths and waitresses who brought large brown teapots to the table, along with plates of assorted cakes. Thanks to the march of progress, this was now a video-shop with a top shelf specialising in kinky tapes with titles like *Naked Sex Dwarfs* and *Naughty Schoolgirl Romps*. But it was still possible to find a decent cup of tea in the Three White Feathers, across from the Two Magpies. It wasn't a patch on the Randolph, of course, but the scones weren't bad, and the fruit cake was renowned.

She hesitated when she saw that Graham Blacklaws was in there, taking tea with his mother. Catching sight of her, he leaped to his feet. 'Come and sit with us,' he called. He seemed relieved to see her, so much so, that Cassie hoped he wouldn't remember that she had landed him with the bill for her lunch only a few days earlier. Anyway, who was he to talk, a man who snitched roses from a dead woman's garden? Although she didn't say so, this was a lucky meeting: she had already decided that a further quizzing of Graham was in order.

'Thank you.' Cassie smiled at Bitsy, who stared glassily back at her. Bitsy had been a merry widow for some thirty years, the merriness originally a consequence of losing her husband but nowadays increasingly reliant on vodka. It was a pity that she was in attendance but with any luck she would shortly fall into an alcoholic semi-stupor.

They chatted inconsequentially for a while about the funeral and the flowers and how John Harris was bearing up. Cassie unwisely asked how the *Messiah* was coming along and Blacklaws gave her a run-down on his rehearsal schedule and the various remedies he used to alleviate the symptoms of a sore throat, should one occur, most of them involving honey and two or three including oil of peppermint. As soon as Bitsy's head began to droop, Cassie said: 'You know we were discussing Naomi Harris's will the other day.'

'Yes.' He frowned, perhaps remembering her unpaid-for lunch, and pushed his glasses further up his long nose.

'You said that she had arranged to come in and change it,' Cassie said quickly.

'That's right,' he said, in his guarded solicitorial fashion.

'It can't hurt now for you to tell me in whose favour, can it?'

He rattled his legal feathers, fluffed them out and displayed them for a moment. 'Professional discretion . . . entrusted to me as . . . breach of client . . . seal of confidentiality . . .'

'But now she's dead, it no longer matters much,' Cassie said, hoping she was pressing the right buttons.

'Then why do you want to know?'

'Just nosy, I suppose.'

'Very true.' He picked up a teaspoon from his saucer and examined it censoriously.

'I thought it was interesting that she should have wanted to change it. She wasn't given to impetuous decisions, was she?'

'Heavens, no.'

'So her reasons must have been quite important.'

'Mmm.' He tugged at the hem of his mother's skirt, which was beginning to ride up over her knees.

'C'mon, Graham. I know she told you over the phone. And I absolutely promise not to tell anyone else. As you know, she and I were—' Cassie swallowed hard on this lie but continued just the same, '—we were pretty close friends, and I wondered whether the person she had in mind as her new beneficiary was the one she told me about just before she died.'

'Who was that?'

'I don't want to tell you because she asked me to keep it to myself for a while.'

'Ah.'

She had him now. She could tell by the way he was chewing on his lips, wondering whether the divulging of his client's words could be construed as an indiscretion. 'Was it to do with someone very close to her?' she said, arching her eyebrows significantly.

'Very close,' he said. 'About as close as you can get.'

'Someone she felt she owed an obligation to? Even a debt?'

He nodded, at the same time picking up his cup and scrutinising the underside of his saucer. The stolen rose in his lapel was not looking in the best of health.

Cassie smiled. 'I think we're talking about the same person, aren't we?'

Graham stared at his mother, who lay with her head back against the back of the sofa, breathing softly through her mouth. He lowered his voice. 'I have to admit that I was flabbergasted when she first told me, a couple of months ago,' he said. 'I advised her in the strongest possible terms to check and double-check on the claims of this young – uh – person before making over half the estate in the event of her death. Which, as we know, occurred much sooner than anyone might have expected.'

'Claims? I understood that this – uh – young person didn't want or need her money,' Cassie said. She was particularly proud of the hesitation.

'Well, yes. I know that. But you can't be too careful.'

'It wasn't as if the suggestion that she change her will came from outside. I understood that the decision was entirely hers.'

'I know that. I was just—'

'Then claims is not quite the word, is it?' Cassie felt a certain indignation on the – uh – young person's behalf.

'Perhaps not.'

'Anyway, she was going to change her will in the young person's favour, is that right?'

'Indeed.'

'But killed herself before seeing you.'

'That's right.'

'One last question, Graham.'

'You haven't joined the police force, have you, Cassandra? You sound jolly like one of those women chief inspectors they have on the telly.'

'Ha, ha, Graham. Very droll. No, I just wanted to know who currently stands to get Naomi's money when John Harris dies.'

He stared at her as though she had just disclosed that she was not wearing any knickers. 'You can't seriously expect me to—'

'I could find out from your senior partner, if I wanted to. Mr Symons plays bridge in one of my fours,' said Cassie. Although the latter half of the sentence was true, the first half was almost certainly not. 'All I wondered was whether it was Harris's to dispose of as he thought fit, or whether Naomi had made further provision for her estate after his death.'

Graham looked sulky. 'The estate then reverts to her next of kin,' he said.

'And who is that?'

'A man called Francis Benson. Some kind of stepbrother – or half-brother. The son of her father by his second marriage.'

'Ah. And where does Mr Benson live?'

'In Ross-on-Wye.'

'Do you have the address?'

'If you mean will I give it to you, the answer's no.'

'Why? What harm can it possibly do?'

'He owns and runs an enterprise called Benson's Bookshop: I'm sure you'll have no difficulty in finding it in the phone book.' Graham tapped the side of his nose and gave a significant smirk. 'You didn't hear it from me.'

'What?'

'I didn't tell you, all right?' He tapped again, this time producing a hollow sound from the inside of his nostril.

'I see what you mean.' Though Cassie didn't really. It seemed off of Naomi to want her money to go to the son of the father who abandoned her. But perhaps until Lucy appeared, there was no one else. 'Did you tell the police about this?'

'Not really.'

'What does that mean?'

'They didn't ask, I didn't tell them. They seemed fairly certain that she killed herself, and there wasn't much reason to believe anything different. Nor is there now. Look,' Graham said, 'Could we talk about something else? All this has been an appalling shock. Mother and I had been playing bridge with her, too, only a few days before the discovery of her body. Mother's still stunned by the news, poor old thing.'

'So I see,' said Cassie.

It looked as though there could be no question that Naomi had been planning to leave a substantial amount to Lucy. The person most likely to wish to prevent her from doing so had been John Harris. But perhaps this Francis Benson was also worth taking a look at. Especially if he didn't know about the existence of Lucy. Perhaps John Harris, instead of being the perpetrator, was even a potential victim.

★ ★ ★

The grandfather clock was chiming the second of eight mellow strokes when Philip Mansfield's motorbike stopped beyond the hedge which bounded Honeysuckle Cottage's front garden. Cassie opened the front door to him before he had time to knock. He accepted a whisky and slumped down on one of the two sofas in the sitting room, his long legs stretched in front of him. He was still wearing his Armani suit but had changed his black loafers for knee-length aviator boots.

'You look depressed,' Cassie said. In fact, he looked almost elderly, the hair and the boots cruelly anachronistic.

'Wouldn't you?' He looked at her angrily. 'My life's completely lost direction, now that Naomi's dead. Everything's been swept away.'

'But you hadn't known her that long, had you?'

'Long enough. And in that time I had something to work for. To hope for. Now—' He jerked an angry shoulder in a half-shrug and pulled at his whisky. 'I don't mind saying I had a hard time keeping my hands off that smug bastard this morning.'

'John Harris?'

'Who else. Did you see the way he was flirting with all those smirking bitches?' Mansfield's face was vicious. 'Mine-hosting it all over the bloody place at his own wife's *fun*eral? I nearly lost my breakfast.'

'Calm down,' said Cassie. 'He wasn't that bad. And those women aren't bitches.' She thought about it. 'Not *all* of them.'

'All I could bloody think of was how much Naomi would have hated the whole thing. She wasn't really sociable: I think that's why she enjoyed playing bridge, because she could get out and meet people, but not have to make conversation.'

'That's very astute of you.'

'It's not something I've just pulled out of the air, you know. I *loved* her. We were going to live together, for chrissake. I thought about her, what made her tick, why she was the way she was.'

'You started to tell me once that she was abused as a child.'

'Yeah.'

He didn't want to talk about it, but Cassie persisted. 'Do you mean she was sexually molested?' When he gave an unwilling nod, she said: 'Who was responsible?'

'Her stepfather, the bastard. Her mother's second husband.'

'What happened to him?'

'God knows. It went on for years, until her mother found out. Then it was Goodbye, husband Number Two.' He drew a finger across his throat. 'Matter of fact, I'm not sure he didn't do time for it.'

'She was lucky, then.'

'You call that lucky? Remind me not to go to the race track with you.'

'Some mothers actually encourage it. Or at least condone it. Or when they find out what's happening, accuse the child of lying, or, even worse, tell her it must have been her fault in the first place. What that must do to a bewildered little girl I can hardly bear to imagine.'

'It wasn't something Naomi would ever talk about.' Getting up, Mansfield fetched the whisky bottle and refilled both their glasses.

'Did she ever mention her real father's second family?'

'She did talk about them, once or twice. I seem to remember there was a son. She'd been down to visit them several times. They lived near Shrewsbury or somewhere.'

Did John Harris know any of this? He hadn't mentioned it earlier. Naomi seemed to have compartmentalised her life to a more than usual degree. 'Were any of them at the funeral?'

'No idea. I wasn't exactly going round taking names for my Christmas card list.'

Cassie took a decision. 'Did you know she had had a child? A daughter.'

'Yeah.' He did not seem particularly interested. 'Gave it up for adoption, she told me. Must be well over twenty years ago, now.'

'Did you know that she had recently tried to get in touch with her?'

'I believe she did say something about it.'

'Do you know if she succeeded?'

He gave her a long look which it was impossible to decipher. The bank robber had had exactly the same wide kitten's eyes. 'No,' he said. Cassie could not tell whether he was lying or not. Nor what the implications might be if he was. It was something she could come back to.

'Do you have any idea what her maiden name was?' she asked.

'Why?'

'Because I want to know,' she said flatly, refusing to be intimidated by his hostile stare.

'Benson,' he said.

'What about the stepfather's name?'

'Dunno.'

'She never mentioned it?'

'No. Why would she?'

'Is he still alive, do you know?'

'Haven't a clue.' Perhaps sensing that she was growing increasingly impatient with his brusqueness, he added: 'She never said he wasn't. But maybe she didn't know. He wasn't exactly someone she'd want to keep in touch with, was he?'

Cassie changed tack. 'Tell me about Edinburgh. Did you get any further on the prostitute thing?'

Some of his usual animation returned. 'As a matter of fact . . .' He reached into the breast pocket of his jacket and brought out a small notebook. 'I won't go into all the reasons I gave the hotel for wanting to know. But they had a record of phone calls made from his room which I was able to obtain.'

'For ready money, I presume.'

'A not inconsiderable sum changed hands,' he said with assumed primness. 'I thought it was a reasonable investment. Anyway, I telephoned the numbers and one of them was this bird who sells her favours for cash. But not a prostitute. At least, if she was, she's pretty high class.'

'How do you know?'

'Because I went round to her place, didn't I?' He adopted a high-pitched Miss Jean Brodie accent. 'Eh, good efternoowun, Mr Mensfield, and whet cen Ay do fairr yeou.' Maggie Smith did it much better.

'And what could she?'

'She confirmed that Harris had spent one of his free afternoons with her. But only one.'

'Bonking, do you mean?'

'Actually, I don't think so.'

'What's the problem, then? He didn't tell the police where he was so he must have wanted to hide it.'

Mansfield dropped his eyes and blustered a bit. 'Actually, I think I got the wrong number first time I rang. She wasn't on the game at all. This bint's married to a minister, and Harris is a former boyfriend. All terribly innocent – unless your husband happens to be a Wee Free Churcher. Strange men spending the afternoon in the manse while the minister's oot of toon? What a scandal.'

'I'm not exactly sure what conclusion we're drawing from this.'

'That he spent the first of his free afternoons with her and, for her sake, he doesn't want anyone to know. However . . .' He poked a finger at Cassie, '. . . according to her, he didn't spend the *second* afternoon there. By the way, I brought that bill you asked for. From the Rivabella Restaurant.' He took it out of his wallet and handed it over. 'As you see, one prosciutto con melone, one lasagne, one bottle of extremely mediocre wine – which I did *not* finish – one green salad. And one lemon sorbet to end with. I may say I've tasted better.'

Cassie scanned the bill. 'Look,' she said, handing it back.

'What at?'

'Anything strike you about it?'

'Nothing at all, except that it was bloody daylight robbery.'

'There's no indication anywhere that you were eating at lunchtime,' she said slowly.

'What?'

'I mean you could have been eating in the evening. Dammit.' Cassie exasperatedly chewed her lip. 'I should have asked you to go back and eat dinner there too. Just to make sure.'

'What are you on about?'

'Don't you see? If Harris had lunch there, early, he could easily have then got down south to do – whatever he did. And when the police asked him what he was doing, he simply presented them with the bill as proof, not that he'd eaten lunch there, but that he'd eaten dinner.'

Mansfield snatched the piece of paper from her. 'You're absolutely right.' He examined it again. 'There's not even a code which might indicate that it was evening rather than midday.'

202

'And if he paid cash, there wouldn't have been a credit card receipt which might have shown the time and date.'

Mansfield looked at her, his expression eager. 'Do you think we've got him?'

'I'm afraid not. I was talking to a colleague of his at Naomi's funeral, who seems to be able to place him in a cashmere sweater place on the afternoon that you've got earmarked for his trip down south. And he also mentioned Harris going to eat at the Rivabella with some Americans.'

'Oh no.'

'And frankly, I'm still not convinced that he's guilty. But if he is, this could be extra ammunition, if nothing else.'

'One more fucking nail,' Mansfield said with relish, 'in his fucking coffin.'

♦ 14 ♦

Quite what she thought she would accomplish by driving across the county to Ross-on-Wye, Cassie wasn't sure. Probably nothing. But if it achieved little else, it would at least stop her from brooding over her contretemps – OK, her break-up – with Walsh. Less selfishly, she felt more and more strongly that she owed Naomi Harris something, though she found it difficult to say exactly what. After due consideration, she came up with friendship. Naomi had yearned for it, and not known how to ask for it. If she herself had been sensitive enough to look beyond the prickly persona into the lonely heart, Naomi's life might not have ended when and how it did. Paying a visit to Francis Benson was an attempt, however futile, to make some reparation.

Enquiries led her down a side street to a small bookshop with the name Francis W. Benson painted above the window. A sign affixed to a plastic hook dangled on the glass pane of the door, informing the public of the shop's opening hours; inside, a man standing behind a till set on a narrow counter glared suspiciously at her as she pushed at the door and went in. He wore brown corduroys and an open-necked check shirt under a navy blue sweatshirt on which large gold letters spelled the words NOTRE DAME and, underneath them: *Fightin' Irish*.

Although he could not have been older than the late twenties, furrows already ran down from the corners of his thin mouth and frown-lines were deeply engraved between his eyebrows. Like so many bookshop owners, he seemed irritated by the presence of a paying customer on his premises.

'Yes?' he said discouragingly.

'Mr Francis Benson?'

'Yes.'

'You don't know me . . .' Cassie began.

'Quite right, I don't,' he said brusquely, interrupting her. 'Should I?'

'Not at all. I'm a friend of Naomi's.'

The lines above his nose grew heavier. 'I don't know any Naomi, either.'

'She seems to have known about you,' Cassie said. 'I believe your father was married to her mother before marrying – uh – *your* mother.' She fell silent in the face of his inimical frown.

'What do you mean?' His voice did not encourage the exchange of genealogical information. 'There's some mistake here. My father was only married once, and that was to my mother.'

Could Graham Blacklaws have been wrong? But he knew that Benson lived in Ross-on-Wye. And Mansfield had more or less confirmed it. Besides, their information would have come from Naomi herself. Who had, presumably, kept tabs on her absconding father, once she was old enough to do so. More importantly, did she, Cassandra Swann, have the right to pass on information which until now had apparently been concealed? She looked at the hostile face of Francis W. Benson and came to a decision.

'I think you're the one who's mistaken,' she said. 'I have it on the highest authority that you are named in Mrs Harris's will as the reversionary legatee.'

He stared at a pile of copies of the latest novel by Dick Francis. Picked one up. Examined the photograph of the author on the back cover. Put it down again. He stalked out from behind the counter and turned over the notice on the glazed door so that it now informed the public that the shop was temporarily closed. Facing her, he stood with his back against the door, the corners of his mouth turning down like a frog's. 'My mother has no idea,' he said.

'No idea of what?'

'That my father was previously married. She's a devout Catholic. She'd never have agreed to marry a divorced man. He told me before he died that although he had lied – even though it was by omission rather than commission – he never once regretted it. Theirs was an extremely happy marriage, Mrs – Uh—'

'Swann. And it's Miss.'

'—Swann. I would not like my mother's memories of my late father to be in any way tainted.' There was an irritating whine in his voice which made her want to slap him with a rolled-up newspaper.

'So you *do* know who Naomi Harris is?'

'Yes.'

'Did you ever meet her?'

He hesitated. 'She came here once, after my father died. To the shop. She told me she wanted to get to know me. She said she – she had no family of her own. I wasn't particularly welcoming, I admit.' He pulled at the collar of his shirt. 'I couldn't see how she would fit into our lives.'

'Our? You and your wife, is this?'

'Me and mother. I'm not married.' There was no need for

him to add that the likelihood that he ever would be was remote. Cassie wondered if she should introduce him to Graham Blacklaws.

'Do you know what happened to Naomi after your father left her mother?'

He held up a hand as though he were back in the classroom. A telephone number was written across it in red ink. 'Excuse me, but you've got that entirely wrong.'

'How do you mean?'

'His first wife left *him*. She was like that, apparently, one of those pretty feckless women with no sense of moral duty. She ran off with another man. A colleague of my father's, as it happens.'

'What did your father do?'

'What *could* he do? He was a gentleman: he agreed to a divorce.'

'I meant, what was his job?'

'He was a librarian.'

'So the colleague was one too?'

'Yes. In a library near Shrewsbury, I think it was. Rather a nasty bit of work by all accounts. A womaniser.' Benson's lip curled as though this was the most heinous of sins. 'Knowing his reputation, my father wasn't too keen on his daughter being brought up by him, quite frankly, but although he tried to gain custody, it wasn't granted. And then he moved down here and met my mother. After that, he decided it would be less disruptive if he stayed out of the child's life.'

'And much more convenient.'

'What do you mean?'

'If he was trying to pass himself off as single, how would he have explained away a small child to your devout mother?' Cassie's cynicism was perfectly obvious.

'He planned to say that he had been left a widower,' Benson said. He glanced at a small crucifix set above one of the bookshelves. 'Look, I know this all sounds as though he didn't behave terribly well, lying and so forth. But I assure you he wasn't that kind of man at all. It all weighed terribly heavily on his conscience.'

'Not heavily enough, it seems. So Naomi never saw him?'

'As far as I know.'

'That's very sad.'

'Is it?' He started to lift his shoulders in a bored shrug then, catching Cassie's eye, thought better of it. 'Yes. I suppose it is. But I imagine she was young enough when he left not to miss her real father. To – you know – be able to bond with the new chap.'

'Depends on how you define bonding. The new chap sexually molested her.'

'What?'

'Abused her.'

'You mean . . .?' His throat bulged and subsided, further increasing the batrachian similarity. There was no mistaking his shock.

'Oh yes,' Cassie said. 'Penetration. The full works.'

'How perfectly frightful. I had no idea.'

'How could you, when you had nothing to do with her after your father had rejected her?'

'Oh dear. And then when she came here, I—'

'—rejected her again.' Cassie's eyes were cold. 'Even though you were the only family she had.'

'Poor woman.'

'And in spite of all that, she made you a beneficiary of her will.'

'I . . .' His eyes shifted again to the crucifix. 'I don't know what to say.'

209

'Did you know about the will?'

He bent and lifted a stack of books from a cardboard box at his feet. Holding them in his arms like a shield against his body, he shook his head. 'No.'

'I wonder why I don't believe you.'

Instead of answering, he began placing the books in a space which had obviously been prepared for them on the shelves. Putting her head on one side, Cassie read the title. *Die Me A River*, by Tim Gardiner. On the shelf above there were three copies of *Sophie's World* by Jostein Gaarder. Which reminded her of something; something she had noticed. Or maybe not noticed.

'I think,' she said, 'that Naomi wrote to you and told you about her will. I think she hoped that you would respond in some way. I think she had to pretend to herself that she wasn't buying your interest. And I wouldn't be surprised to hear that you didn't even bother to reply.'

'That's not true.'

'What isn't?'

'I did write.' He caught the side of his lower lip in his teeth, realising too late what he had admitted.

'So you knew that you stood to inherit.'

'Yes,' he said guiltily. 'I did. Not that anything comes to me until her husband dies. He has a life interest.'

'Did you know how much she was leaving?'

He debated lying again, then said: 'Quite a lot.'

'And of course, even though the husband can't fritter it away, he could still make inroads on what you might rightfully think was *your* money, couldn't he?'

'What exactly are you insinuating?'

'Remember that film called *Kind Hearts and Coronets*? Where Dennis Price bumps off everyone standing between

210

him and a dukedom? And Alec Guinness plays about ten parts?'

'What about it?'

'Nothing, really. Except that if anything happens to John Harris, we'll all be looking at you with considerable attention.'

Panic flared like a damp firework at the back of his eyes. The furrows lengthened down either side of his face. 'I presume that's meant to be a joke,' he said. 'Though, if you ask me, it's one in singularly poor taste.'

'Poor taste: ah yes. There's a lot of that about,' said Cassie. 'Abusing a position of trust isn't in particularly good taste, either. Which brings me to another question. Do you know what this colleague of your father's was called? The one his first wife ran off with?'

'No.' Benson fussed again among the piles of books on the floor beside his counter.

'I'm sure you could remember if you tried really hard.'

'How can I remember something I never knew?'

'You're a very poor liar, Mr Benson.'

'I'll regard that as a compliment.' Benson stared bad-temperedly at his watch. 'Look, Miss Swann, if there's nothing else, perhaps you could leave me to get on with my job.' He bent again to the boxes at his feet.

Cassie said. 'Or perhaps I could nip along to your house and ask your mother. She might have old letters or something which could—'

He straightened so rapidly she heard the vertebrae creak. He raised his hand again. 'Don't!' he wailed. 'Please don't involve her.'

Mother must a hell of an old besom, to be capable of arousing such terror in her grown son. Did she insist that he raise his hand before she let him speak? A blurred image, like an old polaroid photograph, of a small boy cowering in spectacles and overlong school shorts appeared briefly at the back of Cassie's mind. There was more than one kind of abuse. Parents had such power over their offspring, and were able to wield it so ruthlessly: she tried to imagine herself treating a child in the way Naomi had been treated, or Lucy. Or perhaps even Francis Benson.

She softened her voice. 'I really need to know,' she said, even though she was not quite sure what she could do with the information.

'I'll try and find out for you,' gabbled Francis. 'I'm sure Dad told me the name once. Or maybe it was Mrs Harris – Naomi. Somebody did, I know. But just keep my mother out of it, *please*.'

'I'll ring you tomorrow to see if anything's come to mind, OK?'

He nodded sulkily. As she turned to the door, he spoke. 'I'm truly sorry that I wasn't nicer to Mrs Harris. When we came back from holiday and I read about what had happened, the suicide and everything, I was appalled.'

'We all were.'

'But I mean, she was my stepsister. Or half-sister. And I more or less turned her away.'

'Something you'll have to live with, Francis.' Cassie stood outside, holding the door open. 'Mind you, there's some doubt about whether it was suicide.'

'What?' The disagreeable face dropped into even deeper lines.

'They think it might have been murder.' It wasn't a lie, not really, since she didn't specify who "they" were.

'Murder?' Benson's voice rose to a squeak. 'Not suicide at all?'

'That's right. Scarcely bears thinking about, does it?'

Making her way back to her car, Cassie sat for a moment and thought about motivation. If Philip Mansfield was right in believing that Naomi had been murdered, but wrong about attributing the deed to her husband, Francis Benson made an extremely plausible suspect. Suppose he had, in fact, kept up with Naomi, talked to her, or at least observed her. Suppose he knew that she was thinking of changing her will. Not only would her death before she could do so bring him one step closer to a considerable amount of money, it also pre-empted the chance that she might leave him out this time. And even prevented the possibility that she would, on some future occasion, blow the gaff regarding the late Mr Benson's first marriage, thus making life hell for poor Francis. If he was involved in any way, letting him know that there were doubts about the verdict would at least keep him nervous. And nervous men, as she knew from a close reading of the Pandora Quest oeuvre – several chapters, anyway – make mistakes.

It was not until she was pulling out of Cheltenham that she noticed the white car behind her. A Peugeot. But was it the stalker's or did it belong to some perfectly innocent person going about his or her lawful occasions? Although she peered into the rearview mirror, she could not make out who was behind the wheel. Nor could she read the numberplate without running the risk of driving into a ditch. The white car stuck with her as she headed homewards but she was no wiser as to the driver's identity as she pulled off the motorway in the direction of Market Broughton. If it was her stalker, what on earth was he playing at? Why didn't he do something more concrete than follow her? What exactly did he want? Was he Tony Sutherland or not? Why hadn't she been sufficiently on the ball to take down the number of his car at Naomi's funeral?

On impulse, since she was that side of the county, instead of going straight home, she turned left and drove towards Bridge End. She was still unconvinced of John Harris's guilt. She certainly did not credit herself with the kind of hunch-creating sense of intuition that enabled her to be certain about anyone's character. She knew all too well how easy it was to leave a false trail, spray a false scent. It's part of our natures to pretend to be other than we really are. Few of us are necessarily what we seem.

John Harris was pottering in the garden when she drove in through the white-painted gates. He looked up, surprised, at the sound of her engine and then came walking swiftly across the thick green lawn towards her.

'Talk of the devil,' he said. The daylight was unforgiving, emphasising the lines around his eyes and mouth, and the extent of the grey in his thinly spread hair.

'Were you?'

'Well, I've just left a message on your machine, asking you to ring me. Not more than five minutes ago. So you can't have come in response to my call.'

'No.'

He led her into Naomi's kitchen – it was still hers, even if she was dead – and made coffee from a jar. 'Why did you come?' he asked.

'What did you want to talk to me about?'

'Mmm.' He played with his teaspoon. 'Thing is . . .'

'Yes?'

'Naomi had this . . . What happened was that years ago, Naomi . . .'

'Are you going to tell me she had an illegitimate baby?'

She had never seen a jaw drop. She did so now. John Harris's mouth hung open as he stared at her in astonishment.

'How in the world?' he began, then shook his head. 'Oh. I suppose she must have told you. But she told me she hadn't mentioned it to a single person, except a hint to her solicitor.'

And Philip Mansfield, her lover. 'She didn't tell me,' said Cassie. 'Is that what you wanted to talk to me about?'

'Yes. You see, just before she . . . died, Naomi told me she wanted to change her will. At the moment, I'm her sole legatee, at least, I have a life interest, but she planned to rewrite the will so that this . . . child of hers, got half her estate.'

Cassie tried to maintain a neutral expression. Was this some deeply subtle game played by a murderer? Bluff and counter-bluff? By announcing that he had been aware of Naomi's intentions, he was almost inviting the accusation that he was the person with the best possible motive for bumping his wife off before she could carry them out. 'What's the problem?' she said.

'I'd really like to see that this girl – it's a girl, apparently – gets her moral rights. The trouble is, I haven't the faintest idea what her name is, or where she lives or anything at all about her.'

'And you think I do?'

'I was going to ask,' Harris said humbly, 'whether you'd look into the matter for me. I'd be willing to pay you, of course.'

'Why me? There's a private investigation agency in Bellington.'

'You, mainly, because you were a friend of Naomi's. I don't really want to talk about her private affairs to some stranger. And you've been involved with one or two delicate matters like this in the past, haven't you?'

'Sort of.'

'So what do you think? Would you try and find her for me?

I'd like to feel that Naomi's last wishes were carried out. She – she didn't have all that happy a life, when all's said and done.'

Cassie wondered if he was speaking the truth, whether he was genuinely what he appeared to be, a man in some distress, trying to make amends for past mistakes.

If she was right, there was nothing to be lost in telling him about Lucy.

If she was wrong, Lucy's life could be in danger.

She went for it. 'I don't have to look for her,' she said. 'I know her, I know who she is.'

'That's amazing.'

'She was actually here, in the house, at Naomi's funeral. She was the girl with the scarlet punk hairdo.'

'That was Naomi's daughter? Why didn't she come and say something?'

'Because she felt uncomfortable. She didn't want to come to her mother's home, knowing that she would never meet her mother after all. They'd only just got it together.'

'I know. Naomi told me. But surely—' He looked briefly bewildered, and then shook his head. 'I'm forgetting everything at the moment. Sometimes can't even remember if I've had breakfast until I see the dirty dishes on the table.'

'Do you know anything about the baby's father?'

'Um . . .' He glanced away. 'Not really. Naomi didn't like to talk about it. It was one of those areas you simply steered clear of. She told me about the child when we first met, and giving it away and so on, and after that the subject was never mentioned again – until very recently, that is, when she said that she'd traced the baby, not that it was a baby any more, of course.'

'You said Naomi had had an unhappy life. Molestation, was it?'

He nodded unwillingly.

216

'By her mother's second husband?'

'Mmm. That's right.'

'Do you know his name?'

'I used to. Why?'

'I'd really like to know.'

He rose from his chair. 'She didn't take his name, of course, when her mother remarried. I'll look among her papers. It won't take me a minute to find out.'

The white Peugeot reappeared as she turned back onto the main road leading to Bellington and then Frith. He must have been waiting for her. The knowledge made her drive more recklessly than was prudent on a road which offered few chances to overtake. This was the Cotswolds, rural England at the start of the harvest, and speed was constantly impeded by tractors turning, haycarts lumbering, horseboxes ambling along at walking pace.

It was close to six o'clock as she came into Frith, past the village green and the crisp-bag clogged pond. A BMW was standing outside the Old Dower House; a BMW meant Charlie Quartermain and Charlie meant safety. Without thinking further, she pulled up behind it. Killing the engine, she opened the door of her car and stepped onto the grass verge. But the white car, some yards behind, suddenly veered off to the left before she could note any further distinguishing details. It was him. It had to be him. Or did it? He had never displayed any reluctance before to be seen, so why now? She stared at the corner which he had taken. Should she follow him, turn from hunted to hunter? But what if she was wrong, and it was someone else? Before she had time to do more than dither, the handsome front door of the house was wrenched open.

''Ello, darlin',' boomed Charlie.

'Charlie!' Cassie said, warmer than usual. 'How are you?'

There was silence for a moment. Charlie looked puzzled. Probably because he wasn't used to a show of enthusiasm from her when they met. He said: 'Are you going to come in? You could give me some advice. Decorating tips and that.'

'The name's Cassandra Swann, not Laura Ashley.'

'Classy bint like you ought to have some idea on how to do up this kind of a house.'

'How many times do I have to tell you, Charlie, I'm not classy.'

'You are to me, darlin'. Premier league.'

Cassie didn't know why she was arguing. She'd have *paid* to go round the house, even with Quartermain. 'I'd love to come in,' she said.

Charlie seized the moment. 'How about dinner afterwards?'

'Why not?' said Cassie, reckless with relief at being somewhere safe. 'Sounds good. Where did you have in mind?'

'Burger Chef? Chinese takeaway. The Conservatory? The choice is yours.'

'Phew. That's a hard one.'

He opened his mouth to make some stupid comment, and then closed it again. She pretended not to notice.

He stood aside at the top of the graceful steps and she went into the wide panelled hall. 'The Conservatory, I think,' he said. 'Nothing but the best for my girl.'

'I am *not*—' Cassie too swallowed her words: Perhaps they were both learning. 'I'll have to go home and change.'

'I'll drive you there and wait.'

'Fine. Now, show me round your house, Charlie.'

♥ 15 ♥

'Drunk? Who's drunk?' Charlie roared, as he slapped a credit card down on the saucer which contained the bill.

'Me, for a start,' said Cassie.

'It takes more than a couple of bottles of wine to get me rat-arsed, darlin'. With a build like mine, I'd have to drink at least a barrel of the stuff.'

'You're forgetting the gins we had to start with. And the cognacs we ended with.'

'Nah. Much too good to forget. And anyway, they was Armagnac, not cognac.'

'Either way, I'd still prefer to get a taxi home,' said Cassie. God. Why did she always sound like Aunt Polly whenever she said something like that?

'If you'd feel easier, girl, let's do that. Here!' he shouted at the maître d'hôtel, causing the other diners to start nervously. 'Order us a taxi, there's a good head-waiter chappie.'

Cassie stared at her plate. What she would have liked was a discreet – or even totally over the top – neon sign which flashed on at regular intervals and said: HE IS NOT MY PARTNER. She had already ascertained that no one she knew was in the restaurant, but in the limited society of rural Cotswoldshire, everyone knew everyone else and even as she winced, word was probably spreading that Cassandra Swann had been seen dining with the most appalling fellow.

'By the way,' said Charlie, leaning his massive arm on his elbow, which promptly slipped off the edge of the table.

'What?' hissed Cassie, embarrassed, though only Aunt Polly could really have hissed a word which contained no sibilants.

'I was passing your way the other day. Couldn't help noticing you in your sitting room, talking to a pretty boy with a lot of hair. What was he doing round your place?'

'Not that it's any of your business, Charlie, but he's called Philip Mansfield. He's—'

'Mansfield? Blimey, that's rich.'

'So's he,' said Cassie coolly.

Charlie raised his eyes to the ceiling. 'Go on, then, let's hear it. What tale did he spin you? MD of some electronics firm, was it? Or computer whiz kid with his own headquarters in Silicon Valley?'

This was close enough to what Mansfield had told her that Cassie felt her face grow red. 'Do you know him, then?'

'I'll say I know him. Was I right? Or is he putting himself about as something new these days – a sky pilot, for instance? Or – don't tell me – manager of a privately-funded hospice?'

'How do you know him?'

'Last time I come across him, he was operating this scam out of Derby: some kind of medical insurance scheme for miners or industrial workers or something.'

'You mean he's a crook?'

'A conman, darlin'. Or p'raps I should say con artist, because he's one of the best. Mansfield, eh?' Laughter rumbled deep in Quartermain's belly, sending ripples of movement through his chest. 'Real name's Terry Collins.'

'But—'

Before Cassie could decide whether Charlie was telling the truth, and if he was, what the significance of the truth might be, one of the men who had been seated at a table on the other side of the room came striding over.

He seized Quartermain's hand. 'Charlie,' he said. 'Hope you don't mind me butting in. Heard your voice and couldn't resist coming to say hallo.'

''Ello, Freddie.'

'When are you going to be coming our way again?' said Freddie. He was fleshy and youngish, his ample belly straining at a waistcoat of many colours.

'Cassandra,' said Quartermain. 'Can I introduce Freddie Mounceford?'

Freddie nodded at Cassie. 'How nice,' he said vaguely. 'Look, Charlie. M'wife would love to have you to dinner. Give us a ring, won't you?'

'Defretly,' said Charlie. 'Count on it.' And then, as Freddie nodded again and moved back to his table, added to Cassie, speaking out of the side of his mouth: 'Not on your nellie.'

'Why not?'

'Because the food'll be lousy, the house'll be freezing and the wine'll be rubbish,' said Charlie. 'Though the port isn't half bad.'

'Who was he, anyway?' The name had been faintly familiar to Cassie.

'Freddie? Oh, some minor nob. Lives in one of those big country mansions with a crap central heating system. Talk about brass monkeys: last time I stayed there, my balls nearly dropped off, it was so cold.'

'You surely don't mean Lord Peckeridge, do you?'

'That's the feller. Only it's more like Pecker-itch, if you take my meaning. Nudge, nudge,' said Charlie predictably. 'Say no more.'

Freddie Mounceford, Umpteenth Earl, formerly of Eton, Christ Church and the Household Cavalry, was one of the country's more colourful young peers, and frequently featured in the tabloids, either going into Bow Street Magistrate's Court or coming out of Marylebone Registry Office.

Before she could ask how Charlie and the Earl came to be such chums, the waiter arrived with the credit card form. Charlie started to scrawl messily across the bottom then stopped. ''Ere,' he said. 'What happened to this bill? It's shrunk.'

'The Armagnacs,' said the man.

'What about them?'

'Lord Peckeridge insisted on paying for them.'

'Jolly decent of the lad.'

'And your taxi's arrived, sir.'

'Thanks.' Quartermain left a generous tip. As he and Cassie got up to leave, he shouted across the restaurant to Mounceford's table: 'Thanks, Freddie!' Mounceford tipped his glass in silent greeting.

In the taxi, Charlie rested his arm across the back of the seat and for once, Cassie did not shy away, but instead, leaned against his comforting bulk and closed her eyes. It had been a good evening. However annoying he might be, however embarrassing, Charlie was, she had to admit, good company. For some time they had discussed the Old Dower House and how they would furnish it or, to be more accurate, Charlie asked Cassie how she would furnish it and either agreed or disagreed. They spent some time on the kitchen, Charlie talking in terms of handmade units in oak or beech, Cassie arguing passionately for a real country kitchen with good pieces in stripped pine, and an absolute minimum of modern fitted stuff. When he stopped making unfunny jokes and lewd comments, he could be very amusing. As a master mason of considerable renown, he was fascinating on the subject of his own specialist field of expertise. He had told her that one of his current projects was the restoration of gargoyles on the chapel of one of the Oxford colleges. As his arm dropped to draw her closer, she recalled the same arm draped around the frail shoulders of Professor Richardson. His college. Robin, her godfather's, college, too. He smelled nice. Manly. 'Mmm,' she said, snuggling up against him, feeling the coil of wine and the brandy, even the gin and tonic they had had at the start of the evening, in her bloodstream. She felt soft and languorous. She felt a warmth towards her fellow beings. Even towards Charlie.

'Mansfield,' she said suddenly, straightening up as she recalled Charlie's words.

'What about him?'

'Are you sure you're right about him? You only saw him through the cottage windows, didn't you? He's told me all sorts of things about – about a recent murder case.'

'Murder, eh? That's not usually his line.'

'He certainly knows his way about a computer.'

'I didn't say he wasn't smart,' said Charlie. 'Just that he's a crook. Take it from me, anything he knows about computers he learned inside. Seen his muscles?'

'Yes.'

'When he's inside, he spends hours in the prison gym.'

'But I'm rather invo—'

'Let's talk about it another time, all right?'

'I suppose,' Cassie said reluctantly.

On their arrival at Honeysuckle Cottage, she was mystified to hear herself saying, 'Are you coming in for a coffee or something?' She knew better than that, didn't she? She knew what Charlie would assume.

'No coffee, thanks,' Charlie said. 'Something will do fine.'

While he dealt with the taxi driver, she went up the path to the front door, almost tripping over some wretched beetle which was blocking the way, and put her key, with a little difficulty, into the lock. By the time she had opened the door, Charlie was behind her. In the darkened passage, she stumbled again on the uneven flagstones, and he caught her before she landed.

'Whoopsy daisy,' he said, just the way her Gran used to when she was a little girl.

She turned in his arms. He kissed her. She kissed him back. His mouth was warm and firm. 'Charlie,' she said.

'Oh, Lord, Cassie.' He held her very tightly.

She slid her arms under the jacket of his suit and felt the tremble of his big body. 'Charlie,' she murmured. It was like being in Harry Swann's arms again, in the safe days before the world turned upside down. Quartermain had always reminded her of her murdered father, but the emotions rising in her now were far from daughterly.

She tried to pull away. Despite being half-pissed, she had enough sense to be aware of the dangers if she were to give in to her baser instincts. And the instincts currently surging, threatening to overwhelm her, were base in the extreme. Absolutely fundamental. Elemental, even. But he was kissing her again, harder this time, and she was joining in, melting, the pit of her stomach hot as fire, flowing like candlewax against him.

He scooped her into his arms as though she weighed no more than a duvet, and carried her through the lighted sitting room to the door which hid the boxed-in stairs. As she passed, she reached out a hand and flipped off the switch.

'Charlie,' she murmured again, and heard the sound emerge from her mouth less as a word and more like a moan of desire. Somehow, she simply didn't care.

'God, I love you,' he said, his mouth tender against the back of her neck.

'Do you?' She was three-quarters asleep.

'As much as it's possible for a man to love a woman.'

'Why?'

'I don't know.'

'I'm always horrid to you.'

'I don't mind.'

'We're chalk an' cheese.'

'Both full of calcium.'

'What's tha' mean?'

'We're similar. The same.'

'I don't love you,' she said, lips barely moving, sunk into the warmth of the bed, the strength of him curved around her, lost in an erotic haze.

'Yes, you do.'

'This is a one-off, Charlie.'

'Is it?'

'Mmm.'

He moved in closer to her, squashing her against his chest. 'Feel that.'

'This won't happen again.'

'Wanna bet?'

'I mean it, Charlie. 'S only because I'm drunk.'

'Tell me you didn't enjoy it with me.'

'I'd be lying.'

His mouth nibbled her lips. 'Sssh,' he said.

★ ★ ★

225

She woke in the morning to find sunlight streaming in through the open windows. Leaf patterns flickered on the bedroom walls. The room was so silent that she could hear a lark, miles up in the brilliance of the day. Her head thumped rhythmically, as though small men in clogs were doing authentic local dances all over her brain. Her stomach churned. Her mouth was as dry as shoe leather. Yet, unaccountably she felt good. Until she remembered why. Charlie. Oh, Lord above. What had she done?

Might be better to do a Scarlett O'Hara on that one.

Listening, she could hear nothing. He was not a man who moved silently about the place. Last time he had stayed here – sleeping in the spare bedroom – he had broken half the crockery in the house. Yet today there was only the lark, and in the distance, cows lowing, and the faint sound of a car horn on the road to Frith. Had he gone?

After a while, she carefully swung her legs over the edge of the bed and got gingerly to her feet. She brushed her teeth, keeping her eyes away from her reflection and then slowly made her way downstairs. On the table was an ill-spelled note in Quartermain's ungainly hand. *I diden't want to wake you or I'd have brought you some tea. Thaks for giving me such a wonderful fanttastic time.*

She blushed. Couldn't help it. His voice came back to her, urgent but gentle, speaking words not in the throes of passion but as he held her quietly in the safety of his huge embrace. 'I love you, I love you.' Over and over again. 'I love you,' until she drifted off again into sleep.

Oh, she thought. If only I loved him back.

Filling the kettle, she plugged it in at the wall, then opened the back door. What a wonderful day it was. A glorious beautiful almost-autumn golden day.

She stepped across the grass towards the offices of Bridge the Gap, and saw that the door was slightly open. Was Natasha here already? She called out but there was no answer. She pushed the heavy door, then stopped, choking on the petrol fumes which billowed around her as she stepped inside.

For a moment she stared, disbelieving. She blinked. This couldn't have happened. But it had. The room had been systematically trashed. Everything that could be broken was. The trestle tables had been turned over and the legs smashed with something heavy until they broke. All the new stock lay piled into heaps in the middle of the floor; petrol and paint had been poured over it. The thick emulsion colours had curdled together in a coagulated rainbow on the slate tiles: magnolia and salmon, apple green and butter yellow. The pretty white table cloths were ruined, the basketfuls of wrapped packs of cards, score sheets, and leather card cases. The baize tops of the card tables had been scored and torn, their legs snapped off at the hinges. The porcelain dishes had been flung to the ground and lay in pieces. Pages had been ripped from the books and strewn about the room.

The shock was so huge that Cassie, at first not believing what she saw, had to lean against the wall in order to remain upright. What had happened here? A bomb? An earthquake? It was only gradually that she realised this was not some random act of God but the deliberate work of man. Someone had broken in during the night and inflicted all this damage. What she could not understand was who. Or why. Was it someone with a grudge against the business? Or was it someone attempting to frighten her?

Was it the stalker? Was that why he had waited for her, followed her to Frith? Had he waited there too, watched her set off with Charlie, maybe even followed her to the restaurant and known they would be there for long enough for him to vandalise the place in comparative safety? He seemed the obvious suspect. She was going to have to track him down.

If she knew the why, she would know the who. Or even vice versa. It didn't matter much which. But when she found out . . . She straightened up. Turned her back on the debris. Walked back to the kitchen in order to telephone the police. As she lifted the receiver, a thought struck her. She laughed ruefully.

'Jeez,' she said. 'That's one hell of a cure for a hangover.'

'His name was Chessington.' The voice did not identify itself but Cassie recognised the faintly aggrieved tones.

'Thank you, Francis,' she said.

'Robert Chessington. Haven't got an address.'

'That's OK.' She didn't need one. What Benson had just told her only confirmed the information she had been given yesterday by John Harris, which included an address.

She marched up the divided concrete runway which led to Tony Sutherland's garage, avoided a cruelly pruned standard rose and aggressively pressed the doorbell. He needn't think he was going to get away from her this time. She was prepared to stand on the doorstep until sundown, if necessary. Her blood was up.

Insistently, she pushed the bell again, this time holding her finger on it. After a while, she glimpsed movement through the stained glass of the upper part of the door but she kept on ringing until the door was wrenched open. The angry house-holder standing in front of her in pyjamas and dressing gown was no one she had ever seen before. Which cleared up one thing. Even if he was the person responsible for doing over her premises, he was definitely not her stalker.

'What the bloody hell do you think you're playing at?' he said.

'Mr Sutherland?'

'Ringing like that.' A cornflake clung to the braided lapel of his dressing gown. There was a napkin in his hand. She had obviously caught Tony Sutherland at breakfast, although it was now nearly lunchtime. 'Yes, that's me.'

'Where were you between the hours of six and midnight last night?' she demanded. She had already explained to the police that the damage must have been inflicted on the converted outhouse while she and Charlie Quartermain were out at dinner. Her bedroom window looked out over the back of the cottage, and had been open all night: one or other of them would surely have heard something if the vandalism had taken place after they came back from the restaurant.

'What business is it of yours?' Sutherland had palely bellig-erent blue eyes surrounded by what looked like alcohol-reddened whites.

'The police are investigating an incident which took place near Frith last night and you're a suspect.'

If he was startled by this information, he did not reveal it. He adopted a sneering expression. 'And you're from the police, are you?'

She didn't have the balls to lie. Not about being a police officer. There were penalties for things like that. 'Not exactly.'

'Then what the f—'

'I'm the person to whom the incident happened. And I damn well want to know if you're involved.'

'Well, I'm damn well not,' retorted Sutherland. He made to shut the front door but Cassie stuck her foot in the way.

'You run a bridge supplies business, don't you?'

'Used to. So effing what?'

'But not any longer?'

'No.' He peered at her. 'I know you, don't I?'

'Certainly not.'

'Your face – I've definitely seen it before. You a gardener?'

'Not in the sense you mean.'

'Bridge,' he said, snapping his fingers. 'That's it. Saw something about you once in that freebie thing that comes round on Fridays. Swann, is it?'

If you want anonymity, live in a city, not in a sparsely populated rural area. 'That's right.'

'And didn't you write to me about something recently? Setting up your own business, wasn't it?'

'Yes.'

His hostility dropped away. 'If you want my advice, don't. You'd be just as well off tearing up ten-pound notes and flushing them down the loo. And it's a lot less hassle.'

'Oh.' Cassie found herself somewhat nonplussed. It looked as though Tony Sutherland was something of a non-starter as a suspect for the vandalism on her premises. And he certainly wasn't the stalker.

'Look,' he said now. 'Why don't you come in, have a cuppa, I'll tell you a hundred better things you could get into than a bridge business. And you can tell me what all this is about?'

'Well . . .'

He grinned lasciviously. 'If you're worried about my intentions, I've got a very respectable lady friend on the premises, and we both have the best kind of alibi for last night for whenever it was you said. If you catch my drift.'

Difficult not to, really.

'And one for this morning, too, if you're interested,' he added.

Perhaps the red eyes were due to lack of sleep rather than alcohol. God, these old folk. No shame at all. No wonder the country was going down the tubes.

'No thanks,' she said, turning away.

'Good luck,' he said.

She walked back to the road. So Sutherland was nothing to do with anything. But she knew there had to be a link some-where between the stalker, the damage to her property, Naomi's death, Lucy, Mansfield, John Harris. Didn't there? Five or six weeks ago, she hadn't known any of these people, Naomi was still alive, the stalker non-existent. Something, some incident, linked them to her, she was sure. Blotched yellow leaves lay heavily under the plane trees which lined the street where Sutherland lived. Autumn-coloured chrysanthe-mums were beginning to bloom in the gardens. On the garden hedges, swollen spiders laid their elaborate webs.

She sat in her car, suddenly depressed. It seemed that no matter where she turned, she came up against a brick wall. She turned the key in the ignition and listened to the pulmonary wheeze which emerged from the vents. Something would have to be done about it, and soon. On top of that, she was going to have to replace the front tyres before she found herself being fined for driving illegally. In a town, she could have done away with the expense of a car; in the country, it was no longer a luxury but a vital necessity. The bus services had been run down to a virtual standstill, and there were no trains. The car was a lifeline to the outer world. Troublesome, money-eating, worrying – but nonetheless a lifeline.

It took her nearly two hours to reach the north Nottingham suburb where the man she now knew to be Naomi's stepfather lived. Though the brick was redder, the street was very similar to Tony Sutherland's, way to the south. With one essential difference. There had not been policemen standing about further down the road. Nor wasp-striped police tape keeping people away from the front entrance to the house. A small crowd was standing staring up at No 29: Cassie parked and strolled down towards them.

'What's going on?' she asked.

'There's been a murder,' a woman said.

'Who's been killed?'

'Mr Chessington,' said the woman.

'*Robert* Chessington?' Cassie had difficulty taking in what she was being told.

Tears sprang into the woman's eyes. 'I've lived across the way from him for more than twenty years, and there's never been anything like this before.'

'Well, there wouldn't be, really, would there?' said Cassie.

'And now someone's murdered him in his bed.'

'Do you mean literally?'

'They found him at the foot of the stairs, apparently. With his head bashed in.'

'How frightful. What happened: did he disturb a burglar or something?'

The woman turned to a man on her other side. 'They said nothing had been taken, didn't they, Larry?'

Larry was short and plump, with a wisp of monkish grey hair ringing an otherwise naked scalp. 'That's right. And there's plenty there for them to steal, if they'd wanted to. The house was crammed to the attics with antiques. Furniture, silver, glass, that sort of thing. He was something of an expert. Travelled all over the place, buying and selling. Used to have his own shop.'

'I thought he was a librarian,' Cassie said.

'This was after,' said Larry. After his prison sentence, presumably, if Philip Mansfield (or whoever) was right. At that point, his career up the ladder of librarianship must have come to an abrupt halt. 'He took early redundancy and set up his own business. He told me once that was what he'd always wanted to do.'

'And now someone's killed him,' said the woman.

'They've no idea who's responsible, I suppose?' asked Cassie. 'No suspect helping the police with their enquiries?'

'Not as far as I know,' said Larry. 'But it's a bit early for that. They only found him this morning.'

'While we were still asleep in our beds,' wailed the woman. 'Nowhere's safe these days.'

'When did it happen?'

'That's the dreadful thing about it,' said Larry. 'They think he's been there for some time. A week or more. He might have been there even longer if his cleaning woman hadn't come back from a fortnight's holiday and found him this morning.'

'Doesn't bear thinking about,' the woman moaned. 'I had people in for supper on Saturday, and to think that all the time, poor Bob was lying there . . .'

'Were you friends of his?'

'Larry was,' said the woman.

'Drank together down the pub from time to time,' agreed Larry. 'And we both supported Nottingham Forest, went to matches together.'

'Did you know his wife?'

'Poor old Sheila, yes. And the girl. Sheila's, that was. Nathalie, was it?' He looked at the woman for confirmation.

'Naomi,' she said. 'Left home at seventeen and never came back. Not that I ever knew her, because she'd taken off before we moved in, but Sheila often used to talk about her.'

'Poor old Sheila,' said Larry.

It sounded as if Sheila had stood by her man. If Philip (aka Terry?) had been telling the truth about that bit at least, perhaps Naomi had simply preferred to believe that her mother had divorced the man who had been abusing her. Or had Naomi been lying to Philip (or Terry)? It was very confusing.

'Bit of a handful, that Naomi,' the woman told Cassie. 'No better than she should be, if you know what I mean. Went with the boys, so Robert told us. And then she goes and gets herself in the family way.'

'Did she marry the father?'

'Oh no, none of that for young Naomi. Wasn't interested in being made an honest woman of. Refused to say who was responsible. Bob wasn't best pleased. Or so Sheila said. Respectable man with a respectable position. Not what you want, really, is it?'

Respectable, my ass, thought Cassie. Unless child abuse was considered decent in this suburban avenue, acceptable as long as you kept it behind the parlour curtains and the oak front doors and pretended not to hear the screams or see the tears. Wife beaters, child molesters, pornographers, paedophiles: this was exactly the kind of community where they were able to pursue their obsessions, knowing that no one would pry, that once they stepped into their parquet-floored halls and closed their leaded-light doors behind them, they were free to act as they pleased, just as long as they didn't cause embarrassment to the neighbours. And now Robert Chessington, that respectable man, had done just that by getting himself murdered.

'What happened to the baby?' she asked.

'Baby?' The woman looked blank. 'Oh, I think it was stillborn. Something like that.'

More lies, probably on Sheila's part this time.

'Charles Rennie Mackintosh,' said Larry. 'That's the fellow.'

'What is?' said the woman.

'That Bob specialised in. That *art nouveau* stuff. He had two or three pieces in his house. Chairs with tall backs, that kind of thing. I'll bet they're worth a packet these days.'

Two policemen in dayglo-yellow body jackets were emerging from the house now, looking more like sherbert lemons than cops. Both of them carried black plastic garbage sacks. A policewoman hovered behind them in the porch, watching as they marched down the drive, then turned and went back into the house, leaving the door open so that the watchers in the road could see the stairs at the foot of which Robert Chessington must, earlier that day, have been discovered.

'Presumably the – the body's gone,' said Cassie. 'He's not still in there, is he?'

'Took him off this morning. An ambulance arrived.' The woman stirred. 'Well, I'd better get back. There's not much to see here, when all's said and done, and I've got things to do.'

'Me too,' said Larry. They both nodded at Cassie and then walked across to the other side of the road where they conducted a short conversation before entering their own gates, three houses apart.

Cassie returned to her car. So Naomi's stepfather had been murdered. Over a week ago. As, very possibly, had Naomi herself. Was the same person responsible? And if so, what was the motive? There was no point asking further questions of the police or the other neighbours still standing around in the road: the answers she wanted could only have been supplied by Chessington himself. But a connection was there. Had to be.

Was it the money? Money was often a prime factor when violence was done. For a while she had wondered whether Chessington had been responsible for killing Naomi. But he could have had no financial interest in Naomi's estate. It was obvious that Naomi had had nothing to do with him for years. Even her husband couldn't say whether he was alive or dead. And now he too was dead.

She put the key into the ignition but for the moment did not turn it. She was reluctant to return to the cottage. There was a long drive ahead of her and, at the end of it, only the ruined remains of the bridge business. Natasha, horrified but practical, had organised a team of professional cleaners to come in and deal with the worst of the mess; nonetheless, Cassie would rather stay away until the clean-up was finished. The best thing to do would be to go back and cadge a bed for the night from someone. That way, she'd be close at hand, but uninvolved. The question was, which someone? Kathryn? Or Charlie?

So far today she had managed to avoid thinking about last night. Or, for that matter, early this morning. During both of which she had been – what was the word? – engaged with Charles Quartermain, master mason and, she was forced to admit, master lover. Walsh's lovemaking, she now saw, was mediated more through what she had thought was her own love for him than any love he might have felt for her. The fact that she had taken his defection with such equanimity had made her reassess her feelings for him. Was she simply a shallow, sex-starved woman who had slept with him because she was desperate to find love before it was too late?

Frankly, no. She *had* loved Walsh. That was nothing to be ashamed of. And at some deep level, she had always been aware that his feelings for her had a more physical basis than hers for him. For Charlie, on the other hand, she felt nothing, absolutely nothing. And yet in spite of that, in spite of his bulk, in spite of the fact that he irritated her beyond bearing, last night had been – well, wonderful was the only word for it.

Thank God she had made it clear to him that had she not had a little too much to drink she would have never allowed him into her bed. Charlie might not be a gentleman by birth or breeding but he had the right instincts; he would never take advantage of a momentary lapse to come on to her again.

Which, when she thought about it, was kind of a pity.

♠ 16 ♠

All the way back, she considered Philip Mansfield. It was
something she realised she might usefully have done much
earlier than this. He had certainly had the means and the
opportunity to murder Naomi. His insistence that John Harris
was the guilty person now took on a more sinister slant –
deflection away from the real killer. If Charlie was right – and
she had learned by now that he usually was – the man was a
crook, a thief. No wonder he had reminded her of the
banged-up bank robber: the guileless eyes and virtuous
expression were a dead giveaway. Having taught bridge inside
the prison for so long, she ought to have learned by now that
only the guilty dare to look so innocent. But what could
Mansfield's motive have been? And what precisely had he
been after by courting Naomi? It would have been optimistic
in the extreme for him to expect that she would have named
him in her will, besides being a very long-term scam. At
forty-one, Naomi could not have been expected to die for
another thirty-five years or more. Perhaps he had hoped for
nothing more than a comfortable life with her, living off her
money.

Or perhaps he had hoped to be named in the will and then to
do something about coming into his inheritance rather sooner

than the natural course of events might have predicted. Whatever his intentions, Cassie found a wall of cynicism raising itself between her and any idea that he had genuinely been in love with Naomi. Despite the quivering lip, the filling eye. No question, she had swallowed the shtick, hook, line and sinker, but now that she knew what he really was, she could see that it was all part of the act. The ability to be convincing was the major item of the conman's stock-in-trade.

Or was she doing him an injustice? Looking back, Cassie saw that her conversation with Graham Blacklaws could have been taken more than one way. Both of them had rather coyly referred to *the – uh – young person* . . . as though they were characters in a Victorian novel, but for her part, she had been talking about Lucy. Blacklaws, on the other hand, might well have been referring to Philip. And if so, that surely provided a motive for Mansfield (or Collins) *not* to murder Naomi – or at least, not until she had changed her will. It was at least worth putting a phone call through to Graham, in order to clarify the matter.

On the other hand, there was the remark Naomi had made to Anne Norrington, about having your dearest wish come true, only to find you didn't want it after all. Was that a reference to Mansfield? Had she come to realise that moving in with him was not going to be the answer to her prayers? Had she discovered that not only his feet but probably his entire body was made of clay? If she had, and had told him so, it was possible that he had killed her in a fit of frustrated pique. Careful planning had gone into Naomi's death. Was Mansfield capable of organising such a cold-blooded execution? The answer had to be that he was: he was a conman, he must be used to setting up his scams, researching his victims, disguising his impostures with enough pedigree that he'd check out, if any of his proposed fall-guys had the sense to put the eye on him.

But was he a murderer?

Supposing that was what Naomi had done: had him investigated, and found that he wasn't the sort of man it would be sensible to invest in, either emotionally or financially. Suppose she had told him so. What would his reaction be? Cassie found it hard to believe he would kill. For Naomi to discover that he was a trickster, in it for what he could get, would be yet another betrayal; for Mansfield, it would be no more than another scheme which hadn't worked out.

That still left the question of why he was so insistent that John Harris was behind the murder – if murder it was. Was there a further link between Mansfield and Harris, and if so, how could she find out? Once he knew that he'd been rumbled, if he was innocent he'd have nothing to lose by telling her the truth. That was the upside. The downside was that, if he *was* the murderer, he'd very likely take strong exception to being unmasked. In which case, she'd be nuts to confront him. Especially on her own.

Which led unavoidably to thoughts of Charlie. If only she could go for him. If only he didn't fill her with revulsion and fear. Well, fear. She had to admit she hadn't felt too much revulsion last night. Quite the opposite. She would never have thought a man so big could have been so gentle a lover. Natasha had said something about that, hadn't she, claiming to know for a fact that big men were wonderful in bed? It was a point she must take up with Tash some time.

It wasn't until she came off the M1 at Junction 22 and turned onto the M29 that she noticed the white Peugeot behind her. The visor above the driver's seat was pulled down, obscuring the person behind the wheel, but she knew who it was. She wondered why she did not feel fright. That was what she guessed she was supposed to feel. By now she should be pale and haggard. She should be losing weight (in her dreams!), sleeping badly, fingertips dripping blood from her bitten nails. Instead, she felt empowered. Invigorated. What the hell did he think he was playing at? What kind of a pathetic wimp was he, that he couldn't come right out and confront her with whatever she was supposed to have done? At the next lay-by, she wrenched her wheels to the left. If he followed, good. If not, she would have time to note his licence plate. And once she had that, he'd better watch out. She saw him slow down, hesitate, realise that one way or another she was going to be able to take down his number. He floored the accelerator but it was too late. She'd got him. And he knew it.

If this was a Tim Gardiner book, she would now simply have to telephone her chum at the Yard and he would identify the owner of the car for her, thus leaving her free to run into yet another absurd situation from which only the chum would be able to rescue her. It was a bit more difficult in real life. Unless she went to Charlie. Charlie had mates all over the place, high and low. Charlie would find out who the guy was, and no question asked. In doing so, he was bound to come to the wrong conclusions about her, see her request as an excuse to get in touch with him again or something adolescent like that. Was it worth the hassle?

She decided that yes, it was. She wasn't going to be able to get on with her life until this lunatic was off her back. She found a pen and a scrap of paper in her bag, and wrote a short note for Charlie, asking for his help, adding that it was urgent. As she came into Frith, she parked in front of the Old Dower House and put it through the letterbox then drove on home.

She did not see the white Peugeot again.

She parked her car in front of the shed-cum-garage. There was no sign of the cleaning people, no sign of life anywhere around the cottage except for the white cat, which came sidling up to wind itself softly round her legs. She bent and scratched behind its ears while it purred and wheedled. 'No milk for you,' she said. 'Not until you've decided where your loyalties lie.'

She let herself in through the front door and found the card which Philip Mansfield had given her when he first showed up at her door. He answered the telephone on the third ring. Behind him she could hear the sound of a televised football match. 'Cassandra Swann here. How's it going?' she said.

'How's what going?'

'You can't have forgotten. Aren't you trying to prove that John Harris killed his wife?'

'Oh, that.'

'Yes, that.' What had happened? Had he moved onto a new scam or what? 'Look, I've found out something else which might be important.'

'Have you?'

'Why don't you come round and discuss it?'

'I'm a bit tied up, actually, Cass.'

'Are you really . . .' she left a heart beat then added '. . . Terry?'

'You what?'

'I'll be at home from six onwards,' she said, and put down the phone.

Her next call was to Blacklaws's office in Market Broughton. She asked to be put through to his assistant and when Anthea came on the line, said: 'Hi, it's Cassie Swann. How's the aerobics class going?'

Anthea groaned. 'Don't ask. Last week I put my back out trying to do a jumping jack and I've been hobbling round with a stick ever since.'

'You should take up something safe, like bridge.'

'I might very well do that.'

'Call me when you make up your mind. Meanwhile, I want to ask you something. I'd go to Graham but I've already pumped him twice and if I ask him any more questions I'll be forced to go and hear him sing in The *Messiah* at Christmas.'

'What's wrong with that? I happen to think he's got a very good voice, actually.'

'I know that,' Cassie said quickly. 'It's the chorus which gets me. All those screeching sopranos.'

'I'm in the chorus,' said Anthea, her voice belligerent. 'A soprano, as it happens.'

'Well, of course, I didn't mean *all* of them scree—'

'What exactly did you want?' Anthea's tone made it clear that Cassie could swing in hell before she'd prise any information out of her.

'I was wondering,' Cassie said humbly, 'whether you knew in whose favour Mrs Naomi Harris had been intending to change her will. I think she was planning to include either a girl called Lucy Benson, or a man called Philip Mansfield.'

There was a long cold silence.

'Please, Anthea.'

More silence.

'I'll come to the *Messiah*,' said Cassie.

The silence grew icicles.

'And bring a friend. *Two* friends.'

'Do you promise?'

'Absolutely swear.'

'It'll mean looking at his notes.'

'I really appreciate it, Anth.'

'I'll have to call you back.'

'Fine.'

Replacing the receiver, Cassie rolled her eyes. Lawdy, lawdy: when would she learn to be discreet? How could she have guessed that Anthea sang? Or that she'd got the hots for Graham? From the disparaging way she'd always referred to him while struggling in and out of her scarlet leotard, Cassie had assumed she took a pretty dim view of the man. She looked at her watch. Two hours before she could conceivably justify taking out the whisky bottle. Two hours before Philip Mansfield was likely to show up.

He arrived at six-twenty. He had changed his hairstyle: it was now slicked back, Wall Street style, and tied into a cunning little ponytail. The leathers had given way to a well-cut navy suit: he wore a stiff-collared shirt with silk knots at the cuffs and a discreetly opulent tie.

Cassie gave him a drink and sat down opposite him in the sitting room. She had already decided not to beat about the bush. 'Win a few, lose a few, huh?' she said.

'I'm sorry?' Even his voice had changed. The brash self-made man had given way to the top executive of some international conglomerate, used only to the best, whether it be cars, hotels or women.

'You didn't quite get it together with Naomi Harris, did you?'

'I'm not with you.'

'Knock it off, Terry. You know exactly what I mean.'

He gave her his long slow look, then laughed. 'OK, so I lost out there.' The MD's voice vanished. 'How was I to know the poor old girl was going to pull a trick like that? An overdose, for Gawd's sake.' He leaned forward. 'How d'you know my name, anyway?'

'I have friends,' said Cassie. 'And sources which I do not intend to reveal.'

'You don't mean that cop friend of yours, do you? I wouldn't want him poking his nose into my girlish secrets.'

'Not him. Someone much more . . .' Cassie paused. What exactly was Charlie Quartermain more than Paul Walsh? '. . . reliable,' she finished.

'Nothing to do with the filth?'

'Nothing.'

'That's all right, then.'

'Is it? I want to know what you were hoping to gain from Naomi.'

'Gain?'

'Once she'd moved in, what did you want her to do?'

'I was hoping she'd set me up in my own little business.'

'I thought you already had one.'

'What's that?'

'Computers? In Chipping Camden? The Bill Gates of the Cotswolds, wasn't it?'

'Oh that. Nah, made that up, didn't I? These days, it's so easy. Give 'em a business card, yeah, and they assume it's legit.'

'Why Naomi?'

'Rich old bird like that? Ripe for the plucking, she was. Hadn't had any for years, liked a bit of rough. I can always tell.' He smiled, unrepentant. 'The leathers and the boots, all those zips and buckles. They love it. And all she had to do for it was share out a bit of the lolly.'

'Aren't you ashamed of yourself?'

'Why? I didn't do nothing. Gave her a good time, for the

first time in her life. Made her feel as though she was worth something. What's wrong with that?'

'Nothing, I suppose.' In a conscienceless way, he had a point. A sad thought struck her: had Naomi gone with Mansfield/Collins in the desperate hope that he might prove more fertile than John?

'As a matter of fact, I rather liked the old dear.'

'I wish you'd stop referring to her as old. She wasn't that much older than I am.'

'Yeah, but you're young at heart, Cass, and poor old Naomi had never been young in her life.'

'Whose fault was that, I wonder?'

'That sodding stepfather of hers. Robert Chessington, ex-librarian, so-called antiques dealer.'

'You knew him, then?'

'I made it my business to find out. Always be prepared, that's the secret of success in my line of work.' He shook his newly-sleek head. 'What a bastard, eh?'

'Did you know he was dead? That someone murdered him?'

Blood leached from behind the weatherbeaten skin. 'What?'

'Yes. More or less the same time as Naomi died. Funny, that. A bit of a coincidence, wouldn't you say?'

'Don't look at me, darling. I didn't have nothing to do with it.' A touch of the ex-con's whine, a sound Cassie was familiar with, had crept into his voice now. 'It's not my game, murder isn't. I don't mess with that kind of crap. Not my sort of thing at all.'

Although this was a man who made a living out of telling lies, a man, indeed, whose whole existence was based on falsehood, Cassie believed him. Mansfield might be a callous criminal, playing on the sad inadequacies of unhappy women, but he was unambiguous, his aims transparently clear. Inside his head were none of those dark places where the compulsions to murder lurked.

'Then why were you so keen to nail John Harris for murdering Naomi?' Cassie asked.

He shrugged. 'I still think he did it. And then I thought, if I could prove it, I could lean on him a bit. Make a bob or two. Not that blackmail's my usual line, but you gotta be versatile.'

'That's *so* immoral.'

'Somebody killed her, that's for sure. I saw her only a couple of days before she took off for Wales and—'

'How do you know when that was?'

'I can read. I worked it out from the newspaper reports. They weren't too sure of the time of death, but give or take twenty-four hours, I could see when she must have left home. And there was that parking lot chappie: he knew when her car arrived in Aberystwyth or wherever, so, like I say, I knew I'd been with her two days before that. Take it from me: she wasn't about to do herself in at that point. No way.'

'Why do you say that?'

'She was really lit up about something. Dunno what. She wouldn't tell me. But even though she was giving me the brush-off in no uncertain terms, you could tell she was all excited.'

Cassie considered him. 'Have you ever thought about going straight?'

He sighed. 'Like to, wouldn't I? But easier said than done. Once you've got a record . . . That's why I was dead keen on old Naomi. Thought she'd see me right. And don't get me wrong: fair dues and all that. I'd have looked after her, made her happy.'

'As long as she paid.'

'Of course. What do you think? I'm in business for myself, same as everyone else, right?'

'What went wrong between you then?'

He looked shifty. 'Who says anything did?'

'I do.'

'She wasn't stupid, I'll say that for her. She only got the dicks onto me, didn't she?'

'A private investigator, do you mean?'

'Right. One of them Philip Marlowe types. I caught someone going through my garbage and I knew that was it. The end of the line. Curtains for Philip Mansfield. But she was good to me, was Naomi, and when I heard about her dying like that, I thought it was worth stirring things a bit. Not just for my sake, either. I owed her one.'

'So where now, Terry?'

'Here,' he said, showing alarm. 'I don't know where you got hold of that piece of info about me real name, and I don't want to know. But keep it to yourself, right?'

'Right.'

'I mean, I got things in the pipeline. I don't want them going off the boil, do I?'

'What sort of things? I mean—' Cassie gestured at the suit, the hair. 'You've rather revamped your image, haven't you?'

'I don't want to say too much,' said Terry. 'Not at this stage. But there's this bird, yeah, thinks I just dropped down from heaven. If I play my cards right, I could really land on my feet. And what's more . . .' Here Terry grew a trifle misty-eyed, '. . . I think I'm in love.'

'With what?'

'What d'you mean? Her, of course!'

'Is she rich?'

He smirked. 'The fact that her old man left her with a pocketful of sovs's got nothing to do with it.'

'Save it for someone who might believe you,' said Cassie. 'And, although I disapprove of you strongly . . . good luck.'

Someone had murdered Naomi. But why? Over a second and even a third whisky, Cassie pondered the problem. What motive could there be? Still sulking, Anthea had rung back, to reveal – though not before exacting every milligram of brown-nosing grovel she could – that Naomi had indeed wanted to come in to discuss with Graham Blacklaws the changing of her will to include Lucy Benson. There were few details, since Anthea was taking the information from the notes Graham had made in his record book, but it seemed that John Harris's position would not have changed much. There was no mention in the notes of Philip Mansfield. Nor Terry Collins.

'What about the reversionary legatee, if that's the right phrase?' asked Cassie. 'This Francis W. Benson bloke.'

'Presumably he would have only got half after John Harris's death, instead of the lot,' Anthea said coldly. An unforgiving nature, obviously.

It was a motive for Benson to do away with Naomi. On the other hand, he almost certainly didn't know of Naomi's intentions. Although she might have informed him after the new will was drawn up, she was unlikely to have done so beforehand. Especially after his unfriendly reception of her. And there was something else, something he'd said, which knocked him out of the running. What was it?

She tried calling the number Lucy had given her but no one answered and the answering machine wasn't functioning. As she replaced the receiver after her fifth or sixth try, the phone rang. It was Charlie. 'Hello, Cassandra,' he said, his voice hollow.

'Charlie. What's the matter?'

'How do you mean?'

'You don't sound like your usual self.'

'How do I sound, then?'

'Quiet.'

'Mmm.'

'You're all right, are you?'

He gave a huge rumbling sigh. 'About as all right I could be, in the circumstances.'

'What *are* the circumstances, Charlie?'

'I've had a taste of paradise, haven't I?'

There was no point being coy. 'Oh, Charlie . . .'

'And now nothing less will do me.'

'I *told* you. It was – I was drunk. Otherwise it wouldn't have happened.'

'You're saying I'm the kind of bastard who takes advantage of a girl who's over the limit.'

'I didn't say that at all.'

'Or do you mean the only way you'd get into bed with me is if you were pissed. Is that it?'

Pretty close to the mark, actually. 'Of *course* not,' she said. 'I'm just not in the habit of sleeping with every Tom, Dick or Harry who takes me out for dinner.'

'I see.'

He sounded so sad that, despite the dangers, she found herself rushing in to comfort him. 'I'm not saying it wasn't wonder— that it wasn't nice,' she explained. 'I've told you before that it's not a good idea. You and me, I mean. We just aren't each other's type.'

'You're my type, girl.'

'We wouldn't get on. I'd make you terribly unhappy.' Jesus, how did she get into this situation anyway?

251

'Never.'

'Look, we've had this discussion before. It never comes to anything.'

'OK. I won't push you on it.'

'Thank God for that.'

'What I rung up about was, I gave this mate of mine a bell—'

'I knew you would, Charlie.'

'—And he got hold of the info you was after.'

'That's brilliant.'

'Got a pencil? You can write this down.'

'Let's have it.'

'The owner of the vehicle is called Peter Johannsen, and his address is . . .' Charlie spelled it out to her.

'Thank you,' she said. 'I'm very grateful.'

'Look, Cass, who is this bloke? Not the sod that's been following you round, is he?'

If she told him, Cassie knew that he would try to take over. His intentions would be good, but this was something she wanted – *needed* – to handle herself. 'No,' she lied. 'Just someone I'd like to get in touch with.'

He seemed to buy it.

When she had replaced the telephone, she looked at the sheet of paper on the kitchen table. Peter Johannsen. 15 Cremorne Gardens, Crowthorne, near Leamington Spa. So, after all these weeks, she had him pinned down, reduced to a name and address. She could find him, confront him, banish him from her life. Yet there was a curious feeling of pathos about it. He should have been called Mandragora or Beelzebub, he should have come from the Mountains of the Moon or Gehenna. Cremorne Gardens was so banal a location; Peter, so ordinary a name. Now that she had him contained within the words on the paper, she felt no sense of urgency. One thing she was very clear on: she wanted Johannsen to suffer. Two could play at that game. Driving up to his house, asking him what the hell he thought he was playing at, would not be sufficient. When she had decided how best to handle him, she would make her moves. Until then, she wouldn't worry about him.

It occurred to her that it might be a good idea to bring Lucy into it. They could work out a game plan, discuss tactics and strategies which could in turn help Lucy with her appalling father. She dialled the London number of Bancroft & Unwin. When the switchboard operator answered, she asked to put through to Lucy Benson.

'Which department?' the woman asked, using the standard adenoidal approach. Never mind efficiency or politeness: if you didn't speak through your nose, you could forget a career as a telephonist.

'Um . . . I'm not sure,' Cassie said.

'One moment.' Without any warning, the operator's voice was replaced by a raucous electronic rendition of *Doh's a Deer, a Female Deer* from *The Sound of Music* which had Cassie wincing with pain. Only partly because the bloody tune would now stay in her head for the rest of the week. Her ear bounced and hummed. Dammit. This was an operator who was not only rhinologically challenged, but sadistic as well.

She returned after Cassie had been brought back to doh, reh, me, fah for the second time. 'No Lucy Benson,' she snarled.

'I know she works there,' said Cassie.

'Not here, she doesn't, madam.'

'Where else, then?'

'We got branches. Perhaps she's in one of them. Rio?'

'What?'

'Maybe,' said the operator, with nasal contempt, 'she works in Rio de Janeiro. In Brazil.'

'Are you trying to be funny?'

'No, madam.'

'How would I find out which branch Miss Benson's attached to?'

'Don't know, really.'

'There's no central computer? No database of employees?'

'Not as far as I'm aware.'

'Thank you *so* much for your help,' Cassie began but was cut off before she had completed the sentence.

She rang the number of the Francis W. Benson Bookstore in Ross-on-Wye. 'It's Cassandra Swann again,' she said cheerily.

He didn't sound too thrilled to hear from her. 'Yes?'

'You told me when I saw you that you'd been on holiday.'

'That's right.'

'Where did you go?'

'What business is it of yours?'

'Now, now, Francis. If you won't tell me, I can always ring your mother.'

'Oh, all right,' he said ungraciously. 'We – mother and I, that is – went to Majorca for a fortnight. We go every year. Anything else you want to know?'

'Yes. The date you left and the date you came back.'

He told her.

'That's a pity,' she said.

'Why? There's nothing wrong with Majorca at that time of year, whatever the snobs would have you believe.'

'The thing is, I really had you tagged as the murderer, but if

254

you were away, you can't have been, can you?'

   'The murderer? What the hell are you talking about?'

   'The person who killed Naomi.'

   'But – she committed suicide, didn't she?'

   'The jury's still out on that one, Francis. See you.'

   'Oh God,' he said fervently. 'I do hope not.'

♣ 17 ♣

Why had Lucy lied about working for the London head-quarters of Bancroft & Unwin? And what else might she have lied about? Until now, Cassie had taken her at face value; today she saw that might have been a serious mistake. As she drove through the country lanes to have coffee with John Harris, she thought about Lucy, readjusting her recollections of the girl, modifying her perceptions, recalibrating details which gradually, as she grew nearer to Bridge End, began to take on a different and alarming perspective.

John Harris was considerably less forlorn than when she had previously seen him. This morning he looked plumped out, glossy as a bantam. There even seemed to be more hair than usual stretched across his shiny scalp.

'Cassie!' he cried.

'How are you, John?'

'Getting on, I suppose. Managing. Surprisingly well, actually. Come into the kitchen, my dear. I've got coffee brewing.'

The house had already lost its pristinity. There were dust balls on the rich parquet of the hall, a pile of badly folded underpants and vests on a chair in the kitchen, muddy welling-tons standing by the Aga. The vacuum cleaner waited at the bottom of the stairs; there were dead flowers in the vases. It was much more like the milieu in which Cassie herself moved, and made Harris appear more human and therefore more likeable.

'Naomi would have a fit,' he said guiltily, moving newspapers from one side of the kitchen table to the other. 'Look, would you prefer to be more formal and go into the sitting room?'

'This is fine.'

'I'm afraid I'm letting things slip a bit. If it wasn't for Anne, I'd be up to my ears in old milk bottles and dirty washing.'

'Anne?'

'Anne Norrington?' He put his head on one side. 'You know her, don't you? She plays bridge with you, she told me. And with Naomi, of course. Or used to.' He looked momentarily confused.

'She's giving you a hand, is she?'

'Most kind,' said Harris. 'A really nice woman. An excellent cook, too, which poor Naomi . . . And she's a wonderful artist. She showed me some of her watercolours the other day when I picked her up. Very talented, I thought.'

'Picked her up?'

'I was taking her to a concert at the Music Rooms, in Oxford, and we had dinner beforehand,' explained Harris.

'Ah.'

'It probably seems a bit precipitate, but as Anne points out, we're none of us as young as we were.'

'Quite.'

'*Carpe diem*, she tells me, and I've been doing just that. Seizing the day. I'm sure you can understand, can't you?'

'Probably the best thing you could do,' said Cassie, feeling at least a hundred years old. Was he going to ask for her blessing? Her permission? Her gaze fell on the pile of newspapers.

Harris noticed. 'Do you remember asking me about Naomi's stepfather?' he said, reaching an arm out to remove the top two or three copies.

'Of course.'

'I could hardly believe my eyes when I read that someone had broken into his house and attacked him. It seemed so odd, when we'd been talking about him only the day before.'

'I don't take a newspaper.' It was one of Cassie's economies, designed to make her feel virtuous and thrifty.

'Then perhaps you didn't know about him being killed.'

'I didn't read about it, no.'

'Oh goodness. I'll show you.' He scrabbled some more, opening the *Daily Telegraph* and showing her the lead story on the third page. 'They found him in his hallway, dead. Someone had hit him from behind and then pushed him down the stairs. Isn't that terrible?'

'I don't know, John. Is it?'

'Well, you know . . .'

'From what I've heard, someone should have eliminated him years ago.'

'You're right. It's a sad old world we live in, isn't it? The way parents treat their children these days takes some believing. Not all parents, of course. I mean, take Anne, Anne Norrington . . .'

It looked as though he'd already taken her himself. Cassie listened while he praised Anne's children, waxed eloquent about their obvious love for their mother, their upbringing, the fact that they were decent lads and a credit to her. 'Doing really well, too. Dan's at university, studying journalism, you know, and Tommy's thinking about going into the army. I've pointed out the drawbacks, but of course, it does provide a safe career structure and is excellent training for civilian life when you've finished your stint.'

Cassie stifled a yawn.

'Such a contrast to this bloody man, Chessington,' said Harris, happily unaware of how transparent he was being. He picked up the newspaper again. 'Um, look, Cassie, there's something I wanted to tell you – that's why I invited you over. It wasn't something I really wanted to say over the phone.'

'What it's about?'

'I don't really know why I think you're the right person to tell, but I've got to share it with someone, and for obvious reasons, I can't tell Anne. And with you being Naomi's best friend and so forth—'

'I was no—' Oh hell. What did it matter? Let it go.

'—It seemed fitting that you were the one. You see, she made me promise never to tell a soul, ever, but now all this has happened – her suicide and Chessington being killed – it seems important somehow that someone else knows.'

'Why?'

He seemed unhappy. 'It might be significant, you see. I was hoping you'd be able to advise me on the matter, because I seriously wonder whether it's not something I shouldn't inform the police about.'

'What is?' Or did she mean 'What isn't'?

'The thing is, if Chessington had simply died, I probably wouldn't feel it necessary. But since he didn't just fall down the stairs but was knocked on the head first – in other words, was murdered – it might be my duty to pass the information on. I don't know. Naomi would be so mortified if anyone found out.'

'John . . .'

'I could swear the police to secrecy, couldn't I? They do that sometimes, don't they? Withhold evidence if it will incriminate the innocent? Or at least, behave with discretion about it.'

'John,' Cassie said again, louder this time.

'Yes, I'm wittering a bit,' Harris said. 'It's all rather embarrassing – one doesn't like talking about such matters, even if it's not hushed up the way it used to be.'

'What isn't?'

'Incest.' He looked reflective. 'Though I'm not sure if you call it incest if the relationship isn't one of blood. Child abuse, anyway.'

'If you mean about Chessington and poor Naomi, you already told—'

'No, it's more complicated than that.'

'Tell me about it.'

He drew a deep breath. 'Oh dear. Poor Naomi. How she would hate – You see, Chessington wasn't simply Naomi's stepfather.'

'What else was he?'

'He was also the father of her child.'

Cassie felt cold. 'No,' she whispered. 'Oh Jesus. No.'

'I'm afraid so. At his insistence, she had several abortions – she's always believed that's why we couldn't have any children – and then she refused to have any more. They gave the baby up to a couple that her parents knew who couldn't have any of their own, but it all came out, the abuse and so on, though nobody else knew about him being the father of the child.'

'Except the mother.'

'Of course. Which is why he went to prison, after Naomi left home. It's a dreadful story.'

'Horrible. *Horrible*. Don't these bloody men ever think about anything else but their dicks?' Cassie said savagely.

261

'Don't they ever think what they're doing, the lives they're destroying just so they can get their end away? Hurting, traumatising, dominating some helpless quivering *child*, just to make themselves seem bigger than they are? And not just once, but for years.'

'Don't, my dear.' Harris reached across and took her hand. 'Don't lump us all together.'

'I'm sorry. But when I think of the misery . . .' She was choking with fury. 'After hearing about this, if someone else hadn't done it, I'd have willingly killed Chessington myself. When you think what Naomi must have gone through.'

'I know. And with her own death taking place so shortly after, it did occur to me that, you know, there might be some connection.'

Cassie scarcely heard him. Chessington. What were the implications of this fresh piece of information? There was only one question which really required answering. Her heart ached. 'Oh, Lucy,' she said softly.

'I know. I keep thinking of that poor child,' said Harris. 'What a dreadful thing for her if she ever found out.'

Maybe she already had. Maybe she had done something about it. 'I must go,' Cassie said, pushing back her chair.

'But what do you think I should do?' Harris said. 'About passing this on to the police?'

'Nothing. Not yet.' Breathing space was needed. Room for Lucy. Cassie sucked in a huge breath. 'Look, since you asked my advice, I should keep it to yourself for the moment. Let me think about it. As you say, Naomi would be so upset if this got out among her friends. And the police investigating the Chessington case may already have enough clues without you having to give away Naomi's secrets.' Time. Time. The word banged like a clock inside her head. Time for

Lucy. Time to buy time. She stood up.

'Must you go?' Harris said. 'Anne's coming.'

'I'm sorry. But I'm really devastated by what you've just told me. Especially knowing Lucy as I do.'

Or as I thought I did. What has she kept from me? What has she done?

Harris got to his feet. 'If you're sure . . .'

'Yes.'

'I'll see you out then.' As they passed the open door of the drawing room, he said: 'You were so good to her, Cassie. I wondered if there's some little memento you'd like to have. Something of hers to remind you of happier days.'

On the mantel was the glass egg which Lucy had picked up. 'What about that,' she said.

'Perfect. Take it.' Harris gave it to her. 'Naomi loved that. We bought it on holiday in Mexico. She often sat here by the fire, holding it. I shall like to think of you, her close friend, doing the same thing.'

Let me out of here, Cassie thought. Was this history in the making, or what? Her sense of self swam and shimmered like a celluloid dissolve. There was nothing she could do to prevent the construction of the legend that Cassandra Swann and Naomi Harris had been *such* good friends. Not only would it become part of the local mythology, but she would find herself colluding in it. The truth would blur, had already done so, would be half-remembered, then half-forgotten. The fact that she had not even liked Naomi would be airbrushed out of the picture, a fact inconvenient, unfitting.

Lying on top of the pile of books on the coffee table was *Sophie's World*. 'Oh,' she said. 'I wondered where this had got to. I didn't see it here when I came round before.'

'What?'

'Naomi bought a copy in Oxford, but—'

'I've only just got it,' said Harris. 'Anne recommended it, so I bought a copy at the bookshop in Bellington.'

'But there was another copy. Naomi had one. I saw it.'

'She probably gave it to someone.'

'That must be it.' Cassie could have laid bets that she knew who the recipient was. That the book had been handed over in person. The knowledge only increased her anxiety.

'By the way, I'm meeting Naomi's solicitor early next week,' said Harris. 'To see if we can sort out this business with the will. I'd like that poor little creature to have what she's morally owed. It can't make up for the past in any real sense, but it might be helpful to her in the future.'

He stood in front of her, his image slipping before her eyes, as though she was seeing him through a prism, not the bloated arrogant person she had always thought him but an earnest, worried, slightly dull man, trying to do the best he could. Cassie wondered what kind of a desert his married life had been. Surprising herself, she bent and kissed his cheek. 'I hope it all works out.'

'What does?'

'You and Anne,' she said. As she walked to her car she heard his protestations that he didn't know what she meant, he hoped he hadn't been giving the wrong impression, he and Anne weren't . . . 'Oh yes, you are,' she said.

And, for the first time, saw him smile.

Lucy. Why hadn't she seen it before? What a difference a few facts could make. Details came rushing towards her, a time warp in reverse, their force increasing as each one added to the information already held. It was so obvious, when you thought about it.

Lucy.

Where was she? Cassie had tried to telephone several times last night and again this morning, without success. The answering machine was still switched off, making it impossible to leave a message. It seemed imperative that she find her, talk to her, if nothing else. Perhaps it was too late. She thought of the lives destroyed. Naomi's first, of course, and now it seemed there was little hope for Lucy.

She recalled the rosebud-splattered dress Lucy had worn at Naomi's funeral: she knew where she had seen it before. Sweat broke out on the back of her neck as it came to her, Naomi uneasy on the sofa in the Randolph's reception area, the shopping bags beside her seat, spilling out their contents, roses on fabric overflowing from a plastic carrier, books. Sadness filled her. Why can things never be the way they ought to be? Why is there so much pain? She remembered Lucy saying that it had been a present, that the giver had said the dress would suit her. She had also said that she and Naomi had never met. She couldn't have known that Naomi would bump into someone she knew in the Randolph, someone who would later recognise the dress and realise that Lucy had been given it by her mother.

The way Lucy had gone through the manor house came back to her. Picking things up, touching, grasping door handles, holding objects like the glass egg in her hand. Just in case . . . just in case the police caught up with her, asked her about the death of her mother. She must have been in the house before; it might even have been her who had picked up the telephone when Cassie rang. Perhaps she was lurking about when Cassie arrived, thinking up her plan even then, swinging into the house, pretending she believed Cassie to be the mother she claimed she had never met. A fine piece of acting, that, as were the tears and the despair. No wonder she had been so unsurprised when Cassie suggested that it might have been murder, not suicide, had accepted the idea so easily, pointed the finger at John Harris. How easy it would have been to drive off with Naomi to Wales, or anywhere else, drug her with her own medication, confuse her, and then, as Mansfield had suggested, get her to write a suicide note and persuade her to lie down in the boot of the car before taking the train back. Or perhaps she had come to the house, dealt with the logistics of crushed pills, pen and paper, whisky, before persuading Naomi to go for a drive. The motivation was not hard to find: she hadn't wanted Naomi's money, she'd wanted revenge. She would have seen Naomi as the one responsible for what had happened to her. She had demanded a life for a life. A death to compensate for the ruins of her own existence.

And Chessington: was that her work, too? Had she found out who her father was and dealt with him as she had dealt with Naomi? The two defaulting parents paying for the ugliness they had doomed their child to?

Cassie wished she could find it in her heart to condemn the girl. Coming to the turn-off towards Bellington, she slowed down. If she carried straight on, she would be driving towards Oxford. She remembered Lucy saying once that, when she was really depressed, she liked to wander round the Pitt Rivers Museum. Was it worth a try? Deciding it was, she put her foot down and headed towards the city.

It was sheer chance that Cassie noticed her. The Pitt Rivers had been almost empty. A few Asian anthropology students wandered between the glass cases, a North Oxford mother with four small boys in tow examined the shrunken heads, a shaven-headed youth in denims was paying suspiciously close attention to the firearms. But there was no Lucy.

Cassie walked down Parks Road towards Broad Street, thinking she would buy a sandwich at the King's Arms, giving no more than a cursory glance at the people ahead of her. Only as she looked again did she realise to whom the small rounded skull with its shock of chocolatey-ginger hair belonged.

'Hey, Lucy!' she called. But Lucy did not hear her and as she continued along the pavement, Cassie broke into a run, at the same time shouting: 'Wait! Lucy!'

This time Lucy heard. She stopped outside Wadham and turned round. When Cassie caught up with her, she said, with indifference: 'Oh, hi.' The shadows above her cheekbones were the colour of undiluted whisky, all the more startling against the unhealthy paleness of her face.

'Where have you been?' Cassie said, gasping slightly. 'I've been trying to contact you for ages.'

'Have you? Why?'

'Because I've been worried about you.'

Lucy merely nodded.

'Lucy.' Cassie shook the girl's arm. 'Come down from wherever you are and talk to me. Why haven't you been in touch?' She was fully aware that she sounded more like the girl's mother – or, if not like Naomi, then at least as though she had some parental rights over her – than as though she were simply a concerned friend.

'Sorry.' Lucy gave a brief smile which faded as swiftly as breath on a window pane. 'I've had a lot of business to attend to recently.'

'I'm sure you have.'

'Yeah, well . . .' Lucy's eyes slid beyond Cassie to the traffic in the street behind her.

'You don't look at all well.'

267

'Don't I?'

'In fact, you look as if you haven't had a square meal for days.' Cassie surveyed her critically. 'Let me buy you lunch.'

'OK.'

Cassie looked at her watch. 'We could drive out to the Trout. It won't be as crowded as the centre of town.'

Lucy hesitated for a moment, then smiled, though not directly at Cassie. 'Why not?' she said. Her eyes followed something in the road. 'My car's just round the corner, I managed to find a place in the Broad. Why don't I drive you out there and bring you back here after?'

'Good idea.'

The two women walked together to Lucy's VW. Neither spoke. Lying on the front passenger seat was a copy of *Sophie's World*. Cassie held it in her lap as they headed up the Woodstock Road towards the roundabout at the top.

'Have you read this?' Cassie asked.

'Not yet.'

'Did Naomi give it to you?'

'Yeah.'

'What's wrong, Lucy?' Cassie said. Stupid question.

'Nothing.' Stupid answer.

'Something is.'

Vigorously Lucy shook her head. 'No.' Only everything. 'Quite the opposite, really.'

'You're sorting out some of your problems, are you?'

'In a manner of speaking. But probably not the way you mean.'

'Have you got a new boyfriend?'

'I've never even had an old one, Cassie.' Lucy's voice was hard.

They reached the top of the Woodstock Road, and took the

268

left-hand turn down to Wolvercote and Godstow.

There were empty tables on the terrace of the Trout Inn. Yellow leaves drifted slowly down from the trees on the opposite bank of the river. A peacock strutted. On the uneven stone flags, sparrows quarrelled over crumbs. Cassie sat Lucy down so that she could watch the water tumble and sparkle over the weir below the bridge and went inside. When she came out with a tray, Lucy was staring into the river. 'I can see why people have to weigh themselves down,' she said, as Cassie slid the tray onto the wooden slats of the table.

'How do you mean?'

'With stones in their pockets. Like Virginia Woolf did. It would be so difficult to drown yourself, otherwise. Almost impossible, I should think. The instinct to survive would force you to keep coming up for air, wouldn't it?'

'It's not something I've thought about a great deal,' said Cassie brusquely. She handed over a plate. 'Eat this.'

'I'm not really very hungry.'

'Eat it, Lucy.'

The girl began to pick languidly at cold chicken, lifting a lettuce leaf as though it weighed several tons, breaking off a morsel of cheese.

'What are you doing with yourself these days?' asked Cassie.

'Nothing much. Drifting.'

'You've left your job, haven't you?'

Lucy's jaw tightened. 'What do you mean?'

'I called your firm. Bancroft & Unwin.'

'Why did you do that?' demanded Lucy. 'Who gave you the right to spy on me? What makes you think you can check up on me like that?' With each question, her white face grew more flushed and her voice louder.

'I wasn't spying. I just wanted to find out where you were.'

Cassie put a hand on the girl's knee but she jerked it away. 'Lucy, believe it or not, I'm worried about you. I care about you. I want to make sure you're all right.'

'Well, I'm not.' The girl's voice was ungracious. 'And the way things are, I'm never likely to be, either.'

'I've told you before, get some professional help. You might not believe it, but it is possible to get over traumas, whatever you think now.'

Lucy laid both her arms on the table top. In the amber autumn light, the skin on the inside of her arms was so absolutely bloodless that the white scars across her wrists showed up clearly, the faint raised lines dramatically conspicuous. 'Depends on the traumas,' she said.

'Let me help you.'

'I'm beyond help,' said Lucy. 'Beyond saving.' She flashed her smoke-brief grin at Cassie again. 'Don't worry about it. It's not your problem.'

'None of us live in isolation, Lucy. You and I are friends, aren't we?' With foreboding, Cassie sensed in her companion a despair that might now be too deep for curing, too weighty to be lifted.

'Are we?' The question was not meant to be aggressive, merely wondering.

'We are. So if you have a problem, then it's my problem too. That's what friends are for.'

'My problems aren't exactly the sort you can share.' Getting up, Lucy picked the granary roll off her plate and took it over to the low wall which ran along the terrace. She sat sideways there, tearing off bits of bread and flicking them down into the river below. She looked so like her mother that Cassie caught her breath. Perhaps if Naomi were still alive . . . 'Have you ever thought of looking for your real father?' she said carefully.

'I already did.'

'Did you find him?'

'Yes.'

'How?'

'Before she . . . I made my mother tell me who he was. Naomi, I mean.'

'You went to see him, didn't you?'

'Yes.'

'How did he take it?'

Lucy turned and looked full into Cassie's eyes. 'He laughed. He asked what I thought I could do about it.'

'Is that all?'

'Not quite.'

'What else?'

'I told him. What I could do about it, I mean.'

'And what was that?'

Lucy didn't answer. Cassie had not really expected her to. She could see it all so clearly, the girl in the dark hallway, the man's mocking laughter, the agonised accusation and the cruel response. Perhaps she had picked up some weapon, or brought one with her and, seeing it, he must have retreated up the stairs, perhaps not even then believing the seriousness of her purpose, still treating her with contempt, until he got to the landing and found her behind him. Perhaps he had tried to remonstrate, but it was too late as the blows rained down upon his head, as he was violently pushed, as he fell forward into space. Maybe he knew a moment's remorse as he tumbled to his death. Maybe not. Perhaps the fall hadn't killed him, perhaps the girl had run lightly down after him and smashed at the frail bones of his skull until she was sure he was dead.

Lucy turned back to the water below her and leaned outward so far that Cassie half-stood, uncertain, alarmed. For a moment, there, she had been afraid that Lucy would throw herself down. 'You don't want to talk about it,' she said.

'No.' Instead, Lucy jumped to her feet. 'Shall I get us another beer?'

'Take the money from my bag,' Cassie said.

'I'll pay.'

'It's my treat.'

Lucy opened Cassie's bag. Scrabbled about. Stared down into it. Grew absolutely still.

'What's the matter?' said Cassie.

The blood had vanished from Lucy's already pale cheeks. Her lips were almost invisible against her white face. 'This,' she whispered. She held up the sheet of paper on which Cassie had written Peter Johannsen's address. 'What's this?'

Cassie reached for the paper, but Lucy pulled away. 'I was going to tell you about him, when you were telling me about your father hassling you. Someone's been hassling me, too. That guy.' Cassie nodded at the sheet Lucy was holding up in the air like a flag. 'He's been following me for weeks. I'm pretty sure he's the person who just trashed my business premises. I think he's dangerous.'

'I know.'

Cassie frowned. 'You do? How?'

'Because I know him well.'

'Who is he?'

'He's my father,' said Lucy. 'My adoptive father.'

♦ 18 ♦

They were walking round the University Parks. Leaves slid through the mellow light to lie damply on grass of an almost hectic green. Modern slabs of science labs rose above the trees. The cricket pitch markings had faded, signalling the end of yet another summer. A few late punts still meandered, pursued by marauding ducks. 'He sort of thinks you're Naomi, you see,' Lucy said.

'Why on earth should he think that?'

'I told him you were.'

'*What*?'

'Well, not quite. It was Naomi really. She was worried about him knowing her real name, so we used yours. If she had to leave a message, she called herself Cassandra Swann. Then I'd know, you see, that it was really her.'

'You had no right to use my name,' said Cassie. They stood side by side on the hump-backed bridge looking at the thick green river between the willows. Final comprehension drifted like tumbleweed across her mind.

'I know. I can see that now. But at the time . . . I was kind of desperate and Naomi thought that you wouldn't mind, if you found out. She said you were the only person she knew who would understand.'

'But how could he intercept your messages? You don't live with him.'

'He knows stuff like that. He's into electronics in a big way.'

'Do you mean he taps your phone?'

'Or else he's got some kind of bugging device installed somewhere in my flat. I know for a fact that he's broken in more than once.'

'How?'

'Because he's made sure I do. Left notes on the table, moved things about, taken things of mine and then returned them.'

Was this the truth, or another of Lucy's distorted fantasies? 'You do know it's illegal to do that, don't you? You don't have to put up with it.'

'Right, yeah,' said Lucy wearily. 'So how do I stop him? How do I prove it's him stealing my knickers and tearing pages out of my books and making soup out of the sugar and the flour and the – the eggs.' She rested her elbows on the bridge-railings. 'You've just got no idea.'

'He must be insane.'

'Tell me about it.'

'Are you saying that this man, Peter Johannsen, has been tracking me, following me, frightening me, just because he thinks you're my daughter?'

'Yeah.'

A puffball remained in place for a moment, attached itself to part of Cassie's brain, made sense. 'The only time we spoke, he accused me of trying to take something away which was rightfully his. Did he mean you?'

'I told you he's always been possessive. And he feels he owns me.'

'But you've both put me in considerable danger. Or at least, under considerable stress.'

'I'm really sorry. I don't think either Naomi or I have acted very rationally over the past couple of months.'

'But surely if you had explained to him who I really was, he'd have stopped.'

'Maybe. But I can't talk to him. Can't even bear to see his face.'

These were waters too deep for Cassie. She lifted her shoulders and dropped them, trying to ease the tension which spread like a yoke across the top of her spine. A ascetic-looking man was calling across the grass to a recalcitrant dog, his well-bred tones piercing the yellow afternoon. 'Did you like Naomi, when you finally met her?'

Lucy bit her lip. 'I thought I told you I'd never seen her.'

'And we both know that you were lying, though I don't know why you should have done.'

'I was frightened. She'd gone off in such a state.'

'She gave you that dress, didn't she? When she met you at the Randolph Hotel?'

'Yes, the first time I met her. How do you know that?'

'Life has a way of taking its own course, however many plans we make,' said Cassie. As they came down from the bridge and strolled towards the duckpond, she explained that she had been in Oxford that afternoon, when Naomi waited nervously for the daughter she had not seen for more than twenty years. 'We thought she was meeting a lover, but it was you she was expecting.'

Lucy began suddenly to cry. She bent over as though bitten by a sudden cramp. 'She was so kind,' she sobbed. 'She'd brought me all sorts of stuff: books and clothes and things. But the terrible thing was, she didn't like me.'

'How do you know that?'

'I didn't, at first. It was after.'

'After what? After you visited her at Bridge End?'

'How do you know I . . .' The question fizzled out, as though the answer didn't really matter much. Which, in all the important ways, it did not. Shabby drakes darted at each other across the surface of the pond. Beautiful comical things: oh sure. Also aggressive, predatory and very male.

'When we went round the place together, I wondered why you kept picking things up and putting them down,' said Cassie. 'Now I realise you were trying to cover your tracks, and there was only one reason why you'd want to do that: because you'd been there before. That's when I realised who had killed poor Naomi.'

'She didn't like me,' said Lucy again. 'I couldn't handle that.'

'Did she say so?'

'She didn't need to. I could see it in her eyes. And then she started saying that she was going to change her will in my favour. I tried to tell her that I didn't want that, I wasn't interested in her money. But she insisted. She said it was the least she could do to try and make up for . . . everything. And the awful thing was, she was right.'

'What do you mean?'

'It *was* the least thing, the easiest thing she could have done. But I wanted her to love me. And she didn't. She pretended she did, but I could see she didn't.'

'She did, Lucy. She just didn't know how to show it.'

Poor Naomi, unused to demonstrative affection, always so stiff in company, so stilted. It was easy to imagine how hard she would have found it to express her delight in finding Lucy again, after the long separation. She was so unused to love. And Lucy, too, would have been hesitant, too gauche to know how to handle such an awkward situation. Too ready to assume she was unlovable.

276

'She didn't love me,' Lucy sobbed.

'You're wrong there,' said Cassie, trying to keep her voice steady, trying not to be moved by what she knew were false tears, faked grief. 'And don't forget that she was as much a victim as you were.'

'How could she have been? She wasn't given away at birth, like I was.'

'She was abused the way you were.'

'Who by?'

'Didn't you realise who Chessington was?'

'He was my real father.'

'He was also Naomi's stepfather.'

'Her stepf . . . I – uh – I didn't realise that.' Lucy's voice wavered. 'I kept asking her who my father was, but when she finally told me, she didn't explain that.' She picked up some pebbles from the gravel path and threw them into the pond. The ducks rushed excitedly across, treading on each other in their eagerness to snatch at what they thought was bread.

'Her parents split up and her mother married this Chessington. When the mother discovered what he'd been doing, she called in the police and he did time in prison for it. By which time, of course, you'd been born. She'd have only been sixteen or seventeen. How could she have kept you?'

'How long did Chessington get?'

'Four years.'

'I'm serving life.'

'So was Naomi.' Cassie was thinking fast, trying to work out whether there could be anything other than a tragic ending to the train of events which had begun years ago in the dust of some provincial library, when a pretty woman, bringing back an armful of books or attending some office function with her husband, had fallen in love with a librarian.

'Lucy,' she said gently, 'you'll have to face the fact that you're not going to get off scot-free. You realise that, don't you? But John Harris is trying to see that you get the money that Naomi wanted you to have. It'll be more than enough to cover the cost of a good barrister. And society is much more aware these days; much more sympathetic to the kind of trauma you've been through.'

'What?' The small pinched face screwed itself up into an expression of disbelief. 'I don't quite . . .'

'Naomi,' said Cassie. 'And Chessington.'

'What about them?'

'I know you felt you had good reasons for what you did. And, as I say, you'll get help.'

'Whoa. Hold on here.' Lucy held up a hand. 'I'm not following all this.'

'You did kill them both, didn't you?'

'*Kill* them?' Lucy looked as if she had suddenly found herself keeping company with a rabid skunk. 'I didn't even know that Chessington was dead.'

'Are you sure?'

'Of course I'm bloody sure. Jesus. Are you out of your mind?'

'But—'

'I know I'm screwed-up,' Lucy said, 'but I'm not completely nuts. I agree that I'd give my left tit to know that Johannsen was dead. But I'm not going to be the one who does something about it.'

Could she be believed? Cassie wasn't sure.

'I also agree that what you've just said about Chessington doesn't exactly fill me with gloom and despondency,' continued Lucy. 'Did you say someone killed him?'

'Smashed in the back of his head and pushed him down the stairs.'

278

'I hope it hurt.'

'You tell me.'

Lucy stared. 'You seriously believe I did it, don't you?'

'Didn't you?'

'*No*. I already said I didn't.' A glitter came into Lucy's eyes. 'But if you thought I did it, why would you believe me if I said I didn't? How do you know I won't kill *you*, now that you've uncovered my guilty secret?'

'Don't be silly.'

'You really thought I'd killed Naomi, didn't you?'

'I had to ask,' said Cassie. 'I wanted to be sure.'

'And are you sure now?'

'Of course.'

'Is my say-so sufficient to convince you?'

'Yes.'

'Oh really?' Lucy's voice was soaked in sarcasm.

'I needed to know,' explained Cassie, 'before we try to work out what's the best thing for you.' She was ashamed of her own prevarication. Had she truly believed Lucy capable of murder, of double murder, or had she simply recognised the possibility that she might have been? Whichever it was, the two were identical in the lack of emotional support she herself had displayed, the confidence in Lucy she had clearly not shown. What empty spaces in herself there must be, what deserts of selfishness. No wonder she was incapable of sustaining a relationship with anyone. No wonder her brief marriage had failed. Caught between the values of the Vicarage and the pub, she had failed to grasp either. She could feel her own grief rising like floodwater.

'We?' Lucy said coldly. 'What do I have to do with you?'

'Whether you like it or not, we're linked. You and Naomi involved me, without asking me. You brought this Johannsen into my life and now you and I are going to get him out of it. And out of yours, too. I think we should work out what we can do about him. And make things better for you.' Cassie ignored the mutinous expression on Lucy's face. 'I don't know anything about you, what you really do, whether you're an accountant or not, whether you even went to university. You've told me a number of lies; it would be better if you started telling me the truth. And when I know it, I'm going to the police.'

'About . . . *him*?'

'Of course.'

'I can't,' Lucy said. She stood with clenched fists, staring up at the sky. 'I couldn't face it, having everybody know that I was fucked by my own father. I couldn't stand up in court and go through it all. I've managed to get clear of him, I can't dive back into all that . . . *stuff*.'

'If you have to, you will. You're not really clear of it, Lucy. You know that yourself – you've said as much to me. It'll be an ordeal for you, I know, but I'll be there, I'll . . .' Cassie's eyes filled with tears. 'Please,' she said, her voice breaking. 'Let me help.' The way I should have helped Naomi, she thought.

'Even if I went through it all, giving evidence, the whole shtick, how do we know anyone will believe me? How do you know it'll work?'

'I don't. But it's worth a try.'

Lucy was obviously undecided.

'Isn't it?' Cassie pressed. 'Isn't it, Lucy?'

'I suppose so.'

'You can come and stay with me again,' said Cassie.

'And we'll fix Johannsen, right?'

'Ri-i-i-ght.'

'Yo, baby,' said Lucy, but her voice was uncertain. She took

Cassie's arm as they walked back towards the alley leading into Norham Gardens. 'Now tell me how we're going to do it.'

Natasha's Dr Zhivago phase seemed to have passed. When Cassie and Lucy arrived back at Honeysuckle Cottage they found her slinging white paint at the walls of the converted outhouse. She was wearing headphones. '*Born in the USA,*' she warbled tunelessly, slapping paint, swaying inside white painters' overalls which were much too big for her, long black hair tucked up inside a baseball cap with FASHION CAFE embroidered across it in red. '*I was born in the . . .* oh goodness! What a fright you gave me, Cassie. Couldn't you have warned me?' She pulled the headphones off so they hung around her neck.

'How could I?' protested Cassie. 'You were too busy hanging out with Springsteen.'

'I'm making a start on getting things back to normal,' said Natasha. She looked beyond Cassie to where Lucy lagged behind. 'And who is this?'

Cassie introduced them. 'She's coming to stay with me for a while. We've got some things to sort out.'

'If you need any help with the painting . . .' Lucy said.

'Whenever you like. There are spare paintbrushes and rollers in the little place at the end, and some spare overalls,' said Natasha.

'Cool.'

'Cassie, I found a letter for you lying on the floor in here when I arrived this morning,' Natasha said. 'It's on the table in the kitchen. A bill, I should think, from the cleaning company.'

It wasn't. Inside a long white envelope with her name hand printed on it in neat capitals, she found a sheet of paper folded three times. THIS IS JUST THE BEGINNING, she read. And under that, shadow printed: SHE'S MINE.

Johannsen. He'd obviously used a laser printer. Which meant that, as far as identification went, there was no hope of tracing the message back to him, unless he'd left his finger-prints on the paper. In the olden days before computers, the idiosyncrasies of manual typewriters were as effective as DNA profiling in pinpointing on which machine an anonymous note had been typed. Provided you knew where to look in the first place, of course. If you could then positively prove that the owner was responsible for the typing, you'd got your man. Which reminded her of another thing which annoyed her about Tim Gardiner's books: when an unsigned letter provided Pan-dora Quest with a vital clue, it was always written on an old Imperial, as though none of his characters had ever heard of modern technology.

Cassie didn't need fingerprints or dodgy lower case e's to know who was behind this. She wondered if Johannsen would leave her alone if she pointed out to him that she was not Lucy's mother, and that nobody was trying to take the girl away from him: he'd alienated her sufficiently himself. But even if he stopped bugging *her*, there was still Lucy to be considered, to be compensated. And worse than that was the possibility that his obsession with his adopted daughter might turn more violent as he realised that there was no way she would ever have anything to do with him again.

Another thought struck her. Perhaps he was perfectly well aware that she was not Lucy's biological mother, but was nonetheless determined that she would not take over Naomi's place in Lucy's affections. Perhaps he had already struck once to prevent this and would strike again if necessary.

Facts would have to be gathered, of course, but it was perfectly possible that he was the one who had faked Naomi's suicide. In fact, the more she considered it, the more logical the notion became. He could so easily have arranged to meet Naomi, perhaps giving the excuse of discussing Lucy with her. He could have organised all the rest, the whisky, the pills, even the note. He could have driven to Wales – he already spent a great deal of time driving around so an extra journey wouldn't have fazed him – or persuaded Naomi to drive him, and left her dead or dying in the boot of her own car, before travelling back to his own home. Excitement filled her. Of course. All she had to do was either prove it herself, or persuade the police to investigate him.

But if they turned up nothing, or if they could show categorically that he was not the murderer, he would still have to be dealt with. The question was, how?

The glimmering of an idea occurred to her. Would she and Lucy be able to get him to incriminate himself? As far as the sexual abuse went, Lucy's word might not be enough, but strengthened with the evidence of his break-ins, his buggings, his threats and the damage done to the offices of Bridge the Gap, it ought to be enough to put him away. Briefly, she thought of Paul Walsh. If Johannsen agreed to come to the cottage, should she ask Paul to come round? A hundred *films noirs* did quick-time through her head: the lonely PI walking down deserted rain-slick streets, shadows falling on white faces, cigarette smoke curling in saloon bars where the drinks were cheap and the women cost plenty, while the villain incriminated himself in the last reel and was duly led off in handcuffs. Would it be that easy with Johannsen? It seemed unlikely that he would go in for violence: the whole point about child abusers was that they had no guts. Why else would they only dare to bully the defenceless? How ineffectual did you have to be that you only felt capable of attacking a child?

What moral responsibilities had you abrogated in order to justify such actions?

Cassie had seen the nonces in the nick: furtive, runty men for the most part, who shuffled back to their isolation wing, too frightened of retribution to live among the ordinary prison population. But Johannsen hadn't been like that. She wondered what sort of a man Chessington had been. Perhaps fathers were in a different league from the scoutmasters and Catholic priests and all the other emasculated wimps who got their kicks and their self-esteem from abusing children.

She woke instantly, terrified. Someone was trying to lift the latch of her door. She lay rigid in the darkness, listening. Had Lucy, asleep in the spare bedroom, heard it too. Was it Johannsen? Cautiously she raised herself up on her elbows and stared intently at the slab of wall which contained the door, but could make out nothing in the deep rural blackness. She heard it again: the cautious scrape of the hasp against the bracket in which it rested.

There was nothing on the bedside table which she could use as a weapon. All she could do was wait until he was inside the room, then scream for Lucy. Between them, the two of them could surely see him off. She reached a careful hand towards the switch of the lamp, hoping she wouldn't find herself fumbling for it and thus give him warning that she was awake.

There was silence, then she heard a whisper in the dark, soft as a slug. 'Cassie. Cassie.'

Sweat was cold between her shoulder-blades, her mouth was dry.

'Cassie, are you awake?'

A floorboard creaked as the intruder moved towards her bed

and brushed against the trailing duvet.

She opened her mouth and screamed. 'Lucy! Lucy!'

'Jesus!' It was Lucy's voice. 'What the hell are you doing? I'm right here.'

Cassie found the switch and fumbled on the light. 'What are you – I thought it was bloody Johannsen.'

'I just wondered if I could come into bed with you. I'm cold, I'm feeling so . . .' Lucy's chin trembled. She wore a tiny little nightdress of red spotted cotton; her hair stuck up in chocolatey spikes. She could have been six years old.

Anguish moved in Cassie's chest. How could anyone have violated such a small, defenceless thing? It was like torturing a kitten or tearing the petals off a rose. She pushed back the duvet. 'Come on then,' she said.

Lucy climbed in and unselfconsciously snuggled against her. Feeling the knobs of her curved spine, the thinness of her limbs, Cassie was aware of a rush of feeling which she could only imagine was what parents experienced for their children: the certain knowledge that it would be worth dying to safeguard this hapless, helpless creature's well-being. She reached under the lampshade and switched out the light. 'I hope you don't snore,' she said.

'I don't know whether I do or not.'

'You'll have to go back to your own bed if you do.'

'It's a deal.'

Cassie turned over on her side away from Lucy, aware that the girl was lying on her back, and sleepless. Who was she, this Lucy? What were the mysteries she concealed in the secret garden where she spent most of her time?

She felt a timid touch on her back. 'Are you still awake, Cassie?'

'No.'

'There's something I've got to tell you,' Lucy said. 'Something I should have said before.'

'What is it?'

'You know you accused me of murdering Naomi?'

'Well, not exactly.'

'But you were right. I did.'

'Oh Lucy.' Cassie turned over towards the unseen whisper in the dark. 'Oh, no.'

The girl's cold hand folded round Cassie's arm. 'I didn't want to. But all the same, I killed her.'

♥ 19 ♥

'I kept pushing at her. Going on and on about it. Saying I could never forgive either of them. That she had no right to conceal who my father was, that I had a right to know. That the two of them were as responsible for the mess I'm in as Johannsen was.'

'This was when you went to Bridge End?'

'Right. That first meeting at the Randolph, we didn't go into much of that, although I kind of hinted at things. And then she wanted me to come to her house, so she drove over to Oxford early that day – the one where I first saw you – and picked me up, because there's no way of getting there except by car and mine was at the garage and wouldn't be ready until that afternoon. She said she'd take me back there after lunch, so I could pick it up. She was so thrilled to have me, showed me all round the place, told me about her roses and things, the new carpet they'd just laid in the drawing room, how she was going to have the conservatory enlarged – oh please,' Lucy said, shaking her head violently, 'I didn't go to talk about domestic crap. I wanted to get down to the nitty-gritty, the *real* stuff. She made some coffee and took it into the drawing room and while she was still faffing round with milk and sugar, I started telling her about Johannsen and what he did to me for all those years.'

Poor Naomi. So eager to make a new start with her lost daughter: what must she have felt, hearing this? 'How did she take it?'

'It was dreadful. She went a funny colour, sort of greyish, and she started shaking. She even slopped coffee onto that precious carpet of hers. Then she began screaming.' Lucy, sitting up in Cassie's double bed, hugged her knees tightly at the memory. 'She put her hands over her ears and shouted that she didn't want to hear this, she couldn't bear it, not after everything else she'd been through.'

'What did you do?' Wrapped in the duvet from the spare room, Cassie thought she could guess.

'I just thought she was being spoiled, you see. Rich woman used to getting her own way, people doing what she told them. And I thought, why should she get away with it? So I went on telling her, screaming louder than she was, told her how I hated him, how I hated her for being so – so *cowardly* as to give me up. I said she should have kept me, I said *I* would have done, if it'd been me. And she said I didn't know, I couldn't possibly know. That's when I started in about my right to know who my own father was.'

'What happened then?'

'She jumped up, she looked terrible, as though she'd aged about twenty years in twenty minutes. She ran out of the room and I heard her upstairs rummaging around and then she came down again, and snatched a bottle of whisky out of that cabinet thing in the corner of the room and then said in this dreadful sort of howling voice that if I wanted to know who my father was, she'd take me to him.'

'What did you say?'

'There wasn't much I could say. She was in a real state by then. I went out after her – she was backing the car out of the garage, all over the place. I offered to drive, but she wouldn't let me. We went tearing out of the drive – she hit something, that pot of flowers, I should think – and out into the lane and . . .' Lucy grimaced. 'God, I thought I was going to die, I really did. I mean she was driving like a total maniac. And all the way to wherever, she kept saying things like she didn't mean to, she hadn't realised, I had to understand that it wasn't her fault. But of course, I didn't realise that her sodding stepfather had been treating her just the way my adoptive father treated me, did I?'

'Would it have made any difference if you had?'

'I think it would. I do, Cassie, I really do.' Lucy's eyes were big with self-censure as she stared pleadingly at Cassie who sat in the raggedy old armchair set under the sloping bedroom roof. 'How could I possibly have known? But if I had, I would have said something, I'm sure. Something about the two of us being in the same boat, that it would make our relationship even stronger to have shared such an experience.'

'And instead?'

'Instead, I just ranted on. I was full of resentment, of hate, even. If the two of them hadn't given me away, things would have been so different. At least, that's what I thought then. But of course now I can see that she couldn't possibly have kept me.'

'So there the two of you were, hurtling through the country-side towards Nottingham?'

'Is that where it was? I honestly didn't know. I was so terrified she was going to smash into a brick wall or something. Anyway, we came to this town after what seemed like hours and she drove like a bat out of hell through these suburban streets. I was just praying for the police to come after us – I mean, most of the time she wasn't even stopping at red lights.'

'There's never a policeman when you want one.'

'So we pulled up half on the pavement in front of this semi-detached house in a quiet nice neighbourhood, and she told me to wait there while she checked whether my dad was there – my real father, she meant. So she marched up to the front door and banged on it and after a bit it opened, and she went inside and she must have been in there about ten minutes – I could hear her screaming at someone but I don't know who – and then she came rushing out again, slamming the front door behind her, and jumped into the car and said he wasn't at home, we'd have to come back later.'

'Then what?'

'She set off again, I don't know where. I was so terrified, not just of her driving but the way she looked. Like a madwoman, her teeth kind of drawn back and her hair all wild. She kept muttering, too. About how useless she was, what a mess she'd made of things, she wasn't fit to live. Awful sorts of things. And then suddenly, I don't know where we were but way out on some motorway, she came to one of those Welcome Break places and she screeched up and scrabbled around in her bag and gave me a great wodge of fivers and things, and told me to get out and take a taxi home.'

'Is that what you did?'

'I didn't know what else I could do. I went in and had a cup of coffee and tried to think what was the best thing to do, and in the end I called a cab and told him to take me back to the garage where my car was, and then I drove back again to Bridge End. I thought she might be back, you see. Come to her senses. So we could talk about it a bit more calmly.'

'So why all the charade, pretending you thought I was your mother?'

'Because . . .' Lucy rested her head on her knees for a

moment. 'I think I knew even then that something really frightful had happened. There was no way she was going to be driving like that for long without having some major accident. I thought that if I pretended I'd never been there that day, never even met her, nobody could blame me for anything, the police wouldn't want me to make a statement or even be able to connect me with her. Why would they?'

'I see.'

The grim details were making sense at last.

Naomi *had* killed herself, after all. Had planned to, as soon as she heard Lucy's accusations. Must have felt that there was nothing else for her to do. She must have gone upstairs to her bedroom and picked up the bottle of pills, collected the whisky, knowing she'd need something to help her swallow them down. But first she had driven to Nottingham, her daughter at her side, and murdered the man behind all her troubles and those of Lucy. It was still conjecture, but with corroboration from Lucy, the police would probably be able to establish the facts. At the moment, there was no reason for the two police forces handling the two entirely separate cases to have made any connections between them.

She would have to contact Paul Walsh. Drop a word in his ear. If she called him, would he think it was just an excuse for her to make up with him? Was it? She could just as well call the inspector in charge of the Chessington case. Naomi must have left fingerprints at his house. It was just sheer bad luck for the police, as far as solving the case was concerned, that nobody had noticed the car driving up, the frantic woman getting out, the girl waiting in the car. Nobody had even heard the screaming, apparently.

'So it's all my fault,' concluded Lucy. 'Isn't it?'

'You were no more than a precipitating factor in something

which was begun years before you were even born,' Cassie said.

'But if I hadn't pushed her to tell me about my real father, none of this would have happened.'

'If it's any comfort, I don't believe that. I knew Naomi better than you did. She wasn't happy. Finding you couldn't have changed that, even though she hoped that it might. It's like wrinkles in the face,' said Cassie. 'Once they're there, you can't change them, or make them go away. Naomi's whole life was so wrinkled with sadness that even finding you again wasn't going to make any difference.'

'But if I hadn't told her about Johannsen raping me . . .'

'You would have to have told her some time. It's not something you could ever have kept secret. And as soon as Naomi heard about it, she was bound to feel even worse.' Cassie kept to herself the thought that if Naomi had not still been weighted down with the chains of depression and post-operative trauma, she might have handled Lucy's revelations less dramatically. But self-blame, self-hatred, damaged self-esteem, were already so much part of her character that the added blow of Johannsen's treatment of Lucy would probably not, in the end, have significantly altered the events which ended with Naomi's body decomposing in the boot of her car.

'Johannsen,' she said. 'He's the one we've got to worry about now.'

They had spent some time the previous afternoon discussing how best to entrap Johannsen. They had decided, almost without debate, that he had to pay for his treatment of Cassie, as well as his long-term abuse of Lucy. It would have been easy for the girl to go the police, with evidence from the psychiatrist she had briefly visited at university. They wanted more than that.

'Ring him now,' Cassie said, glancing down at her watch.

'What time is it?'

'Three-fourteen.'

'He'll be asleep.'

'Good. Wake him up.'

'And when he answers, what do I say?'

'We went through all this last night.'

'I know, but I'm scared.'

'Tell him,' Cassie said patiently, 'that you're going to the police tomorrow. That you're going to shop him. That when you've told them about the things he's done to you, he'll be going to gaol, for sure. That you should have done it years ago but you never had the guts, but now that I'm encouraging you, you've made up your mind.'

'Oh Cassie. I don't dare.'

'Of course you do. I'd do it myself, but you'll be much more convincing. Keep emphasising the fact that I'm encouraging you to go for it.'

'It's like setting a trap.'

'And you're the bait.'

'The tethered goat waiting for the tiger.'

'Exactly. But I shan't let the tiger attack you.'

'If he comes.'

'He'll come,' said Cassie.

'Suppose he arrives with a gun?'

'Where's he going to get one from at this hour?'

'Do you think he'll really try to kill us?'

'He's certainly going to try to terrify us so badly that we'll keep quiet. But it's not going to work. All these years he's kept you from doing anything about the abuse because he knows how to frighten you, but he doesn't frighten me and it's not going to work any more.'

'No. It's not, is it?' Lucy was obviously not convinced. She stretched one of her stick-insect arms towards the telephone.

'Remember, don't get into conversation with him. Just make sure he knows where you are, and who you're with, and then put the receiver down.'

'You're certain this will work?'

'Absolutely.' Cassie sounded much more positive than she felt.

She had been so certain that he would come.

The day progressed from breakfast to lunchtime and on towards the early evening without a sign of him. When Lucy had put down the receiver on her conversation with Johannsen, the two women had sat together in the kitchen, drinking coffee, glancing fearfully at the windows as the night slowly grew lighter. At that pre-dawn hour, both kitchen and sitting room had an artificial air about them, as though the stiff unreal air which filled them had been filtered from a museum. Gradually, the sun rose into a mist which blocked out the hills beyond the back hedge and hung like the ghost of a cloud above the lily pond.

They spent the day in the ruined offices, finishing the paint job Natasha had started, sorting through the pile of damaged goods left behind by the commercial cleaning company in the hope that something could be salvaged, scrubbing areas of the tiled floor which had still not come clean. They worked uneasily, constantly glancing through the open door, listening, nerves stretched.

He didn't come. As the evening arrived, they stood together at the end of the garden, watching the combine harvester work up and down the field over the hedge. Behind it gulls surged and swooped, energetically working the stubbled rows for anything edible they could find. The sun was sinking on the far side of the cottage, gold limning the sagging curves of the ridgepole and dazzling behind the chimneypots. Out in the lane they could hear the shuffle of cows being led to the milking parlour.

'I wish he'd get on with it,' Lucy said. With one hand she clasped the elbow of her other arm and shivered a little. Despite the warmth still in the air, there were goosebumps on her skin.

'He probably wants to scare us by coming at night.'

'But I told him I'd go to the police today.'

'He's probably lurking somewhere nearby and knows perfectly well that we haven't left the cottage all day.'

'That's worse than him not coming at all. Anyway, how does he know I wouldn't ring them first?'

'He doesn't. But he'd know it would make much more sense for you to go in person to make a statement rather than phone.'

Cassie did not add that when she had lifted the telephone from its stand around six o'clock, the line had been dead. She hoped very much that she was right in thinking it was merely a fault on the line and, equally, that the telephone company was already onto it. The alternative explanation was that Johannsen himself had snipped the wires which led from the pole at the end of the lane into the house via a neat hole above the front door, waiting to do so until it was too late to call out the engineers to repair it. So far, she had not been able to check this theory out since Lucy had stuck to her side all day and she did not want to frighten her. Not for the first time, she wished that she owned a mobile telephone. She had avoided buying one on the grounds that although the initial purchase was relatively cheap, the subsequent bills wouldn't be and she couldn't afford any more expenses at the moment. But if she owned one, she would now have been able, if necessary, to summon the police. As it was, she had no choice but to sit here waiting for a pervert and possible homicidal maniac to consign her and Lucy to oblivion. Although she wanted to handle this on her own, with Lucy, because she felt it important for the girl's confidence, and she didn't foresee any real danger, she nonetheless would have liked the choice of calling in reinforcements if she needed to.

'You *are* sure he's gonna show, aren't you?' Lucy said.

'Absolutely. Look,' said Cassie, concerned by the girl's haggard look, 'We can get in the car and go visit someone. Or we could ask a friend to come round, if you like. I know someone who'd make steak tartare out of your adoptive father without even getting out of breath.' Contacting Charlie Quartermain would mean walking down the lane to Kathryn's cottage in order to use her phone.

'We can handle him, I'm not worried about that,' Lucy said. 'I'm just worried that he's got a gun. Suppose that's what he's been doing all day.'

The same thought had occurred to Cassie. They would have no protection against a gun. She laughed loudly. 'Scouring the stews and sewers of Leamington Spa's grimy underworld for a piece? Somehow I don't think so.'

'How did you know he came from Leamington?'

'Because after he'd been trailing me for weeks, I finally had the sense to take down the number of his car. A friend had it put through the computers at Swansea for me. That's why I had it written down in my bag.' Cassie spoke as though she was a teacher at an infant school, using simple words and short sentences.

'I wish he would hurry up.'

The sky was closing in now. Cassie wished she had not tried

to be so independent, that she had rung Charlie earlier in the day, or even taken Lucy down to visit Kathryn. Now, she admitted to herself that she was frightened to walk down the lane in the darkness. On the other hand, were they simply going to sit here all night, waiting like – as Lucy had put it – tethered goats? She stood outside the kitchen door and took in a deep breath of damp air. Johannsen was out there some-where, close by, waiting for the cover of darkness. She fancied that she could smell his malevolent reek under the scent of dying leaves and grass dampened by the evening dews. In the pond, the frogs croaked; a bird called; distantly came the innocent sound of traffic on far roads. People returning home to wives and children, suppers and television. People speeding to meet lovers. People heading for theatres or dinner parties or a night out with the boys. The evening star burned fiercely just above the brow of the hill, other stars were beginning to prickle faintly in the deepening gloom.

She closed the kitchen door and turned the key in the lock, shutting away the world. Common sense told her that Johannsen was not violent but it was difficult not to wonder whether Lucy was right, and that when he came, he would be armed with a gun. She took the girl with her as they checked locks and windowbolts and carefully drew all the curtains. Earlier she had brought in two croquet mallets from the garden shed, and the hockey stick which she had used at school in another lifetime from this.

'What about knives?' asked Lucy.

'If push came to shove, do you seriously think you could use it on him?'

Lucy gave it a microsecond's thought. 'No question.'

'Right.'

At eleven-thirty, they turned off the lights downstairs. At midnight they switched off the bedroom lights, first in Lucy's room and then, fifteen minutes later, in Cassie's. They both crept downstairs and then took it in turns to lie on the sofa in the sitting room, wrapped in a duvet. Despite her obvious fear, Lucy was able to sleep, but Cassie could only pretend as the long hours slowly dragged by. Music would have helped to pass the time, or the television, but she dared not allow the interference of sound, in case it gave Johannsen the opportunity to break in without being heard. One o'clock came and went; two o'clock, three o'clock, three-thirty, three-forty-five. And then, just after four, she heard something, a stealthiness on the grass outside, a sense of held breath, footsteps careful under the windows.

'Lucy.' She shook the girl's shoulder. Bending close, she scarcely moved her mouth as she said against Lucy's ear: 'Wake up.'

'What is it?' Lucy stirred under the billows of the duvet and then sat up, her eyes wide.

'I think he's here. Outside.'

'Oh, my God.'

'Don't worry.'

'Suppose it doesn't work.'

'It will.'

'But if he realises, he won't say anything.'

'Why should he realise? He has no reason to think that we have the skills.'

'But he has to be in the house, if it's going to work.'

'We hope he'll break in. We *want* him to break in. We went through it all yesterday. Breaking and entering is already a crime. And when he does, then we go for it.'

'Oh Cassie. I'm frightened.'

'You're not. Not really. You just think you are. You aren't a little girl any more. He can't hurt you. He has no power. Hang on to that.'

'He has no power,' Lucy said doubtfully.

'You have to mean it.'

'He has no power,' she said again.

Out in the kitchen, metal strained quietly against wood. Cassie had not pulled the bolts across the door, merely turned the key in the deadbolt and snicked down the lock on the Yale. She figured Johannsen wouldn't find either obstacle too difficult to deal with. She was right. She heard him fumbling outside and then the locks turning, the faint chafing sound as the warped door scraped across the uneven surface of the quarry tile floor.

Her night-accustomed eyes saw the shape of him move between the kitchen window and the door to the sitting room, filling the space. He stopped there, listening, while in the darkness she willed him to come on further into the room. Come on, now, just another step, and one more after that. Come *on*, baby.

Baby came. And as he did so, the sitting room door slammed shut behind him, and Cassie turned on the powerful lamp. Its beam, Lubyanka strong, blinded him. He put an arm over his eyes.

'What the hell . . .?' he began, as Lucy, from behind, grabbed him around the knees and butted him in the small of the back, pushing him further into the room so that he fell headlong over one of the two squashy sofas which stood on either side of the fireplace. She switched on the overhead lights while Cassie pulled his arms behind him and began wrapping them in sticky tape from the wide roll she had brought over from the offices of Bridge the Gap. But he was too strong for

299

her, and too quick. He rolled away, falling on all fours to the floor and immediately springing to his feet.

'Now what?' he said, facing her, ready, bouncing on his feet like a boxer, moving towards her in a series of little dancing steps.

Behind her, Lucy, her voice trembling, said: 'Shall I call the police?'

'You won't be able to,' said Cassie keeping her eyes on Johannsen. 'He's already disconnected the line.'

'Then how're we going to . . .?'

'Don't worry about it.'

'Oh,' said Johannsen. 'I think you *should* worry about it.' He looked over at the girl. 'Come here, Lucy.'

'Don't,' Cassie said sharply.

'Come on, Lucy.'

Cassie could feel Lucy's indecision. 'Ignore him!'

'If it's not a rude question,' Johannsen said, bouncing, bunching his fists, grinning, 'what the fuck do you think you're doing?'

'I'm trying to protect a very vulnerable person.'

'Perhaps you don't realise that there are laws against this sort of thing. Alienation of affection, they call it. You gave her up years ago.'

'I did?'

'She's my daughter now, not yours. She belongs to me.' While she was assimilating this – obviously he still thought that she was Naomi, or, at least, Lucy's mother – he leaped towards her. Grabbed her. Spun her round. Yanked her arm so hard behind her that she thought it must break.

Lucy began to scream, a thin, high-pitched wail that sounded more like a baby than an adult. 'Don't. Please don't. Oh, please. Don't!' The sound raised the hairs on the back of

Cassie's neck. It was like hearing something which belonged to the past, the ghost of long-ago pains come back to haunt the present. Was this the sound that the child Lucy had made while this vicious man raped her?

'You've got the wrong person,' Cassie said over her shoulder, teeth gritted against the pain. This operation was going wrong. 'That's been your mistake all along. Lucy isn't my daughter. It's unfortunate for her that she's yours. Though,' she added, trying to pull away from him, struggling against his grip, 'I've been wondering recently just how legal the adoption was in the first place.'

It had been intended as a shot in the dark, designed to do no more than help Lucy free herself from his influence. From his silence, she realised it was a shot which had found its mark. 'What?' he said.

'Not that any of that matters,' she said smoothly, knowing this was something to explore in the future. 'Sexual molestation is still a crime, whether the child you abuse is your legal daughter or not.'

'Sexual abuse, is that what she told you?' There was deep contempt in his voice. 'Is that what that little whore told you?'

'I'm not,' Lucy said. 'I'm *not*.'

'Even when she was only a toddler, she used to get me going,' Johannsen said. He pushed Cassie's arm higher up her back until she gasped with agony. 'Coming down in her little nightdress to say goodnight, sitting on my knee, rubbing herself all over me. Oh, she knew what she was doing, all right. Turning me on like a common prostitute.'

'I didn't.'

'Of course you didn't,' Cassie said. The stabbing pain of her arm was making her head swim. If he pushed it any further, it would break, and that would leave Lucy to deal with him on

301

her own, something she was clearly not able to do. The thought made Cassie forget her own discomfort. She stood still within his grip for a moment, then abruptly moved backwards, taking him by surprise, thrusting against him, using the element of unexpectedness to get him off-balance, so that he staggered slightly, his hold on her loosening.

She pulled herself free, moved rapidly across the room to stand beside Lucy, grabbed the hockey stick. 'I wouldn't come too close,' she said, in conversational fashion. 'I know how to use this.'

'Oh dear, I'm *sooo* afraid,' he sneered. Though he stayed where he was, his eyes were angry.

'Lucy,' Cassie said. 'Now that we've got him safely cornered in here, you can run down the lane to Kathryn's house and call the police from there. She's a heavy sleeper so just keep banging until she answers the door.'

'What about you?'

'I'll be all right. I don't think a man who gets his kicks from raping children is really going to be too much of a problem.' Cassie wished she felt as confident as she hoped, for Lucy's sake, that she sounded.

'Rape? What are you talking about? She consented. Begged for it. Put her hand down the front of my—'

'Go, Lucy,' commanded Cassie.

'You don't believe him, do you?'

'Not a word. Go on, girl. Take my torch.'

Both she and the man heard the kitchen door bang shut and then the sound of Lucy's footsteps running past the window.

For the first time, the man looked uncertain. 'You can't keep me here,' he said, looking round.

'Feel free to leave any time.'

He made a move towards her and she lifted the hockey stick.

302

He swallowed. 'It wasn't rape,' he said. 'She wanted me to do it.'

'How do you know?'

'She asked me to. She used to plead with me to give it to her.'

'Was this before or after you'd threatened her?'

'I didn't threaten anyone. She wanted it. She was as hot for it as I was.'

'At eight years old?'

'She didn't stay eight,' he said.

'If she was so hot for it, as you put it, why do you think she cried every time you came near her?'

'You know what women are,' he said easily. 'They say one thing and mean another. Say no and mean yes. I bet you've done it yourself.'

'The rapist's excuse,' said Cassie. He took a step forward, one arm reaching towards her, and she smashed the stick against his bicep with all the strength she had. He yelled with astonishment and pain. 'Anyway,' she said, 'Whatever definition of "woman" you use, it doesn't cover an eight-year-old child. Nor a nine- or ten- or even fourteen-year-old one.'

'She made me do it,' he said stubbornly. 'I tried not to give in to her. I mean, I knew it was wrong to have sex with her, but she just wouldn't leave me alone. Very highly developed sex urge, that girl. Some kids are like that – there was a case in the papers recently. Don't blame me, blame her.'

'I can't believe you mean this. You're talking about a *child*,' said Cassie.

'Children know about sex. Ask Sigmund Freud.'

'You sick pervert,' said Cassie.

'You're right. I need help,' he said quickly, changing tack. 'I couldn't help myself. Especially with her tempting me the way she did. I did my best to keep away from her, but when she came onto me like that, I just couldn't control myself.'

'Oh God. You're revolting.' Cassie lifted the stick again and he cowered away.

'Please,' he said. 'Don't hurt me. I can't cope with pain.'

'You can hand it out but you can't take it?'

'If you want to put it like that.' As he spoke, his eyes darted round the room, looking for a means of escape, or a way to overcome her.

'I hope you like urine in your tea, and people gobbing onto your supper,' said Cassie.

'What?'

'I hope you like your own company. Or, failing that, that you're prepared to put up with a lot of aggro.'

'What do you mean?'

'When they finally lock you up, you'll find that your fellow prisoners aren't very keen on people like you. They consider child molesters the dregs, the absolute scum of society. And they make their feelings very clear. So you'll have the choice of isolation or a pretty tough existence on the landings.'

Watching him, the way he slowly crumpled, the realisation that she spoke the truth darkening his eyes, she wondered how she could ever have been frightened of him. She had thought him a monster but he was a worm. If she picked him up and wrung him out, he would drip water like a wet teacloth.

'You're definitely going to go to the police, are you?' There was a grovelling note in his voice now which made her feel as though she had smelled rotting meat.

'Too right. And you're going to pay for the damage you did to Lucy.'

'But why should you care? If you're not her real mother, why should you be bothered?'

She stared at him. 'You really need to ask that, don't you?'

'I wouldn't enquire otherwise.'

'I said you were going to pay for what you've done to Lucy. But she's not the only one who's suffered because of you. Naomi, her real mother, committed suicide recently.'

'What's that got to do with me?'

'She killed herself when Lucy told her what you had done to her. I think you owe somebody for that, Mr Johannsen.'

'Suicide? I don't think . . .' His voice shook slightly. 'I can't be held responsible for some neurotic . . .' The bluster died away as he observed the scorn in her gaze, as reality began to invade the fantasies in which he had hidden himself for so long.

Cassie listened. How long would it take Lucy to rouse Kathryn? How soon after that would the police arrive? There was another matter to be dealt with. 'It was you who trashed my business premises, wasn't it?'

'I was trying to warn you off my daughter,' he said.

'What made you think it would work? Make her come back?'

'She's all I've got,' he said.

'But she hates you, surely you know that? She is revolted by you.'

'In time, we could rebuild our relationship. At least, as long as people like you don't try to interfere.'

The ignorance, the arrogance, amazed her. The borders of his private world were, it seemed, impregnable. She listened again. This time she did hear something. So did Johannsen.

'I'm not staying here,' he said. He sprang towards her, as he had earlier, this time ducking under the raised stick with which she tried to hit out at him, shoving her to one side, aiming a vicious kick at her stomach and another at her head. He grabbed the stick from her and swung it at the side of her face, slamming her back against the raised stone hearth, drawing blood as her cheek opened, loosening teeth in her upper jaw. The inside of her cheek felt like mush; there was blood, hot and salty, in her throat. His eyes were wild as he raised the stick again. She kicked out at him with both feet, catching him just below the knee so that his leg gave way and he collapsed on top of her, grunting with pain.

'Bitch,' he said fiercely. His hands came around her throat and she tore at them, trying to scream, trying to knee him in the groin, but he was too strong. He squeezed as she went for his eyes, easily avoiding her stiffened forefingers. Trying to shake him off, she bucked beneath him as though the two of them partook of some brutish coupling. His hands crushed her throat, his face close enough to hers that she could feel the bristle of his jaw. She scraped her nails down the side of his cheeks, sickened as she felt the skin rip, then, as he reared away, his grip slackening a little, she reached down between the two of them and grabbed his balls. As hard as she could, she twisted them. He screamed, letting go of her neck, drawing in sharp breaths. 'Bitch!' he yelled again. 'Let me go!'

He tried to pull away from her but she held on, increasing the pressure, squeezing tighter and tighter, revelling in the sight of his pain. He tried to beat her hand away. He punched her face. He seized one of her breasts and dug in his fingers, but she was beyond feeling pain now, intent only on inflicting it. His face was contorted, eyes glazed, lips pulled back from his teeth as he shrieked from his very heart. Panting, she let go of him. She tried to get up, but he was too heavy for her to push away, especially as one of her arms was now trapped between their bodies.

He rolled away, clutching himself. There was sweat on his

face. 'You wait,' he gasped. 'Just wai . . .' With difficulty, he staggered to his feet and slowly, holding onto the wall, shuffled out of the sitting room. She heard his feet slide across the tiles, and the sound of the back door opening, then closing behind him.

Leaning against the back of the sofa and trying to catch her breath, she didn't make the slightest effort to try to stop him. He wasn't going to go far. And even if he did, she knew where he lived. Eventually she made her own way into the kitchen and walked out into the dawn. Birds were making tentative wake-up noises. The creamy rambler roses filled the air with scent. Small puffy clouds tinged with pink moved slowly across a sky which was already turning from oyster-white to the palest of blues.

It was going to be a beautiful day.

♠ 20 ♠

The saloon bar of the Seven Stars in Frith throbbed with bonhomie. Sound bounced from the low nicotine-stained ceiling, amplifying the shouts and groans from the informal darts match at the far end of the room, the clank of the fruit machines, the soft outer-space whines of the electronic games.

'Graham tells me it's a foregone conclusion that the case will go to trial,' Cassie said. 'The evidence is irrefutable.'

'That's thanks to you.' Lucy looked up at Terry Collins, who was sitting next to her.

The former Philip Mansfield smiled down at her. 'Glad to help,' he said. 'If those tapes help put the bastard behind bars, that's great.'

It said a lot for the education schemes within the prison service that he had proved so adept at rigging up a temporary recording system on the ground floor of Honeysuckle Cottage. Perhaps it had been an asset in his former line of work. As it was, every word that Johannsen had spoken came across loud and clear on the tapes: out of his own mouth, Lucy's adoptive father had condemned himself.

Watching Terry's proprietorial air towards Lucy, Cassie though he might make the girl happy. He obviously had a strongly protective attitude towards vulnerable women; she was inclined to believe in his desire to go straight, and Lucy was going to have money when the legal details had been sorted out. Maybe the nice little business would materialise after all. She had already had a quiet word with him, explained that if he made Lucy unhappy in any way whatsoever, she, Cassandra Swann, would personally break both his arms and then put sugar in the tank of his motorbike.

In addition, rapport had been established between Lucy and John Harris, not to mention Anne Norrington: it looked as though a new, if unorthodox, family unit might be developing. The traditional happy ending. It was exactly what Lucy needed.

The only fly in the ointment was Charlie Quartermain.

It would be a long time before Cassie forgot what had happened after Peter Johannsen had left the cottage. Still trying to get herself together, she heard him make his painful way round the side of the cottage, his groans clearly audible with every step. Her heart was just slowing down to its normal rate when she heard a new commotion out in the lane.

What now? She went through the sitting room to undo the front door and stepped out onto the stone slab of doorstep to see Johannsen crouched in the middle of the lane, his hands protecting his head. Charlie Quartermain was standing over him in an attitude of menace.

''Ello, darlin',' he said cheerfully, as she walked down the front path. 'How's things?'

'Perfectly fine, thank you, Charles,' she said tartly.

'I knew you'd need a hand sorting this bugger out,' he said.

'That's really sweet of you.' The smile on her face was acid. 'But you really shouldn't have bothered.'

'For you, darlin',' nothing's too much.'

'What I mean, Charles, is that I didn't need any help. I had everything under control.' She enunciated each word very clearly in case he had missed the point.

He took absolutely no notice. 'Tried to ring you last night, see, and discovered the phone had been cut off. Decided there was something definitely fishy going on. Thought I'd better come along in case you wanted some help.'

'How utterly adorable of you,' said Cassie sarcastically. 'But your back-up was quite unnecessary. I'm perfectly capable of handling things on my own.' God, he could be irritating.

He gave a smug grin. 'Never hurts to have a big strong man around, does it?'

'Not if you're in the demolition business, no, I don't suppose it does.'

At this point, Kathryn had come racing up the lane, with Lucy dragging along behind her. 'Charlie, by all that's holy!' she cried dramatically, clasping her hands to her heart. 'Thank the good Lord you were here.'

'Yer, well . . .'

'Otherwise who knows what might have happened to these poor defenceless creatures.'

'Which defenceless creatures are those?' Cassie asked aggressively. 'I hope you aren't referring to Lucy and me.'

'Oh poor darling Cassie, where would you be without him?'

'Just a damn min—'

'It was Cassie,' Lucy said. 'She was wonderful. The way she dealt with my . . . with him.' She nodded at the abject figure still cowering in the road. 'She was so strong. I'll never forget it, never.'

'But if it hadn't been for darling Charlie, he'd have gotten away,' said Kathryn.

'No, he would not,' said Cassie.

'The cavalry riding to the rescue once again!' said Kathryn, avoiding Cassie's eye.

'Just call me St George,' Charlie said modestly.

'Would you two listen to me?' demanded Cassie. She didn't know what game Kathryn was playing, but there was no way Charlie was going to take the credit for the night's doings. Not that she wanted credit for herself, either, but if credit was going, let it be to the right place.

Charlie looked over at her. 'Here, girl,' he said. 'You look a bit rough.'

'I feel it, actually.'

'Blood and that,' said Charlie. 'I'll keep an eye on this—' he kicked Johannsen in the ribs, not very gently. '—While you go and clean yourself up.'

'There's no need,' Cassie said again. 'The police are on their way. And anyway he can't go far.'

'If you're going inside, put the kettle on, there's a good girl.'

'Charlie . . .' Cassie's teeth were gritted so hard she was afraid they would crack.

'What, darlin'?'

'Knock it off, will you?' Cassie touched the stickiness on one side of her face. As the adrenalin wore off she was conscious of bruises, of random aches, of wincing tenderness when she moved.

'Seriously,' Charlie said. 'You look like you could do with a handful of aspirin and a stiff drink not to mention a hot bath.' His eyes brightened. 'Tell you what: soon as I've unloaded this bit of garbage, why don't I come and scrub your back—'

'In your dreams, Charlie.'

'—And then tuck you up in bed after? Kiss you goodnight?'

'As *if* . . .' Cassie said witheringly.

She turned and went back into the cottage. Tiredness swept

312

over her. Exhaustion. A desire to weep, though she could not have said why. There was so much to do. And Lucy still to help.

This was not the end, she knew that much.

This was really just the beginning.

A selection of bestsellers from Headline

OXFORD EXIT	Veronica Stallwood	£5.99	☐
THE BROTHERS OF GWYNEDD	Ellis Peters	£5.99	☐
DEATH AT THE TABLE	Janet Laurence	£5.99	☐
KINDRED GAMES	Janet Dawson	£5.99	☐
ALLEY KAT BLUES	Karen Kijewski	£5.99	☐
RAINBOW'S END	Martha Grimes	£5.99	☐
A TAPESTRY OF MURDERS	P C Doherty	£5.99	☐
BRAVO FOR THE BRIDE	Elizabeth Eyre	£5.99	☐
FLOWERS FOR HIS FUNERAL	Ann Granger	£5.99	☐
THE MUSHROOM MAN	Stuart Pawson	£5.99	☐
THE HOLY INNOCENTS	Kate Sedley	£5.99	☐
GOODBYE, NANNY GRAY	Staynes & Storey	£4.99	☐
SINS OF THE WOLF	Anne Perry	£5.99	☐
WRITTEN IN BLOOD	Caroline Graham	£5.99	☐

All Headline books are available at your local bookshop or newsagent, or can be ordered direct from the publisher. Just tick the titles you want and fill in the form below. Prices and availability subject to change without notice.

Headline Book Publishing, Cash Sales Department, Bookpoint, 39 Milton Park, Abingdon, OXON, OX14 4TD, UK. If you have a credit card you may order by telephone – 01235 400400.

Please enclose a cheque or postal order made payable to Bookpoint Ltd to the value of the cover price and allow the following for postage and packing:

UK & BFPO: £1.00 for the first book, 50p for the second book and 30p for each additional book ordered up to a maximum charge of £3.00.

OVERSEAS & EIRE: £2.00 for the first book, £1.00 for the second book and 50p for each additional book.

Name ....

Address ....

....

....

If you would prefer to pay by credit card, please complete:
Please debit my Visa/Access/Diner's Card/American Express (delete as applicable) card no:

Signature .... Expiry Date ....